Were they looking at the beginning of the end times? Brognola wondered

Was the Apocalypse one more riot in Karachi, one more WTC-type bombing away? All the dire missions his people had undertaken, the close calls where calamity could have struck down entire nations if not for the Stony Man warriors, and he couldn't ever remember feeling this heavy, so grim, so troubled.

Where did it all go from there? He couldn't say, but at least he had the best of the best out there, willing to go the distance to keep the fuse of Armageddon from lighting the whole damn planet on fire.

If they weren't enough...

Well, he thought, God help them all. God save the human race.

DON PENDLETON'S

STONY

AMERICA'S ULTRA-COVERT INTELLIGENCE AGENCY

MAN

COLD
OBJECTIVE

A GOLD EAGLE BOOK FROM
W⚡RLDWIDE.

TORONTO • NEW YORK • LONDON
AMSTERDAM • PARIS • SYDNEY • HAMBURG
STOCKHOLM • ATHENS • TOKYO • MILAN
MADRID • WARSAW • BUDAPEST • AUCKLAND

First edition October 2004

ISBN 0-373-61957-X

COLD OBJECTIVE

Special thanks and acknowledgment to
Dan Schmidt for his contribution to this work.

Printed in U.S.A.

COLD
OBJECTIVE

PROLOGUE

Captain Yuri Zhabkov feared he held the key to nuclear Armageddon, and the terror of being the trigger of World War III haunted his dreams each and every night. Not a moment passed these days where he wasn't tweaked in some weird out-of-body experience, wired up on nerves, with agitation, worry, disbelief and horror of the unthinkable shadow companions who stood over his shoulder, grinning skulls that craved nothing but death and destruction.

For himself—and the human race.

It wouldn't be his call, of course, to begin the war to end all wars, but as commander of the Shark-class attack submarine, capable of launching three MIRVs, each fitted with triple 4-megaton payloads, able to vaporize American cities from 4500-plus miles away, he dreaded he was the man who would give the order to fire.

If and when, he thought, it came down to begin the

end. He prayed that the whispers he'd caught from the Spetsnaz goons aboard the SS-SSN torpedo-attack prototype sub were little more than drunken braggadocio, grim killers packed into the six-thousand ton sleek tube who had too much time on the their hands and way too much vodka in the wardroom. When it came to black ops, though, he knew nothing was beyond the realm of possibility. That's what troubled him.

The unthinkable did happen in their world of murder, sabotage and subterfuge, where everyone needed a scorecard to keep track of who was what. And even then no one could be sure.

In his darkest moment of fear and wild imaginings Zhabkov knew this mission had all the earmarks of creating an international incident that would never see the history books, since there might not be a human left standing to pen the nightmare he feared on the horizon.

Perhaps he was getting ahead of himself, he considered, infected by the paranoia and xenophobia common to his countrymen, unsure what the bottom line actually was, or even who was in charge from on high. It was crazy, though, what he might be called upon to do. In fact, it made little sense, other than the fact he was a puppet, and madmen with dreams of obscene wealth and power were the ones pulling his strings. He was a submariner, not a saboteur, much less a mass murderer, but he was on a strict need-to-know.

In the dark, then, the noose dangling over his head. Such was life, he concluded; not much had changed after the czars, the revolution, and only a fool believed the cold war really ended when the Berlin Wall came down. The mission he was undertaking proved Russia was as militant, power mad and paranoid as anything during the Stalin reign. He had the proof of that on board.

With the special night-vision goggles in place, he peered through the periscope, panning the green-glowing horizon, taking in the rising skeletal frames of the drilling rigs. Zhabkov had already pored over the radar pictures from the Video Data Link—VDL—wondering now which were the most susceptible targets. Meaning which would go up in groups of twos and threes, torched by Mk 50 torpedoes, create the most ferocious firestorm, perhaps raze the entire reserve with sweeping infernos. Twelve rigs were mounted on anchored platforms, looming above the choppy waters of the inlet, with another twenty rigs staggered on the permafrost tundra, fifty yards from where the refinery—with all its storage tanks, pumps and pipelines—rose just inside the flat rocky shoreline. There were two derricks perched on the shoreline, where the beach actually sloped into the Beaufort Sea, which could take direct hits. The VDL readouts also showed the reserve was branching out, one kilometer due south, where an additional twenty-three development derricks were in the works. If they blew up three or four derricks, he thought, the environmental disaster alone would wash out into the Beaufort, oil rivers rolling out into the tundra, driving off herds of caribou in sliding, snorting stampedes, maybe miring the lone grizzly or a few moose in quicksand of black sludge, schools of fish suffocating in the poisonous goo in the inlets, estuaries or the sea itself.

Which targets? he wondered. Twelve torpedoes, and practically speaking, considering his own survival naturally, he couldn't quite fathom launching all tubes, just in case an American submarine turned up on sonar on the long, nervous haul back across Arctic Ocean to Base Camp One Bear, and they needed something in reserve if they encountered antisubmarine warfare beneath the polar ice.

Zhabkov looked away from the target area, stripped off the goggles, seeing but not seeing the crew in the combat control room, his submariners manning the sonar and radar, intently watching the screens for any sign of a roving American sub or a helicopter. He wasn't aware he was gently shaking his head until he heard the familiar raspy voice. "Problem, comrade?"

The man moved like a ghost, having crept up on him out of nowhere, it seemed, donning a skintight blacksuit, his buzzcut nothing more than white bristles in the soft glow radiating from the screens, a 9 mm Makarov hanging in shoulder rigging.

"You look like a dog that has just eaten its own vomit, comrade Captain."

Zhabkov peered hard at Lieutenant Colonel Mikhail Kirchenko, then glanced at his submariners, reading the neutral expressions, his crew pretending they didn't hear the insult. He bit down the angry urge to fire off any number of questions for which his troubled soul wanted answers. Before he could say anything Kirchenko snatched the goggles out of his hand, grabbed the manwheel and looked through the periscope, bobbing his porcupine head, grunting.

"If you do not mind my saying so, it is madness, if what I hear is about to happen is true."

There. He'd said it. He waited while Kirchenko took his sweet grim time looking through the periscope, more head bobbing and grunting. Then the chiseled face pulled back, head swiveling, dark eyes revealing the window to the soul of a stone-cold killer when the goggles were removed.

"What is madness, comrade Captain?"

"Attacking this oil field. Creating what could possibly be the beginning of a war between us and the Americans. Not to mention an ecological nightmare that might make the *Valdez* disaster—"

Kirchenko chuckled. "Enough. I was not aware you were such a conservationist. We are not here to save the whales, comrade. We are not interested in flora and fauna and catching salmon. Listen to me—you do not have to understand, Captain. You do not have to like it— do what you must, not what you want. This is your submarine, but you have seen the orders, straight from the naval Spetsnaz high command, need I remind you."

"Yes, I have, and you need not. And when this order is given…?"

"I will look at the VDL readouts, but from what I see

of this reserve, I believe I can select the most appropriate targets with the naked eye."

"And then what?"

Kirchenko pinched the bridge of his nose, squeezing his eyes shut. "You already know what will happen next."

"Yes. You will go up top with a full squad, toss the packages overboard, inflate the motorized rubber outboards by remote. Board them, then go in to the reserve on foot. How many will be enough, Colonel?"

"Are you referring to equipment or personnel?"

"Both."

"As many as I deem fit when we hit the beach. There will be several hostages taken—I neglected to mention that little item, seeing as your nerves are not all they should be."

That felt like another body blow to Zhabkov. Any submarine was notoriously short on space, and every inch of his vessel was already packed with bodies, supplies, state-of-the-art equipment he believed not even the American CIA knew existed.

Zhabkov blew an exasperated breath. "What? How many? And where do you propose we bunk these prisoners?"

"We will make room somehow. We have two more Shark-class submarines on maneuvers in the Arctic Ocean. Should it become necessary, the hostages can be transferred at sea, to conserve on your precious space. I have taken the liberty to radio Tiger Sharks Two and Three and alert them to the possibility of prisoner transfer on open sea. How many, you ask? I have not decided. I will again review the intelligence dossier and determine which scientists and geologists could prove most valuable."

"Insanity," Zhabkov muttered. "A kidnapping on top of an assault!"

"I am growing weary of your bellyaching, comrade Captain. You will do as you are ordered—"

"Or?"

"I will relieve you of command."

Zhabkov froze, caught himself before he launched into a tirade. Better to at least be a puppet, have some control over his destiny and his submarine than relinquish all power to a bunch of raiders.

"This, comrade Captain, will only be the beginning. What you don't understand about all of this is a lot."

"Feel free to clue me in."

"Very well. Russia turned over Alaska more than a hundred years ago to the Americans—1867, to be exact. Sold out for a mere 7.2 million dollars, which comes down to two cents an acre. A very bad mistake in hindsight, since our own country, bankrupt by corrupt politicians, has a serious energy supply shortage. The north slope of Alaska is awash in fossil fuel, and we have every much a right to it as the Americans. The very same price we sold out was the exact same value of the first shipment of crude by tanker. Irony? A slap in our face?"

"You are saying by attacking this reserve the Americans will somehow fall to their knees and allow us access to this Spectron Oil Reserve, perhaps let us tap into the Trans-Alaska Pipeline? Perhaps let us simply walk in and help ourselves and let us set up shop in Prudhoe Bay?"

"Not hardly, but we must make a statement. Item— you do not know that this oil field belongs to us as part of a secret pact with an American company."

"Vertigo International." Zhabkov caught the flicker of surprise on the Spetsnaz man's face. "Yes, I have a few sources of my own."

"So, then, you understand we are receiving assistance from the very Americans you fear so much. The same Americans, but the power whores in Washington who reneged on the Energy Security Treaty we signed with them."

"Because of criminal ties to our military?"

"Alleged."

Zhabkov nearly laughed out loud. The man spoke of corrupt politicians wreaking havoc on his country, when in truth Russia was owned and run by gangsters, many of whom were former KGB agents or military men. "By the power of the sword, you and whoever you work for believe they can blow up and rebuild Alaska in your image, reclaim it for the motherland? What is next? You will sabotage eight hundred miles of the Trans-Alaska Pipeline with explosives? Contaminate the vast wilderness?"

The fire that burned suddenly in Kirchenko's eyes sent a shiver down Zhabkov's spine. The man was insane, but if he was hell-bent on starting what at worst would be a dirty little war, then the men above him were nothing more than devils, seeking to charge straight for the gates of hell.

"You said it, comrade Captain. Now, dive. Sixty meters and hold this position. I will be back when the time has come. The next time you see me, it will have begun. Prepare yourself for that dirty little war."

Zhabkov watched as the Spetsnaz commander took one last look at the sonar screens, then marched off and vanished down the passageway. He felt terribly alone all of a sudden, thinking the whole world had gone mad.

VIKTOR "RUSSO" RUSKAVKA was poised to usher in a new age for the motherland. For too long now his country had played second string to the Americans, especially where matters of energy—gas, fossil fuel and nuclear—were concerned. Too few had too much, he thought, in terms of the wealth and energy that kept their country on top, the rest of the world little more than groveling whelps begging for scraps. There was always the question of military might making right, and that, as far as he was concerned, would provide the key to changing the tide in favor of his country.

So, there were critical matters to attend to, personal and professional, the hour of truth nearly upon them all. But he needed to know where his American counterpart stood.

Meaning could the man be trusted when the heat

blew their way? A legal, political and military firestorm would be touched off when he relayed the order.

Flanked by his Russian right-hand man, with his guards Boris and Ivan scanning the vacant reception area with dark scowls, as if they expected armed shadows to pop out of the offices and bays, the Russian Don of one of the top three Families out of Moscow shoved open the heavy double mahogany doors to the man's office suite.

"I guess manners went out with you people after the death of Rasputin."

Ruskavka marched a few steps inside the doorway, the heels of his Italian leather loafers rapping softly over the polished teakwood floor. He grunted, staring down at the man's full head of black wavy hair, the industrialist striking him as more arrogant and vain each time they met. "Stalin had more so-called manners than that drunken, lecherous scoundrel. If you believe what you just said, then you know very little about my country's history."

"I know enough. And I was always partial to old Rasputin."

"Good to know who your heroes are."

"All my heroes are dead. Bruce Lee, Hendrix, the murdered Beatle, Lee Marvin, Napoleon—to name the shortlist."

Ruskavka kept watching the man. He was maybe all of five and a half feet tall, tipping the scales at no more than a 150 pounds. Stripped down to black bikini briefs, the corded muscles of sinewy iron in his shoulders and back rippled beneath the white umbrella of soft overhead light. Even this late at night, Ruskavka wondered about the sanity of a man who spent most of his spare time on keeping his body a sacred temple of physical and spiritual perfection. Still, it was a sight to marvel at, this American doing not just one-handed push-ups, but using only two fingers. Ruskavka became uncomfortably conscious of his beefy, self-indulgent bulk.

"I saw Bruce Lee do this once," the American industrialist said, bicep popping up and down, no break or even the hint of strain in his voice, his sleek frame sheened in sweat. "I think I could have given him a lesson or two in training. What do you think?"

Ruskavka, ever the paranoid, told Boris to close the doors in Russian.

"I know Russian, by the way."

"So you do," Ruskavka said. "Moscow, we both know, has always been your second home."

"It must be the *blini*."

The Don scanned the Spartanly furnished suite. For a multibillionaire, he wondered again about the mental stability of Max Walker, who had more money than Donald Trump or Bill Gates, but he never indulged in pleasures of the flesh or surrounded himself with the finer trappings of money. The only sign of hospitality was the wet bar in the far corner of the room, and Ruskavka told Ivan to make him a vodka, neat. In the other corner, he noted, barbells and other free weights were scattered around various weight and aerobics machines. In another room, he knew the man had built his own dojo, complete with samurai swords and every weapon of Asian martial arts he could conceive of. The Don wasn't even sure how many black belts Walker had earned, but he was a three-time world karate champion, middleweight. To Ruskavka he was the businessman's answered prayer to their version of Chuck Norris. Then there were the rumors how Walker had sometimes walked the streets of Seattle, late at night, flashing cash, crippling would-be muggers with his bare hands. Fact or fiction? Ruskavka wasn't sure he cared to find out.

The Russian glanced at the bright Seattle skyline beyond the row of floor-to-ceiling windows. The Space Needle was winking back at him from two o'clock. He was aware that far north, past the skyscrapers and the mountains and Canada, the fight for the future was about to be unleashed. He took the drink from Ivan, watched as Walker launched himself to his feet, using only his fingertips as a grenadelike springboard. The American industrialist moved like a cat to a rack near the weights, grabbed a towel.

"Okay, now that you're drinking my vodka," Walker said, toweling off his torso, "I assume you're here to tell me the news. Please. Take a seat."

Ruskavka claimed a seat on the leather couch as Walker walked to the refrigerator behind the wet bar and pulled out a bottle of water.

"There is going to be serious heat when this happens."

"Tell me something I don't know."

Ruskavka studied the man, lifted his empty glass to Ivan. "Do you mind?"

"Help yourself, comrade. It's your party."

"Correction. It's our show, our game to win."

Walker sipped from the bottle. "When?"

"One hour. Certain channels had to be reached for final confirmation. I will relay the order once I leave here."

"So what's the problem? I get the impression you called this powwow to feel out my nerves."

"My American friend, there will be much to be nervous about in the coming days."

"My nerves are in good shape, solid steel, just like the pipelines and drilling equipment I produce and ship all over the world. From where I stand it looks like I should be worried about my Muscovite comrades. Is this a feeler? A way for you to come here, Vlad and Igor the gunslingers by your side, and issue little implied threats?"

"A courtesy call. To make sure we are on the same page."

"We've planned this for a long time. We knew the deal going in, Russo. The rewards outweighed the risks. We want major market monopoly, but that's only the tip of the glacier. You want more money and power than you now have. You want to build your own vast oil fields in Siberia, using my equipment, my experts, my ships. You want to lock up the entire power structure in Moscow in your own vise and maybe proclaim yourself president someday, for all I know, once you apply the energy squeeze and the big boys with all the toys find themselves freezing to death in their own dachas. You want it all."

"And you do not?"

"There's a bottom line with me."

"Which is?"

Walker glanced at Boris as he poured another vodka. "Nothing is ever good enough for the gods. New horizons to conquer, like that."

"I almost forgot. Napoleon is one of your dead heroes."

Walker appeared to ignore the remark. "Problem is, Russo, I don't think it's good for us to be seen together at the eleventh hour. My own security people are seeing G-men all over Seattle these days."

"We already know about the FBI and the Justice Department. It was understood that I would be under their watchful eye since arriving from Moscow. I make no secret who I am." He shrugged. "If they cause us grief, they will be disposed of in prompt fashion."

"Then we understand each other. If it hits the fan, a tidal wave of crap will blow our direction. We simply turn a bigger fan their way and send it back in their faces."

"Precisely. You stand to make tens, perhaps hundreds of millions from this deal, depending on how the exploration goes in the Siberian wilderness."

"You don't listen so good, comrade. Money, I have. The world is what I want."

"Yours—and ours?"

Walker chuckled. "All of it. Let me be clear, comrade. You have access to all sorts of weapons. You bragged one fine night about it in Moscow over twenty or thirty double vodkas, only I had it checked out. Chem, bio, nuke stockpiles—you're a smorgasbord of mass destruction. You're also former KGB, and the list of political and military clout on your payroll reaches from here to the Bering Strait."

"Your point?"

"We're going to need their help, so I suggest you recheck your roster and ask yourself which ones will fold, which ones will go the distance with us when this heat you mentioned is on. Endgame here—we make our climb to the petro top. OPEC is next on the hit list. The Middle East is down the road, but since fifty percent of crude comes to America from that part of the world, we need to find a way to shut off the flow—permanently. Market monopoly."

"So, we will be at war with the world? Everyone is fair game."

"One small step for mankind at a time. You see, one of these days, the oil will stop flowing out of the ground, at least the proved reserves. When that happens, those who have the means to keep all the little people's cars running will be the masters of the human race. Do you know the rate of energy consumption is quadrupling in this country alone, and every six months."

"Fascinating."

"Don't patronize me."

"Never. A question, and I expect the truth."

"I always have, and always will be straightforward with you. I like being able to look at myself in the mirror, knowing I'm a straight shooter."

"Indeed. I ask you now, no matter what happens in the coming days, are we in this together?"

Max Walker smiled over his bottled water. "To the bitter and even a bloody end. Hail Rasputin."

Ruskavka killed the vodka, set the glass on the teak coffee table and stood. "That is all I needed to hear."

"You know where to reach me. I won't run, I won't hide."

"I expected no less."

"Keep me posted, comrade. It's balls-to-the wall time."

"FIRE NUMBER one!"

The solid-fueled torpedo sliced the surface, trailing a frothy wake, a sleek metallic shark with explosive teeth homed in on the first target, an inlet platform about to blow, burn and spew poison into the water.

Zhabkov shuddered, mentally calculating speed and range, waiting it out, then the platform blew in a ball of fire that swelled his NVD goggles, made him wince and turn away from the blinding flash.

His worst fear was realized. The nightmare had begun.

His radioman was telling him the colonel wished to speak with him, the semi-insuborinate bastard throwing in that Kirchenko said it was urgent. The Spetsnaz squad was on the deck now, he knew, twelve raiders prepared to board the motorized rubber outboards, sail in, fan the flames of death and destruction.

Zhabkov slipped on the headset. "Yes."

"What are you waiting for!"

"It will take a moment to make the adjustments, recalculate range and lock onto the next target. Torpedoes are not fired like a machine gun on a swivel mount."

"Watch your tongue with me, comrade Captain! Do it! Quickly!"

Zhabkov gave the order to recalculate, adjust to the target area for the next strike, the fingers of his submariners at the fire-control and action-display terminals flying over keyboards, a vision of the frenzy of the crew loading missiles in the torpedo room flashing those grinning skulls through his mind. Numbers two and three tubes belched their payloads. The vessel didn't shimmy or shake from the launch, but the Shark-class attack sub, he knew, was built for supreme quiet on top of speed. Springs and rubber mounts had been installed, stem to stern, all sound from the vessel itself absorbed into the hull. The Zilkov cloaking device emitted electromagnetic jamming waves, supposedly capable of throwing off enemy sonar, even fouling up spy satellites with blurs and glitches. Whatever was out there, Zhabkov knew they would hear the enemy before the enemy heard them.

He was hardly confident.

In fact he felt ill.

Back at the periscope, he gave the order to fire numbers four, five and six.

At one thousand meters and change, it was a short run for the torpedoes, a handful of seconds, it seemed, and the derricks were torched up in geysers of shooting fire up and down the shoreline. Already the first direct hit, a skeleton swathed in a leaping firewall, black smoke and spurting oil adding to the conflagration, was toppling for the water.

The madness had begun.

Zhabkov groaned to himself. There was no turning back now, the future growing more dark with each torpedo that struck another derrick. He thought about his wife and three children back in Moscow, wondering if he'd ever see them again.

KIRCHENKO HIT the green button on his multipurpose remote, and the valves on the attached air pumps inflated the trio of rubberized outboards. The nylon-wrapped motors bobbed to the surface as the three outboards swelled with oxygen. Slender mooring lines held the craft to the cleats in the sub's hull, anchoring them in the chop as his squad toted their war bags, descending to board. Once aboard, engines were cranked to life, black ski masks slipping over their faces. The weapon of choice was an HK MP-5 subgun, fitted with laser sights, sound suppressors, their hip-holstered side arms the Beretta 92-F. All of them were ordered to communicate in English. Confusion that this was an attack by some American paramilitary force for reasons unknown would fuel the fires of chaos once they evacuated with their catch, but only after mining a number of the storage tanks and pipelines with plastic explosive would they retreat. Death, destruction and the horrified bewilderment of any surviving personnel would also buy them time to return to their Arctic base.

Kirchenko checked the destruction, noting the veritable ring of fire they would slip through to put the master stroke to the operation. The compound was mentally marked in his mind, after days of review of intelligence, both sat and VDL pictures, all of it committed to ironclad memory. His commandos were seasoned pros with any number of black ops under their belts, briefed time and again at the base camp and on the sub. They would claim a beachhead in a cove, smack in the middle of the refinery. From there, a short hike up the rocky slope, begin planting the charges on the way to the personnel building to the southeast, begin the snatch. He lingered on the deck, dwarfed by the conning tower, taking in the holocaust with a feeling of awe and mounting invincibility. A dirty smudge of light was breaking through a low ceiling of cloud cover, marking the onslaught of dawn. There would be no need for NVD goggles, daylight or not, especially since the firestorms were now meshing between derricks in the inlet and on the shore. He heard the chaos in the distance, the panicked shouts of personnel reaching out to sea before he spotted the flailing shadows near the refinery. Sirens wailed and steel groaned as derricks crumbled. The ground and the water were already slick with shooting crude, and the fingers of geysering oil appeared like the arms of some giant black octopus writhing from the ocean depths.

It was time to go.

He gave a moment's gruff consideration to the captain's plight, knowing the man would hold up—or else there would be an impromptu burial at sea. Despite his brief boasting about his own intelligence sources, Kirchenko knew the man had no clue actually what was really taking place here, the intricate web of deceit and subterfuge already spun, and that would allow them to penetrate the reserve, shoot up as many firefighters and personnel as possible while rounding up seven of the best scientists and geologists their Department of Energy could recruit.

And, no, he thought, Captain Zhabkov hadn't the first inkling Spetsnaz was being assisted by a man on the inside of the Spectron Reserve.

Kirchenko hefted his war bag off the deck, slipped it across his shoulder, twisted about and began the short descent down the cleats to join his commandos.

It was time to go to war, or at least take the slaughter to the lambs.

THE FIRST EXPLOSION WAS enough to send Carl Rutgen flying out of his bunk. For months now he had been waiting to earn all the money the mystery Russkie cutouts back in Washington had been handing off the past two years, either in envelopes in the dead of night on some dark country road, or direct electronic deposits in two separate offshore accounts in the lower Americas.

They were coming finally, and he thought it was about time. The Spectron Reserve had been under around-the-clock development for eighteen months, but he had only been assigned ten months back for this stint, when a man from the Department of Energy had handpicked him as head of security. It was a joke really, out there in the boondocks, six DOE spooks gleaned from various intelligence agencies with Beretta 92-Fs, an assortment of Colt Commando assault rifles under lock and key, the idea to keep away poachers, stragglers and the curious Inuit or Aleut Indians who might wander in too close from the tundra. It was a no-muss, no-fuss job—or would have been until now. His part had been defined by the shadow men in no uncertain terms.

He was to hold the science crew at bay in their quarters, then make himself scarce. In short, stay the hell out of the way, or buy the farm when the invaders made their move.

Well, they were shaking and baking now and it was time to aid and assist.

Who and what the mystery invaders were wasn't important, but the ex-NSA man, once in charge of a division called Energy Sabotage and Antiterrorism, almost felt relief. The waiting for it to happen had been the agonizing part.

The head of security at the Spectron Reserve heard the sirens, a blanket of noise that might make it near impossible to speak, unless he was shouting at the top of his lungs in someone's face.

He started the shouting, his handheld radio crackling with the panicked shrill of the plant manager. Ritter was squawking, "What the hell... Rigs One, Five, Six...Oh, my God..."

Another three derricks lit up before Ritter's eyes. Rutgen fell into his role. "Go to the main control room. Shut off the valves, turn off the pumps. Get the fire brigade—"

"I already did that, but it'll take time for the shutdown of crude—"

"I know that, mister! We're going to have one hellacious mess to clean up."

"We're going to have call in—"

The military. Any number of Army and naval stations, he knew, were spread around the vast wilderness, which, he'd once heard Alaskans boast, could be lopped in half and still put Texas down as the third-largest state. It would take time to get the HAZMAT cleanup team from the military on-site, which meant the communications center needed to be taken out.

Rutgen turned to his six-man team. "All of you, get to the personnel barracks and keep them calm and inside. Move it!" Two of them were running for the gun rack. He nearly told them they didn't need assault rifles, it was simply a fire of unknown origins, but figured let them have at it.

Why not, he figured, at least make it look good, give them a fighting chance before they were mowed down.

He sure as hell was staying out of the way of the coming slaughter machine.

KIRCHENKO HIT the concrete deck near the first row of storage tanks running, began triggering his subgun on the fly. Supreme chaos, he found, ruled the predawn hour, firefighters in HAZMAT suits with attached oxygen tanks hooking up the hoses to the water towers, special chemical foam spraying the firestorms from their massive trucks, water geysers hitting the towering infernos nearby in sweeping sprays that would have made a damburst look weak in comparison. His commandos knew what to do and got busy planting the first series of plastique. They made the storage tanks, placing enough charges on four to punch gaping holes in the base, set off explosions they could probably see all the way to Vancouver, but staggering the coming blasts with every other unit. Kirchenko watched as three of his commandos peeled off, as previously ordered, racing for the com center to kill all personnel, cripple anything that could send out the SOS.

In unison with his commandos hit maybe ten or twelve firefighters with long sweeping bursts of autofire, spilling them near their trucks.

The inferno raged on to the west, Kirchenko feeling his flesh plastered to his blacksuit, the heat so intense it sucked the air out of his lungs. Scurrying personnel were chopped up by Kirchenko's subgun fire, spinning and dropping before him, bouncing off pipelines, littering the charge ahead. The colonel burned through two clips, number three locked and loaded. He was surging on, angling down the west edge of the sprawling parking lot, when his com link crackled and he was told the charges were good to go.

It took several critical minutes, but they were clearing the refinery and ground zero, sprinting for the personnel barracks where he saw the members of the security detail flapping their arms, shoving the science workforce back into the white building. Kirchenko hit the button on his handheld radio, touching off the one frequency tied in to all doomsday packages. Pipelines, pumps and tanks, he saw, glancing over his shoulder, flared up in a supernova of intercoursing fireballs. The earth shook, the blasts vomiting out for the parking lot, flying slabs of wreckage pulping eighteen-wheelers, Sno-cats, snowmobiles, SUVs.

The members of the security force, he saw, had their backs turned, Kirchenko having filed away the face of their man on the inside, but if he had to, he'd cut down the guy. In fact, maybe that was the way to go. No point in leaving behind songbirds.

Kirchenko took the sitrep from Khalov, his com link buzzing with the words he wanted to hear.

"Com center disabled. All personnel extinguished."

Something next about their inside man, running away, alive and kicking, gone to ground. Kirchenko had to forget about him, told his com cripplers to link up at the personnel building. He wanted this wrapped in five minutes, on board with their catch and racing back for the sub.

They charged ahead, a skirmish line of hitters, subguns cutting loose on the security detail. They fell like dominoes, white parkas chopped to red ruins, screams lost to the hellish racket of sirens.

A check of the conflagration near the shore, and Kirchenko felt confident the hard part was over. All hands were too busy trying to put out the holocaust. Whatever resistance was on-site was strewed at his feet.

Kirchenko saw the faces of fear in the series of doorways, then bulled ahead to start selecting the saved.

Resistance would be unacceptable. Victory here was his for the taking.

Kirchenko began taking.

CHAPTER ONE

"What do we have, people? Besides what could turn out to be the mother nightmare of all catastrophic international incidents in the last hundred years."

His name was Hal Brognola, and he was entering the War Room at Stony Man Farm. Aside from his duties at the Justice Department the big Fed was liaison to the President of the United States, who sanctioned the covert missions out of the Farm. The Stony Man warriors—Able Team, Phoenix Force and Mack Bolan, aka the Executioner, who operated primarily as a lone wolf when he wasn't in the trenches with the other troops—were backed by the cybernetics wizards and support staff who were the brains behind the muscle comprising the most ultrasecret covert agency on the planet.

Without exception.

Brognola chomped on his unlit cigar, scanning the faces at the table. He had just choppered in from Reagan National to the Shenandoah Valley after spending the better part of a nervous, tense and angry day laying it out for the cyber team here—between redline phone calls to the Man in the Oval Office, trying to get the green light from him to cut loose the troops of Able Team on what the big Fed and the Chief Executive determined was a clear and present danger to national security. For damn sure, they were looking at a disaster nearly beyond comprehension, and the strain and the tension showed in the grim expressions on their faces. Three of the Sensitive Operations Group's best and brightest were gathered at the table, and Brognola had been expecting to see Hermann "Gadgets" Schwarz and Rosario "Politician" Blancanales assembled for the brief. As if reading his thoughts, Carl "Ironman" Lyons, the leader of Able Team, looked up from his intel packet. The ex-LAPD detective told Brognola, "You said it was urgent, you said lock and load, be ready fly at a moment's notice."

"So I did."

"So I sent Gadgets and Pol over to the armory. Cowboy," he said, referring to John "Cowboy" Kissinger, the Farm's chief weapon smith and armorer, "is laying out the goods for the hammer-down as we speak."

Brognola grunted. "Works for me. You can fill them in on the way to Seattle."

Lyons raised an eyebrow. "Seattle? Why not go straight to the flashpoint, Hal? If your suspicions are on the money, we can lop off the head of the viper in

America's last frontier before this thing gets any more out of hand."

"In a moment I'll get to that. And it's already out of hand."

The director of the SOG glanced at Barbara Price, the stunning honey blond woman near his seat at the head of the table. She could have stepped off the cover of any fashion magazine or movie poster and brought the devil to his knees with her beauty. In truth, she was the Farm's mission controller. The big man confined to a wheelchair, courtesy of a bullet to the spine during a long-ago attack on the Farm, was Aaron "the Bear" Kurtzman, who headed up the cyber team. Other than being a genius when it came to theft in cyberspace, Kurtzman made some of the worst coffee this side of hell, and Brognola knew it could choke a saltwater croc.

Knowing some of the score here, and what they were potentially faced with, Brognola knew his nerves were jangled enough, but made a beeline for the coffeepot just the same, feeling the urge for the heavy fuel of a monstrous caffeine fix. Claiming his seat at the head of the table, he gave Price a nod, and she began the brief. Clicker in hand, she snapped on the wall monitor, and the mounted ceiling slide projector brought into focus the first of a series of sat and aerial photos of the area in question.

"Spectron Petroleum and Gas Reserve," Price said, showing a grid map of the reserve from the shores of the Beaufort Sea, outlined in klicks and half klicks all the way inland for the tundra, with derricks, refineries numbered. "Just after 0600 this morning, local Alaska time, six derricks were blown up—torpedoed by a Russian hunter-killer sub."

"And this was confirmed how?" Lyons asked.

"Our antisubmarine-warfare contingent," Brognola said, "operating in the Arctic Sea, the Beaufort and the Bering Strait, but it was the CIA station officers on board a Navy chopper who cut in and decoded encrypted radio com right before the attack between what our intelligence agencies are tagging the Mothership and Hunters Two and Three. What do we know about these subs, Barbara, and where is their present position?"

"Unclear on their exact position, but here's what we know. They're prototype nuclear-powered attack subs, according to CIA and NSA specs. Complete with nukes and twelve Mk 50 torpedoes. Tagged as Shark class, the latest in hunter-killer subs, built in secret on the Chukchi Peninsula. Our side only learned of their existence all of four months ago."

"Chukchi," Brognola grunted. "Right across the Bering Strait, if my mental map serves me right."

Price nodded. "Russia has more than eight thousand nautical miles of Arctic coastline, and they jealously guard the shoreline, supposedly on their side of the international date line. However, 'us' and 'them' have staked claim for years to real estate in the North Pole, setting up clandestine bases, satellite transmission-receiver stations, patrolling the waters of the Arctic above and below the ice. Akira and Hunt," she said, referring to two other invaluable members of the cyber team, Akira Tokaido and Huntington Wethers, "are monitoring NRO, NSA and CIA X-ray sat transmissions now, tracking the subs, trying to pin down where they'll dock. Their guess is they're headed for the pole, where they believe the Russians have an established black-ops base, but we've yet to nail down their final destination. They submerge to more than a hundred yards, we can't track them, unless one of our subs is in the general area. Now, these Shark-class subs are capable, or so we learned, of diving to six, maybe seven hundred yards, able to cut through the water at forty to forty-five knots, but not below a hundred yards. So say the think-tanker ASW experts at Langley."

Lyons whistled. "You're kidding me? I don't know much about subs, Barbara, but I don't think even we have something that can scoot that fast."

"Not even the Los Angeles class," Kurtzman said. "Figure both sides have spent over two—count it—two trillion dollars on claiming the world's waters by submarines since World War II, not to mention we have eighteen Ohio-class subs, each with enough nuke power equalling twenty-three thousand Hiroshima bombs— this from Akira—and the Russians, it seems, just took the edge in the world of sub versus sub. Speed and quiet, that's what you want in a sub, bottom line. That and a mother lode of firepower. These Shark-class hunter-killers have both—or so claims Langley."

"Okay," Brognola said. "What's the score on casualties at Spectron? Likewise give me whatever you have on the environmental damage, Barbara."

Price perused her packet, looked up and told them, "Fifteen firefighters, shot dead by a commando force, believed to total twelve shooters, black ski masks, using HK MP-5s. They were in and out, less than thirty minutes, and they knew what and who they wanted. Clockwork op. The FBI and NSA are on-site now, grilling the work detail, putting together more of the facts. You should know more about the hit, Hal, as soon as we wrap it up here."

"American hardware," Lyons said, nodding. "Slick. Trying to cover their tracks. Classic black ops."

"Well, they failed. The CIA came through on the com crack, or we might still be in the dark. The entire security detail was wiped out, minus the head of security, who was somehow absent from the slaughter."

Lyons grunted. "Somehow absent?"

Price glanced at Lyons, then continued. "Eleven workers, including the plant manager, a number of oil technicians, the radio team, all gunned down. It gets worse." Price paused, then said, "Seven of the best of the Department of Energy's elite science-geology-exploration crew were abducted. Last seen being taken out to sea by motorized rubber outboards, where they board the deck of the hunter-killer sub. Vanish belowdeck, then dive, chug out to sea."

"You're telling me the Russians have declared war

on America?" Lyons growled. "Hit the beach and bagged up a bunch of scientists, for God only knows what reason?"

"Or a renegade faction of the military," Price said. "We believe navy Spetsnaz. Black ops, like you indicated."

"All in the name of oil?" Lyons said. "Pissed off we have more access to natural resources than they do? Won't have hand over the wealth, what? Angry they basically turned over Alaska way back when for what was mere pennies?"

"We're not sure the motivating factors altogether," Kurtzman said. "Washington was on the verge of signing an Energy Security Treaty with Moscow about a year ago, then reneged on allowing the Russians in on the deal to drill on the north slope. Was going to be a joint venture at first. Enter the Russian Mafia, so the floating rumor goes, and the reason Washington pulled the plug on Moscow. Behind the political scenes it put a strain on relations with our so-called ally."

"More on that in a minute, Carl. The damage?" Brognola asked.

Price clicked through a series of sat imagery detailing derricks and storage tanks on fire. "It isn't the *Exxon Valdez* spill of eleven million gallons in Prince William Sound, but it's bad enough. The main valves were closed, but only after the sixth derrick blew. By then they were looking at a veritable floodtide of crude. A sea of ecological poison, in other words."

"I thought all the oil came out of Prudhoe Bay?" Lyons

said. "I must have slept through the past twelve months. When did Congress pass some energy bill to start digging up the north slope and keep the public in the dark?"

"I can only compare it to a dead-of-night deal," Price said. "Energy crunch in California kept the ball rolling, word is this administration also wanting to cut the umbilical cord to our dependence on OPEC. We're learning more about Spectron the deeper we dig around, and we're picking up some bad vibes on the whole deal. Bottom line, the President pushed for further drilling on the north slope, his show, and he got what he wanted."

"Which is presently a nightmare," said Kurtzman. "The AIQ is Tangent Point, just east of Barrow, and west of Prudhoe. The idea was to build a pipeline from Tangent to Prudhoe…"

"And hook up to the Trans-Alaska Pipeline," Price added. "Something like two million barrels per day flow parallel to the Koyukuk River, through untainted pristine wilderness, some eight hundred miles all the way south to Valdez. Our initial investigation into the Spectron reserve indicates there are hopes they can double or even triple that output with further expansion, both out to sea and across the tundra."

"The way you said that about the Trans-Alaska Pipeline," Lyons stated, "you make it sound like the pipeline is a potential target for terrorists."

"The military jumped on this disaster after a distress signal was sent out by the backup com unit in the fire station. And you're right, Carl," Price said, "we're concerned the Trans-Alaska Pipeline could be a target. Military gunship helicopters are monitoring the pipeline, with orders to shoot to kill if any hostiles approach it. Back to the disaster—special fire brigades and HAZMAT teams were flown out of Naval Petroleum Reserve Number Four, Fort Wainwright, Greely, Kodiak and Adak naval stations. As of two hours ago, with the aid of C-130 tankers, the fires were finally put out. But not after a little over one million gallons of crude spilled into the inlet and out into the Beaufort, and they're not even sure how much spilled south across the tundra."

"The conservationists, every environmentalist doomsayer who thinks the sky is falling through gaping holes in the ozone will scream bloody murder," Lyons said. "The natives, too, wanting a few scalps if what I've heard about all the irate objections over plumbing for black gold on the north slope is true. They don't want Uncle Sam up there, with the potential of contaminating the wilderness, killing salmon and so on. Someone—the Russians—just gave them a reason to cry."

"You're right," Kurtzman said. "But this goes deeper and further than a simple exploration for oil."

Lyons raised an eyebrow. "So you say. Why am I hearing some *X-Files*-type conspiracy on the tip of your tongue, Bear?"

"Because there is one," Brognola said, gnawing on his stogie. "That's where you and Able come into play, Carl. I want to be clear on where the Man stands on this, people, before we take this one to the mat. He says our country is at war with enemies of national security who have been the ones declaring all the war up to this point. No more. The gloves are all the way off. The President wants anyone—Arab, Russian or one of our own who is a traitor—to be hunted down and eliminated. Full sanction from here on, whatever it takes, pull no punches—that's straight from the Oval Office. No more trials of international terrorists and criminals, the only justice being the rough-and-ultimate kind."

"I thought that's why we've been here all along," Lyons said. "To do what must be done above and beyond legal limits."

"Exactly. Only these days it doesn't take much for me to convince the Man to cut us loose, not like some of the arm twisting and waiting in limbo I went through in days gone by. Phoenix and Striker are over in Pakistan," he told Lyons. "We believe there is a connection to the trade in heroin between the Russia Mafia—the Viktor 'Russo' Ruskavka Family, to be exact—the Taliban, corrupt Pakistani intelligence agents and military officers, the Pashtun rebels of the northwest frontier of Pakistan…but, that's not your concern, Carl. However, one Viktor Ruskavka is."

"I read the intel, Hal," Lyons said. "And Barbara gave us some of the slide show already. You're thinking the Russian Mafia is tied in to this Vertigo International."

"You saw the slide show, you saw him then, arm in arm, surveillance photos shot by my agents in both Seattle and Moscow, with one Max Walker. Looking happy as pigs in mud, like they're one big move away from grabbing the world by the short hairs."

"According to what I read," Lyons said, nodding at the intel package, "I'd put this Walker on the shortlist for industrial sabotage. Something doesn't look right with the guy, if you consider his hobbies alone. Runs his own weekend-warrior gun club out in the Seattle boondocks, for starters. Then, you have a guy who somehow—no one is sure how—climbed his way up the steel-and-industrial machinery ladder, grooming deals with the eight majors—oil conglomerates—shipping petro chemicals, plastic, drilling rigs, equipment, pipelines from this Spectron Oil Reserve to Venezuela to Oman. Armed security detail, ex-cops with questionable pasts, ex-military types always wandering around in the picture. Not only that, for a simple engineer, with a degree out of Stanford, this guy is every yuppie's version of Bruce Lee and Steven Seagal put together."

"More black belts than you can count," Brognola added. "Three-time world martial-arts champion, owns his own dojo, supposedly a master in every single martial arts you can name. Judo, *bo jitsu,* kung fu, and so on."

"That's not all," Kurtzman said. "Three separate Seattle police reports over the past two years, buried so deep, Akira stumbled over them by accident when he did some fishing on anything that might shed some light on any illicit or illegal activities that would sully his rep. Seems Mr. Walker likes to walk the city streets at nights, alone, flashing money…"

"I got that part," Lyons said. "Three muggers killed by his fists and feet of fury, two crippled so bad they'll never walk again. Ask me, this guy's been watching too many Charles Bronson *Death Wish* flicks."

"He's the real thing. Only he does his killing and maiming with empty hands," Price pointed out. "Pretty much why the police wrote the incidents off as self-defense, cases and lawsuits later filed by the unfortunate recipients of those hard lessons thrown out. We read him as dangerous, perhaps sociopathic. Single, but no playboy lifestyle, he has all the money in the world to buy into any grand Machiavellian schemes, or buy his way out of a jam."

"My people had a line on Ruskavka," Brognola said, "in Moscow. Two years, working side by side with the FBI on organized crime. Wiretaps, surveillance, the whole nine yards. Ruskavka's into black-market weapons of mass destruction when he's not shipping heroin all over the planet. When he came to America some months back we were all over him. Seems he likes the Western way of life more than his dacha. It's more pleasure than business with the guy, the flip side of Walker. You've got the whole rundown on the who and where in Seattle, Carl. I want you and Able out of here in five minutes and on your way after I fill you in on a few more particulars."

"But why Walker?" Lyons asked. "And if there is some connection between a Spetsnaz black ops to sabotage the Spectron Oil Reserve and the Russian Mafia, what does it gain any of them to blow up the place? They're on the verge of starting a world war, or at best, a dirty little covert war, which, the way I'm reading it, the President wants the guilty parties crushed ASAP and this whole ugly mess kept out of the press."

"The answers to a lot of our questions, my friend," Brognola said, "is why you and Able are going to Seattle. My rumbling gut warns me this nightmare hasn't even begun."

"HEY, OLD MAN, you want to join us, or maybe you need help carrying that bag? What gives? You want to bless the ground or something? You lose something?"

Lyons bobbed his head, cocked a grin at the comedian in question. Schwarz was standing in the fuselage doorway of the Bell JetRanger, grinning back. "I got your old man right here," he said, but skipped past the urge to give himself a squeeze, then hopped up into the chopper. He dumped his war bag on the floor, Schwarz shutting the door behind him. Lyons glanced at Blancanales, sitting there, giving him just the kind of look—reading—he ignored. He shot the blacksuit pilots the thumbs-up, said, "Let's hit it. What are you waiting for?"

"So, how do you want play this, Carl?"

Blancanales and Schwarz had lugged two war bags apiece. Lyons figured surveillance equipment and high-tech gizmos were stuffed into a couple of them. Schwarz was already delving inside, detailing the list.

Lyons plopped down in a seat as the chopper lifted off. "We hit Seattle, and we'll just be our usual nice and diplomatic selves."

"Oh, shit, I know that look, I know that tone," Blancanales said, but sported a grim smile. "I hear the doors crashing in already."

"You got that right," Lyons said.

"Okay, so what's the plan?" Schwarz asked, claiming a seat opposite Lyons and Blancanales. "I'm thinking I wasted all my time with Cowboy, picking and choosing the best surveillance and countersurveillance gear this side of God's watching eyes."

Lyons felt as grim as hell. He squeezed his eyes shut, pinching the bridge of his nose. "Give a minute here, guys. Then we'll brainstorm."

He could feel them, watching him, then looking at each other, wondering what the hell, no doubt. Even Carl Lyons, he knew, had his limits. And he'd had enough of the bad guys winning the big ones lately, a bellyful, in fact.

It was time to strike back, like nothing they'd ever done or known before.

God help the animals, he thought. They were going hunting. God might have mercy on their black souls, but he sure as hell wouldn't.

No way, no mercy.

And make no mistake, they weren't taking any prisoners on this one.

CHAPTER TWO

Max Walker believed he had seen the future, and it had come to pass, before his very eyes, live and in color that fateful day when not only had the entire country been changed, but the whole world had stepped into the perilous dawn of a new age. With any luck at all, he figured he would someday be the man of the hour to turn it all back around, steer the world on a new course he and a few fortunate ones he deemed worthy enough to conquer and divide, put it all back on track, break the backs of the new faceless enemies of America—Islam, specifically—bring them to their knees, stake claim to their oil-rich sands. As a warrior, he knew it would take more than good fortune, though, to become the sole heir and lord and master of the fossil-fuel world. It would take nerves of steel, balls of iron, the willingness to shed rivers of blood and, of course, weapons of mass destruction.

Stripped down to black skivvies, he went through his workout on the punching bags, a whirling dervish, high off his feet, coming around and slamming the heel of his foot deep into the painted-on yellow happy face. He imagined that face belonging to one of several low-life punks he crushed to blubbering pulp with his bare hands and feet way back when, going down on their knees, the street punk grabbing himself. No sneak attack, son, he thought. He was a human cruise missile, moving on, two other punching bags—each with a thug wielding a gun or a knife, one white, one black punk, snarling out the mindless rage of the street animal who cared for nothing but his own pleasure through addictions and whatever money he could steal to feed his tawdry existence—he flew into a series of backhand hammer-fists, knife-edged hands to their throats, straight kicks to the gut, upper hands to the family jewels. Take that, he thought. Have a nice day. It damn near reminded him, the only son of an ex-Marine, of how many times he would have liked nothing else but to have stomped the old late and unlamented colonel for all the belts and backhands he'd endured, all the tired old "he'd never amount to rat shit" forever clogging up the memory banks.

Well, that was then, the puny, cringing kid who used to write poetry and while away the days reading comic books was long since dead and gone, and there was a new Max Walker in town, coming of age, on his own terms, kicking ass, corporate and beyond.

In his mind, going back to those beautiful encounters where he clearly separated the men from the boys, the human from the inhuman, he heard them gurgle on their own bloody froth, gagging for air that would never come, lungs sucking in nothing but crimson spittle as the life slowly and in horrific pain drained out of them. He was pumped, fueled on the images of past glory, when he'd done his part to sweep the streets clean of predators, while shaping and fashioning the god he now was in his own image. Of course, he had sought them out, late-night jaunts, a lone white man in a two-thousand-dollar suit, twenty grand worth of Rolex watch in plain view, a wad of cash big enough to choke a horse clearly obvious for what it was as he fell into the role of a frightened executive geek, lost somehow on the wrong side of the tracks and looking to find his way out of the urban jungle as he scurried past the dregs.

An act.

A damn good one, the punks, he recalled, always thinking they had an easy mark, coralling him in some dark alley, pulling a blade or a gun, then dancing to a different tune, especially when they found their balls driven up into their throats or a knee shattered.

He was working up a good sweat, concentrating on his breathing, controlling the swift rhythm of his thrusts, chops and kicks, nothing but a blur in the running mirror of the dojo in the corner of his eye, checking himself out on the sly as bags thudded and the images of punkish agony kept on inflaming and fueling him to greater heights.

"Clap now or later?"

"Up yours."

He was rudely interrupted, the big, beefy ex-homicide detective, Donald Rankin, waddling into the dojo, a cigarette jammed into his yap. The closer the man came, the stronger the stink of whiskey on his breath. Sure, he had called the meeting, and sure, he needed the ex-cop and his pals to keep tabs on any potential enemies, using all their former contacts and connections in the department, on the street, to watch his six. The problem was, he wasn't exactly dealing with the best or the brightest, or these guys would still be on the force.

Walker stopped after a few more spinning kicks, sucked in slow, deep breaths, snapped up a towel off the polished teak floor.

Rankin was grinning at the swinging bags with their painted thugs. "Nice to know you're an equal-opportunity kind of guy. Man in your position, I guess being called racist could be a major hemorrhoid. The doo-rag and the baseball cap screwed on backward are nice touches, but they could give you away, only I don't think Al Sharpton or Jesse will be stopping by to say hello anytime soon."

"I called you here to discuss a little more than political correctness."

Walker led the man out of the dojo, into his office suite, where he took bottled water from the fridge behind the wet bar. "Smells like you need a drink, Donny. Help yourself. I gave the bartender the day off."

"Don't mind if I do."

"A suggestion, my friend. In the coming days, lay off the booze. I don't care what your demons, I need clear heads and focus. You can pass that down the ranks."

Rankin, though, poured himself a glass of straight whiskey, a few cubes, no mixer. "Here's to the future."

And there, Walker thought, pacing around the suite, sipping his bottled water, was part of the problem with America, why he'd long ago seen the future, could have told them all "I told you so." He'd been in a lot of countries, Russia most of the time he was abroad, where people were hungry, angry, poor and sick and tired. Hunger of the soul, he knew, fed an angry pride, could drive a man to greater heights, want more, be more, grateful as all hell when he finally earned his bones, not looking back, but no way ready to lose what he'd sweated his balls off for, even shed some blood to get. The problem with America, the way he saw it, was the country had grown soft, complacent.

The Russians had some of the toughest SOB commandos on the planet, and not even they could stop some of the terrorist attacks he knew had taken place over there—and he had to hand it to the Russians, forever keeping the real ugly stuff Islamic terrorists had done to them under the rug, the world at large never knowing about a few of the more insidious attacks perpetrated by the fundamentalists. It was time for the world, especially America, to wake up and smell the running blood and burning bodies. The future had arrived, and in some respects he compared his own meteoric rise to the top of the industrial heap like a terrorist blitz.

Way back when, as a midlevel engineer and petro explorer for Exxon, there was no way he was going to stand by and let life and all its glories escape, squander his years in suburban purgatory and watch the brass ring swing past, wondering where it had all gone before he had time to think about it, staring at his own shriveled sac fifty years down the road. He had the heart and soul of a lion, and lions didn't go out with a whimper.

Enter blackmail, the sort of pictures the oil-baron hierarchy wouldn't want the wife to see, grooming his own little circle of high-paid leg show back then to seal certain fates. Grease a few politicians, oil the oil barons, break a few skulls here and there, just to let the old guys know he was moving on up. Enter Walker Steel, erected from the plains of middle Ohio. Some Russian Mafia financing never hurt, either, especially when he needed his own armada of seagoing vessels, parked in Elliott Bay, planes, both transport and private to help haul men and matériel to oil reserves the globe over. Yes, he had seen the future, and the big stakes of tomorrow were up for grabs—energy, specifically fossil fuel—who, where and how much that final winner controlled.

He wasn't on top yet, but he could see blue sky above, getting closer by the day—Exxon and Shell cronies in his blackmail grasp, and a few military and political types, friends of friends who had pals close to the President, landing him the contract to put him on the map near Prudhoe Bay.

"There's going to be trouble in the coming days," Walker said. "FBI, Justice, CIA, NSA, who knows. The Department of Energy had contracted my company to build and supply the engineer and scientific brains for an oil field that was attacked. So we can expect an investigation to be heading in our direction. The thing is, I may or may not have to take a trip north to find out for myself if there are any loose tongues flapping all over the place. Now, as head of my security, I expect you to keep a close watch on my office building here, my home, my condo, my warehouses…."

"I've got the picture, Max."

"I don't think you do, or you wouldn't be standing there sucking down my booze, polluting my air with cigarette smoke and acting as if nothing's different. If what I think may happen does happen, this will be no day at the beach."

Rankin scowled over his glass, killed the drink poured another. "You just naturally paranoid, or do you come by all this war talk from some source I don't know about? Maybe your Russian gangster buddies should vacate town for a while, since any heat headed this way could be their doing. You don't think the FBI doesn't know who and what they are?"

"Forget them. My Russian friends and me are partners in something I don't need or have the time to tell you about. However, should the need arise for their security detail and yours to join forces…"

"One big happy family."

"Then we understand each other."

"That it?"

"For now. Stay close. Pass the word."

"We on war footing?"

"We're on notice."

"Mind if I grab some lunch before I brief the troops?"

"After you pass the word. Then you can drive me to an early dinner."

"Keeping tabs on me?"

"We need to discuss security in greater detail."

"No problem. I'll call when I'm back in the neighborhood."

Walker ignored Rankin's grim eyeballing, moved to his desk. He was grateful when the ex-cop was gone, the air no longer fouled by poisonous fumes. He needed time alone to think, plan future conquests.

Someday the world, or the fossil-fuel part of it, would belong to him. Alaska first, then, with the backing of some weapons of mass destruction from his Russian *mafiya* comrades, who knew? If OPEC didn't play ball, there was a chance, beyond nuke, chem or bio blackmail, he might just lay waste to the whole region, nothing but death and irradiated sand. What he couldn't have, no one would, either.

LANDLOCKED Afghanistan, and its surrounding neighbors, Pakistan to the south, and from west to east to the north Turkmenistan, Uzbekistan and Tajikistan—and Brognola wasn't about to forget China on the far eastern tip—were framed on the large wall monitor as the big Fed strode into the Computer Room. He asked Price for a quick explanation of the colored blocks on Afghanistan and Pakistan.

"Yellow are the known tribal areas and terrorist camps. Renegade Taliban, their Pashtun rebel sympathizers in the northern frontier, other known militant extremists pegged down by intelligence. Red are the refugee camps. Blue are our own CIA-Special Forces Eagle Bases near the border with Afghanistan. As you know, India has long since agreed to let us use bases inside their border."

"So I see," Brognola said. "Anybody care to tell me why we haven't heard from Striker or Phoenix yet?"

Kurtzman looked away from his computer monitor, sat imagery of what Brognola believed were terrorist camps on the screen, and said, "Too early, Hal."

"How the hell can it be too early? They landed more than a day ago in Pakistan."

"Details, some legwork and some changes," Kurtzman said.

"What changes?"

Akira Tokaido called out from his own workstation, "There have been a few developments in the past twenty-four hours, Hal."

"What developments, and why am I only hearing about it just now? The way you say that, I'm thinking I'm not going to like it."

"You're not."

Huntington "Hunt" Wethers, the tall, black former professor of cybernetics at Berkeley, wheeled around in his chair as grim as hell and went on to explain. "First, there's the refugee problem that's already thrown a wrinkle our troops' way."

"We already knew that going in."

"We've been trying to sort through it, or simply wait it out until we hear from Striker or Phoenix with breaking news. The Pakistanis," Wethers said, "have long since been worried about the Taliban slipping terrorists in with the refugees, flooding their country with suicide bombers, creating a whole new killing field in a country that's still pretty much straddling the fence with us."

"We knew that when this thing started."

"There was a cell rooted out this morning by the Pakistani ISI in Karachi," Wethers said.

"Three of them, Afghan refugees, loyal members of al-Qaeda blew themselves up," Tokaido said, "when the ISI went crashing through the door of their apartment. The reports we intercepted from the CIA station chief say the blast took out half the block, dozens dead, they haven't even counted up the wounded yet."

"You're saying there's more Taliban or al-Qaeda thugs where they came from? And now maybe the Pakistanis are having serious second thoughts about our people staking out black-ops bases over there."

"On top of that, you have widespread riots and anti-American demonstrations," Price said, "from Islamabad to Karachi, getting more violent by the day. Only three countries have ever officially recognized the Taliban government—Saudi Arabia, the UAE and Pakistan. That's changed. As time goes by the rest of the Islamic world appears to be more and more outraged that the Taliban was overthrown, pissed off about Iraq, calling for more attacks on U.S. soil or against our own overseas. What I'm saying, Hal, is that it may be even harder for Striker and Phoenix to move about the country, much less cross the Khyber Pass and go headhunting for mullahs or the big catch of the day. The whole march in and out, they'll be dealing with extremists, on top of bandits, rebels, marauders, war- and drug-lords in some of the worst and most hostile country on the planet."

Brognola felt his stomach churning. This one, he knew, hadn't even begun to get ugly. The so-called new war, coined by the talking heads on cable, he thought, most of whom wouldn't know a SCUD missile from a Sidewinder, was hardly anything new for the Sensitive Operations Group. It might make all of their jobs a little less worrisome when it came to deniability, what with the ban on assassinations of enemies of the country's national security lifted, but in the end it was hardly any easier.

Truth was, the covert war against terrorists was a

meaner, nastier business than ever, the stakes higher as the body count mounted on both sides. And part of the problem now was that every muck-a-muck journalist was traipsing all over Pakistan and Afghanistan, bringing this new dirty war, live and in color to American living rooms, looking to put their names in lights, grab some awards. Brognola dreaded the thought of Bolan or Phoenix Force being exposed, their faces plastered all over CNN, feared that day could come sooner rather than later, as some gonzo reporter infiltrated one of the covert bases, maybe tracking the warriors back to the Farm and uncovering what they really did. Why worry about something that hadn't happened, though? There were problems enough to keep his stomach rumbling for days, maybe weeks or months to come.

"So spell it out. New mission parameters, what?"

"We're sticking to the original game plan, but with some minor alterations, depending on what happens in the coming hours," Price said. "Phoenix is hooked up with a Special Forces operation here, at Eagle Base," she went on, taking a rolling-ball clicker to outline the AIQ, due south of Peshawar. "Grimaldi is at the helm of one of the CIA's prototype gunships, all set to fly out at a moment's notice."

"What the Company calls the Predator," Kurtzman said, and held out a computer printout, which Brognola went and took and examined.

"Looks like an Apache."

"Looks like," Kurtzman said, "but it has a troop hold

for twenty. Pylons are fitted with six Hellfires, 20 mm chain gun in the nose turret, and a Vulcan Gatling cannon can be mounted and fired from the fuselage. Besides six of those monsters, our guys are planning on going in behind two Spectre gunships, a squad of F-15Es and a B-52."

"More scorched earth on the camps."

"The problem is, Hal," Price said, "as soon as we hit them with a blanket of death from above, they build the camps somewhere else, keep burrowing deeper in the mountains. The Taliban has shifted a lot of their operations from southern Afghanistan to the mountains east of Kabul."

"No bin Laden sightings," Kurtzman said. "But are we surprised? And anyone over there old enough to pick up a weapon is being recruited by both the Taliban and al-Qaeda."

"The Taliban gave us the middle finger way before this all started," Brognola said. "But I think you're about to tell me the Taliban is getting a whole lot of Pakistani sympathy, and they're mounting counteroffensives through the Khyber."

"Exactly," Price said, "which is why Striker originally veered off the original operation to go and dig out any militant conspirators in Karachi first. Whether ISI, army or Taliban thugs, as you put it, who are currently guests of honor of Pakistani sympathizers."

"Root out the vipers first, I understand, find out which Pakistani operatives we can or can't trust. But we have the more pressing problem of high-tech state-of-the-art equipment, and weapons of mass destruction getting funneled from this so-called pharmaceutical company out in the boondocks of the Punjab to the Taliban, who is allegedly selling heroin to the Russian Mafia to finance their war. What's the latest on that?"

Kurtzman shook his head. "If the Taliban is receiving weapons and equipment from the Pakistani army, many of whom, we all know, actually helped to create the Taliban after the Russians went through their own Vietnam—"

"Courtesy, though, Bear, with a lot of help from the friendly spooks at the CIA," Tokaido cut in. "The CIA actually created the Taliban in the first place, something like a billion dollars alone, then you had who only knows how many Stingers, light and heavy hardware dumped off in their laps during the Russian fiasco."

Kurtzman frowned. "Courtesy of the CIA, we don't know really who's doing what. That's Striker's job, or one of them. Worst-case scenario, God forbid, is that some Pakistani sympathizer high up the intelligence or military chain of command somehow gets a nuke to the Taliban. Suitcase variety, or something that can be fitted onto a SCUD, or fired from an artillery cannon."

"Hunt and I are monitoring this supposed pharmaceutical company through a number of satellites that have been parked over that part of the world for some time," Tokaido said.

"We are also in the process," Wethers said, "of working up virtual reality or 3-D digital maps of all AIQS. Pinning it down, from what's where to the number of shooters our guys will be facing."

"I want those ASAP," Brognola said. "And if we don't hear from Striker or Phoenix in six hours, I want them raised for a sitrep. They have vibrating receivers, right, in case they're in a jam, can't talk and know to call back?"

"That they do," Price confirmed.

Brognola grunted, acid from tension squirting around in his gut, but he helped himself to some of Kurtzman's evil caffeine swill anyway. "Incredible. The Russians, our supposed allies, blowing up an oil reserve, absconding with American scientists, and now we're finding out the Russian Mafia is actually financing a Taliban counteroffensive with drug money."

"Afghanistan is the third-poorest country in the world," Tokaido pointed out. "The Russians left that country in utter ruins. They're still finding land mines all over the country, kids blowing themselves up by the scads on a daily basis, something like maybe eighteen, count them, eighteen million land mines still believed unaccounted for. The whole infrastructure of the country isn't even Stone Age. Their only export besides terrorism is hashish and heroin. They're the largest growers of poppies in the world, surpassing even Myanmar. There are something like sixty labs in the southeast and east where the opium gum is refined, then shipped to Turkey, although most of it is transported to Moscow by the Russian military."

"What are you saying?" Brognola asked.

"Maybe while our guys are over there…"

"Kill a few more vultures while they're at it," Kurtzman finished.

"That's a thought. Pass it on whenever we hear from our guys. What's the story on these Russian hunter-killer subs?"

Kurtzman shook his head. "Nothing new. But we're narrowing down a region in the North Pole we think they might dock. Likewise, we're monitoring the Chukchi Peninsula where the CIA believe they were built and bunked."

"Keep on it. Also, I want a background check on this Carl Rutgen. You might want to start by following the money."

"The head of security at Spectron?" Tokaido said. "The sole survivor of the armed detail?"

"Yeah, that guy. Bet your ass, I want to know why he managed to walk away unscathed when everybody else with a piece did all the dying. Lyons caught a whiff from up there, and if the Russians had inside help, Able Team may have to make a trip to Alaska."

Brognola left them to it. He needed to touch base with the Man anyway back in the War Room, and it could be hours before there were any breaking developments. Waiting was always the hardest part, he knew, before the hammer of war dropped, and he could damn well count on a few more surprises along the way.

One thing he was sure of, and it swelled the big Fed

with confidence—there was still hope for a better to-morrow. When the Stony Man warriors launched this one, an all-out assault against the enemies of America and whoever supported them, heads would roll, nothing less than a virtual conveyor belt of slaughter.

THE ABLE TEAM COMMANDOS were gathered at the bolted-down war table in the cabin of their Gulfstream jet. They were now well on their way to Seattle, having used the time wisely, boning up on intel, the packets complete with pictures, background of all key players, their hangouts and hideouts mapped out in sat imagery and ground surveillance provided by Brognola's Justice team. Lyons's foreboding silence was starting to tweak their nerves, just the same, and Blancanales glanced at Schwarz, who kept glancing at Lyons, silently urging him to speak.

"Hey, knock it off with the worried eyes, guys, I'm fine. And, yes, I'm under control, Pol. I can almost hear your thoughts, wanting to know what the hell's eating me." Lyons looked at Schwarz and Blancanales. "You want the truth? Can you handle the truth?" he barked.

"We're all ears, Carl," Gadgets said.

"Okay, here it is. Dirty cops make up the bulk of Walker's security force. Then throw in a few military types, a dishonorable discharge here and there, a couple of spook types with black ops to their credit, or discredit, depending on how much collateral damage they might have inflicted on the natives. I hate dirty cops.

They're less than some child molester in my eyes. They wear the badge, but they're a disgrace to the uniform. Reading all this," he growled, nodding at the pictures and dossiers, "you've got excessive force, you've got a few of them did time for drug dealing, murder and God only knows how much other crap they got away with. I rank them right there with the Russian Mafia our boy Walker is doing business with. I want answers, and I want payback. I'm pulling no punches. Copy?"

Blancanales nodded, saw Gadgets grinning, ready to crack wise, Oh, God, Pol thought, here we go. Gadgets just couldn't let sleeping lions lay.

"So, what's the problem, big guy?" Schwarz asked, still grinning. "I never knew us to be the diplomatic suck-ups you so eloquently in your people-loving way pointed out earlier."

"No problem, smart guy. I just want you guys to understand once we hit Seattle we go hard, all the way, all the time. As soon as we finish chewing the fat here, I'm on the blower to our Justice contact out in Seattle. I want Walker found and watched, ditto for the dirty cops, this Ruskavka scum sucker. I want them to do everything short of walking up to them and painting a bull's-eye on their backs. Then I'm pulling off all Justice Department detail. It's our show, our war to win. This Walker is dirty. Somehow he climbed to the top, and all of us can read between the lines, wondering how the hell he set himself up as the oil-and-steel magnate of the millennium. He has goals, bad ones, I'm sure. He's history, and

I'm turning the heat up on his black-belt ass as soon as I lay eyes on him. We clear?"

Blancanales nodded. "Sounds like a program."

"Damn straight."

So there it was, Blancanales thought. He felt a little easier, but not by much.

God help the bad guys, he knew, once they deplaned. The bloodbath was on the way, and someone was going to drown in it. They just had to make sure the right—or the wrong ones—did all the drowning.

CHAPTER THREE

Vertigo International, the banner name for Max Walker's petro-and-steel conglomerate, was his show, start to curtain call, no problem there, but Don Rankin would be damned if he played second string to Russian gangsters, much less find himself relegated to gofer and chauffeur duty. Playing lackey, he thought, was for some other clown, not the last bona fide, tough-guy dinosaur on the planet. Hell, he could just see it now, Walker forcing him to suck up to the Don, drive him around town, ring up some call girls, show the Russkies a grand old time while they talked their machine-gun-fire potato talk, probably poking fun at him in their own tongue, making him hold back and wait around for them to wrap up some orgy on his clock while they rolled in the hay with American women.

The problem was, no matter what the future held or whatever dirty gig in the wings, Rankin knew he was stuck, forced to do whatever Walker's bidding, and, no, he didn't have to like it—just do it. Take the money and run, then. No big deal—it was the cash he was in it for anyway. If there was life after Walker, so be it. Then again, he knew it was pretty tough for an ex-cop-ex-felon to find work—of the honest variety, at least—in this town. Seattle, a city of not only steep hills and surrounded by water, considered itself one of the more progressive and so-called politically correct cities in the country. It was a town of lumber, fisheries, high-tech aerospace engineering, not to mention the trendsetter for the next generation of wannabe rock n' rollers. Getting work, then…

Well, he didn't fit, never had, not even as a cop. His reputation as a headbreaking so-called dirty cop had preceded him, one reason why he'd pulled a ten-year stint in the big house for assault with intent, bribery and extortion, to name the shortlist of dirty deeds they knew about. He was a known and infamous figure about Seattle, at least, he thought, in the eyes of the D.A., press and every yuppie scumbag and ACLU whine-baller from Elliott Bay to Vancouver. He'd seen his face, career and misdeeds the object of microscopic public scrutiny and vicious pundit critique right before the big fall came, the gavel pounded and he was marched off to do time, stripped of pension, but that was only the least of his worries back then.

On that score, doing hard time, at least his overpaid cheese-bag lawyer had earned enough of his $450-an-hour fee to see he was placed in isolation, since cons generally took out a whole lot of anger—among other nastier and more horrifying scenarios, and he knew there were some fates worse than death—on cops gone bad who found themselves among the general population, fallen angels dropped among the jackals. Being an ex-felon wasn't that big a hassle, actually, almost like a badge of honor the way he saw it, one of the last stand up acts in a society rapidly spiraling out of control, where it was a free-for-all, grab-ass money game out there anyway.

It strengthened his jaded view of the world knowing he had a few former brothers in blue—like-minded fellows—on the security detail who'd done time for extortion, drug-dealing, murder and so on, even a few of the Army guys DDed for various and sundry crimes, usually against a commanding officer, too much testosterone build-up from soldiers, he figured, who didn't respect Colonel Asshole to lead that charge for the hill to begin with. Well, when he spoke, guys under his command had better listen or start looking for work and a new set of teeth. And he had to believe that Walker, a strange dude to say the least, sort of liked his renegade types, guys out there on the edge, desperate and angry, nothing left to lose, which, in and of itself, could pose a whole other slew of headaches. He had to wonder about Walker, just the same, never seeing the man with a woman, not doing much by way of business, either, unless he was holding counsel or the hands of

Russian mobsters. Well, if Max was "that way," hiding sexual skeletons in the closet, that was his business, as long as the cash kept flowing and Don Rankin remained a free man.

It was a strange world, after all, and Rankin figured a year or two more of this nonsense and he could give old Max the kiss-off, retire with a decent nest egg, fly off to Hawaii maybe.

He had just dropped off Walker, then parked the sedan in an underground garage up Madison, a block or so from the Nippon Kan Theater. Walker was getting so paranoid these days that he even insisted Rankin leave behind a couple of the security troops to watch the car. What was he expecting? Ruskavka pulling something treacherous, planting a bomb under the chassis?

Among other things, Seattle was famous for its seafood, but he saw the well-heeled crowd of happy-hour diners was going pretty much for the steak and prime rib and shrimp special. He scowled around as a few suits, guys he figured had never seen a tough day in their lives other than the batteries on their cell phones dying, looked set to sniff the air, wondering what a big, beefy bruiser in a cheap suit jacket—but packing a Glock 17 in shoulder rigging, ladies and gents—was doing lumbering through the dining room, blowing cigarette smoke over their heads, eyeing their women.

He was passing the bar when he heard, "Hey, pal, this is a nonsmoking restaurant."

The skinny bartender in a red frizz-doo, a wanna-be

grunge rocker, he figured, looked as if he wanted to go on the muscle. "I'm with Max Walker," Rankin said, as if that would make everything all right, the red-carpet treatment about to unfurl.

"I don't care if you're with the Pope—lose the smoke."

"Sure thing, kid." Rankin bobbed his head, grinning, found some guy or gal had abandoned a glass of beer to go to the can most likely, and dumped the butt in the foamy brew.

Chuckling, Rankin walked on, Frizzy muttering something, then spotted their table in the back and nearly choked on his own confusion and paranoia. He had been led to believe this was a private powwow to go over security matters, but the Russian Don was sitting up high in the booth, chowing down on a slab of prime rib the size of an elephant's head, licking his fingers. What the hell was this? Was this where the East West alliance got cozy over dinner? Not only that, another table was jammed with four of Ruskavka's henchmen, he saw, all of them clearly packing beneath their suits, tac radios within easy reach, as if they were FBI instead of murderous muscle, the Ivans gorging on a smorgasbord of appetizers, lobster, striploin, calamari, stuffed shrimp, the whole nine yards of fine dining, everything but the dancing girls and the violinist. He tried to keep the distaste off his face, aware Walker, dining on his usual salad sans dressing but with a plate of mussels by his side, was watching him. Walker, he knew, had called ahead to place his own order, a big shot here, always schmoozing the owner and, of course, not bothering, Rankin had noted, to ask him what he wanted to eat.

He wished he'd stopped at the bar for a quick belt or two, but settled in the booth, next to Ruskavka, looking around for a waiter.

"You're not staying, so don't bother to order your usual twenty drinks."

Walker again, getting attitude. "What's the story?"

"We're packing up," Walker said. "I want two jets, fueled and ready to fly out by tomorrow morning. Make the arrangements—you have the number for our pilots."

"Any place special in mind?"

"Alaska."

"Some problem I need to know about?"

"We need to check on a few people up that way, shore up some details about the future with some of our operatives in place, but I thought I already hinted we might have loose lips."

"You did, yeah, but this is all a little sudden."

"Some last-minute business I need to deal with at my home here in Seattle," Ruskavaka said, "calls, and so on, then we'll all be flying out together. I suggest you pack something warm to wear. Some business transactions need my attention, but that doesn't concern you. I will introduce you to my own security team when I'm finished eating, so everyone can become good comrades in the spirit of mutual cooperation."

"I get the feeling I'm being left in the dark, that you guys know something serious is up. What is it? FBI?

Justice Department? I'm feeling heat all of a sudden, I got an itch between my shoulder blades. I mean, hey, if I'm going to watch your backs, I need a little nibble of the menu on what sharks may or may not be swimming our way."

Out of the corner of his eye, Rankin saw the Russian mobsters look up, fidget, forks poised halfway to their mouths, frozen in their seats. He'd been a cop long enough to know when trouble was spotted, heading his way. He was turning, following Walker's dark look when a big guy in a black windbreaker materialized by the table, thrusting out a thin wallet with official-looking credentials.

"Chet Lemon, special agent with the United States Department of Justice. Sit tight, assholes, just shut up and listen. I don't like repeating myself."

"HOW ARE WE SUPPOSED to play this now, Pol? The way Ironman's jacked up right now, I don't think he'll take too kindly to us sitting here with our thumbs up our rears when he comes back and finds our mission not accomplished."

Schwarz watched the two shadows in the Lexus, angled down the garage at the far shadowy end, mentally marking them off by name and dirty deed as he matched them up to the intel package. For whatever reason the pair had been left behind, the big ex-cop-felon, Rankin, having said something to them before wandering for the stairwell of the parking garage. Up to then, the Justice Department stakeout had done an outstanding job, shadowing the Russian Don, his four goons, Walker, Rankin and company here, putting Able Team right on the scent, not a beat missed. The trouble, Schwarz suspected, was the enemy knew they were made, maybe marked for bagging.

Only after listening to the wrath of Lyons, Schwarz knew the only bagging would be the toe-tagging, zipped-up-rubber kind. Not only that, but between Walker's security detail and the Russian Mob squad, the three of them were looking at close to thirty-five shooters, maybe more if there was backup in town. In that regard, they'd come loaded for bear. Everything from side arms to M-16 M-203 combos, MP-5 subguns, SPAS-12 autoshotgun, down to a mixed bag of grenades to Pol's favored Little Bulldozer multiround projectile launcher. Firepower wasn't the problem, nor cover if it came down to flashing around their bogus Justice credentials to cops who might not take kindly to them shooting up the streets of Seattle.

The black Justice Department surveillance van probably didn't aid their cause, either, the enemy surely making it for what it was, paranoid and cautious to a fault, enough antennae on the vehicle to bristle like a huge fat porcupine. But Schwarz liked the high-tech setup in the back, just the same. The minicam on the roof could monitor and record the movements of their enemies, while a miniparabolic mike fixed in the lights on the starboard side could listen in on conversations on the street, the bank of screens just behind Schwarz, who had claimed the shotgun seat. There were wiretapping gizmos, and other surveillance and countersurveillance gear in the back, but the only high-tech finesse Lyons had ordered for the moment was for Schwarz to fix a magnetic transponder to the fender of Walker's sedan. Once done, it would beam a signal to an NRO satellite, via the Farm, bounce it back to a GPS monitor Schwarz had set up in the rear.

The problem was the goons, parked three slots up from the sedan, watching the store, looking edgy, mean.

"We don't have much time before Lyons gets back," Pol said. "But I think I have an idea. Since Carl came here to start a war, why not get it started with a bang?"

"How come I don't like the sound of that? How come I think Ironman's bulldog ways have contaminated the Politician?"

Pol grinned. "Well, if Carl can brazenly stroll right up to Walker and the Russian Mob and announce our presence and our intentions, I think we can help stir up the hornet's nest on this end, see what runs or comes out shooting. Here it is."

And Schwarz listened, grinned, thinking if ballsy down-their-gullets was the way Lyons wanted the action, what Blancanales suggested certainly ranked as an Ironman scenario.

LYONS PUT ON his best menacing face, holding up his credentials. He finally snapped the wallet shut in Walker's eyes, then dumped the packet in the pocket of his windbreaker. A glance over his shoulder, and he told the Russian goons, "Any sudden moves, girls, and you'll be sucking *blini* and caviar out of a straw for the next few months, the only vodka you can get down coming out of a tube in your arms."

"Is there a point to all this, or are you just showing off for the crowd?"

Lyons shot Walker a wicked grin. "You bet your skinny little black belt ass there's a point, Mr. Cool. You're on notice, and me and mine are on war footing. I know all about you and your Russian cronies, how maybe you somehow engineered the attack on the Spectron Oil Reserve, using a hunter-killer sub your buddy's countrymen here coined Shark class," he said. He spotted the slightest flicker in Walker's eyes, knowing he was close to pushing panic buttons all around. "I don't have all the facts yet, but I'll get them, even if it means spilling some Russian Mob blood.

"The thing I don't understand is why kidnap a bunch of American scientists? Don't you clowns in Moscow," he said to Ruskavka, "have that kind of technical expertise? Oh, that's right, your country's broke, everyone's out of work, the only guys turning a buck are Russian *mafiya* scumbags like you.

"And you, asshole," Lyons told Rankin, "I can't stomach the sight of dirty cops. You're lower than snail shit. You and your wanna-be Dirty Harrys are all going down, Rankin, and for the count. No court, no prison, don't you worry about getting tossed back in with all those guys whose rights you violated. Tonight, tomorrow, ten minutes from now, I'll choose the time and place. You won't know when it's coming, but as of this second, I have just declared war. Vertigo International, the Ruskavka Family and Dirty Harry here, eat, drink and be merry, this is your last supper."

"Is this supposed be some elaborate warning, a threat, intimidation?" Ruskavka asked. "Do you honestly think any of us know what you're even talking about?"

"I don't warn, threaten or intimidate, Russo baby. I act. The dumb routine, even for a fat ass like you, doesn't get it. Hey, that looks pretty good, Russo," Lyons suddenly said, eyeing the prime rib, reaching across the table and hauling up the slab of beef with his bare hand. He chomped, chewed, dipped his finger in the horseradish, carrying the barbarian routine to new heights as he ran the sauce all over the meat, licking his fingers, then handling the Don's dinner some more.

Ruskavka, Lyons was sure, was ready to burst with fury, fifteen shades of red crossing his face. Lyons was positive the Don would fly out of his seat next when he dumped the gnawed slab on the plate from five feet across and two up, splashing au jus over Ruskavka and company. Lyons didn't know much Russian, but he was pretty sure the Don wasn't inviting him to stay for dessert with the following outburst.

"Salad—rabbit food. I haven't had that in a while," Lyons said as he fisted a handful of leaves, shoved them in his mouth, chewed, made a face, then spit the lettuce back in the bowl. Walker was now the one who was about to blow up like a rocket. "No dressing? What the hell? I bet you eat quiche, too, all that black-belt biz just a front to cover up a small pair." Using the white linen tablecloth, Lyons wiped off his hands. For the final touch, he snapped up a napkin, made a big show of wiping his mouth, then tossed it on top of the mussels entrée. "Be seeing you."

And Lyons wheeled, ignored the faces of the watching crowd, waiters watching, stunned by the barbarian floor show. What happened next played straight into his game plan.

A quick look behind on the move, and he saw the goons rising, breaking away from the table, shoving a waiter to pursue him outside.

Show time.

The war was just about to start. Lyons could hardly wait. It was high time, way overdue, in fact, to let the bad guys start feeling the pain of all the innocents whose souls cried out for justice.

BLANACANALES STRODE straight for the Lexus, the dirty ex-cops on his dossier growing diamond-cutter stares, eyeballing him, head to toe, looking at him as if he were something they wanted to stomp. Just to keep them feeling uneasy, he let the mini-Uzi in special shoulder rigging hang free, jutting slightly from his windbreaker. Wheeler was the shotgun rider, Hopewell the wheelman. They had been part of what had been tagged by the Seattle media and talking heads on cable as the Seattle Seven. The scandal years ago was pretty much the same dirty crap that went down in L.A. Cops on the take, shaking down drug dealers, busting heads where they deemed necessary or suited their brutal nature. There were a couple of manslaughter raps on their jackets, and Blancanales could only guess at the amount of greasing the skids that went on behind the scenes or in the judge's chamber to see they did minimum time. Rankin had been the ringleader then, and he was back in charge of the savage horde once again.

Dirty, rotten bastards all. Now they were at it once more, eating the innocent, scheming wicked dreams.

Hopewell got antsy first, rolling down the window with the touch of an electronic button, digging inside his jacket.

Blancanales had out his bogus ID, growling as he rolled up to the driver's side, "I wouldn't."

Blancanales held the ID wallet in Hopewell's face. The idea was to block his view, Schwarz, he knew, having already fallen out to do the planting of the homing bug.

Hopewell grunted, made a face. "Rosario Blankenship. Ro-saw-rio. That doesn't sound American to me."

"As American as apple pie, baseball and *Baywatch,* asshole."

Now Hopewell looked as mean as a cobra on the rise, losing the cocky grin. "So, what's your problem? And that subgun doesn't look like anything the Justice Department would issue."

"My problem is former dirty cops who are now working the wrong side of the tracks again. My problem is the Russian Mafia holding hands with your boss, Walker, doing dirty deeds, looking to undermine the American way of life you and your boyfriend there spit on not that long ago. You went for yourselves then, but I guess the more something changes the more it stays the same." He malingered, mentally calculating Schwarz's play.

"You've got a big mouth."

"And you're in a world of hurt," Blancanales said. "Spread the good news. You're going out of business, permanently, and I'm not talking about a walk before the judge and some plea bargain with the D.A. Pass that up the chain of command. Walker's finished. So is the Ruskavka Family. End of story."

They didn't bother to deny it. Instead Wheeler sounded off with a sarcastic chuckle.

"You talk a tough game, Ro-saw-rio. I don't know what banana republic country you're originally from, but I'm thinking America's not going to prove to be 'bery bery' good to you."

The more he stood there, looking at them, the more Blancanales decided Ironman's way was the only way. These guys needed waxing, and not the leg kind, either.

"Stay close, we'll see each other again," Blancanales said. "And we'll see who and what's 'bery bery' good."

He was walking off, slow, trying to keep their line of sight blocked as long as possible, when one of them flung at his back, "Up yours, spic."

Normally that wouldn't faze Blancanales, the dirty ignorant bastards trying to goad him into something rash or even stupid. It didn't really now, even as hot rage swelled his gut. It only hardened his determination to get this war started in full blood earnest.

He saw Schwarz was already hopping back into the van. Good to go, the bad guys would get tracked. Claiming the wheel, he asked Gadgets, "I'm assuming you succeeded."

"You assume correct, even if you know what assume means."

"Ass of *u* and me."

"That would be it. Hey, what's the problem, Pol? You got that look like maybe you're skipping those anger-management classes with Carl again."

"These guys, all of them, need to go."

"I concur."

Blancanales keyed the ignition. "We'll go to the next level up, give them a little more rope. Find a space, back in and wait for them to roll out."

"You and Carl, you guys are starting to make nervous on this outing," Schwarz said, holding on to the dashboard as Blancanales gave it some gas and whipped out of the slot.

IF RANKIN HADN'T seen it with his own eyes, he wouldn't have believed it. The Russian was in a snit, barking out the orders in his native language, the goon squad up and moving. That he understood, the Russian bent out of shape, humiliated in front of Walker and his fellow Ivans, marching out the troops to maybe have an unkind word or two with the big blond guy. And if Chet Lemon, he thought, was G-man issue, or any Fed at all, then he was Mother Teresa.

It was the fear, the look of a cornered animal in the eyes of Walker that held his attention. Tough guy black belt, he thought, looked set to piss himself. Unbelievable, their fearless leader, looking scared and small, the sky falling. Then Walker pulled it together, only Rankin couldn't make it out since Max switched to Russian. Finally Rankin had had enough, growling, "You want to share that?"

Walker glanced his way, then said in English to Ruskavka, "You told them to do what?"

Ruskavka was flapping his arms, slapping at the mess on his silk suit, snarling in Russian.

"Hey, guys, you want to share with the rest of the class or should I take the night off?"

"He ordered his men to kill that Justice Department agent."

Rankin, under different circumstances, would have enjoyed, even raised a toast to himself, seeing Walker in a state of near panic. "That was no Fed, Max."

"I agree," Ruskavka said. "What I would like to know, 'Max,' is how that man knew so much about our business."

"How would I know? What are you saying?"

"I am saying war has been declared on us. I am saying you had better arm yourself with more than just your empty hands. They will not catch a bullet."

Walker, Rankin watched, seemed to weigh something, then nodded. "Okay, then it's time. We skip off to Alaska."

"Not so fast. I need to get to my home. I need to make some calls. I need important documents that I keep there."

"Okay, one stop, then we're out of Seattle."

"And me? I guess I go along for the ride?"

"You'll do more than that, Rankin. You'll earn all that money I pay you for a change."

Rankin bobbed his head, watching as Walker pulled out a wad of cash, slapped some hundreds on the table.

"We are at war, my American comrades. Understand that. And you and I, Max, or you, hinted trouble was coming."

"The way you say that, you make it sound like I had something to do with all this sudden gathering of storm clouds."

"Did you?"

"I'd tell you where to stick it, but I think we've all had enough shame dumped on our laps for one day. Rankin, call downstairs. I want your two men to be ready to blast our way out of the garage. If it's war these guys—whoever they really are—want, it's war they'll get."

Rankin smiled. "God, I love it when you talk that way."

"Skip the smart-ass routine. I saw the way you looked at me, wondering if I've got the real pair for this kind of action. Watch me work. I'm back, I'm ready. Let's get the hell out of here."

CHAPTER FOUR

Some days in recent memory it felt to Carl Lyons as if the whole world had gone crazy, or was poised to spin straight off its axis, all of it flying off into a maelstrom or some dark void of anarchy, the human race devouring itself in religious and ethnic hatred, riots from Indonesia to Karachi to Cincinnati breaking out if the masses didn't like the status quo and were hell-bent to commit suicide in some last raging stand against it all. Mass murder all over the map, guys wiping out their whole families, blowing their brains out or opting for suicide by cop. The threat of chemical and bioterrorism was simply a question of "when" anymore and not "if."

Who would stop the madness?

Given the state of world affairs these days, he often wondered where it was all headed, who had the answers, who would be there to stem the floodtide of evil reaching out its poison, consuming the innocent, slay-ing those people who didn't look or think the way they did or had the money and the power they lusted for or simply because—

At the moment he crushed down the nagging anger he found welling up in his soul, aware he had a full plate of trouble on his six and coming to eat him up, Russian sharks homed in on blood in the water.

His blood.

Still, there was, he knew, an answer, always had been, always would be.

A few good men was all it took to stand up, be counted, and face down evil. If or when that failed, all hope was lost.

No pessimist, doomsayer who saw Armageddon over the next horizon or—God help him sometimes—not one to turn the other cheek, Carl Lyons was damn glad he was still surrounded by the few good ones left standing to carry on the fight. In the end, if he thought about it hard enough, the only friends and family he had, ever would have, were the good people of Stony Man, all of them, cyber team, blacksuits on down through Gadgets and Pol and Striker and Phoenix Force.

Back to real time. He was moving swiftly down the mouth of the underground garage, grimly aware he'd have to shake and bake double-time to make the fourth level where his buddies were waiting, and God help them if they didn't come through with the planting of the homer, since he found himself getting worked up into a real foul mood. He didn't have to keep looking over his shoulder to know the four goons were on his tail—hell, he could damn near feel them, the warrior's mental radar for the bad guys blipping off the screen. Likewise he didn't need to hear any confession out of the mouths of Rankin, Walker or Ruskavka to know he had them pegged for what they were.

Human dog crap.

Lyons still had cop's eyes, and those eyes could still ferret out a bad guy, liar, traitor or worse when they were laser focused and peering into the soul.

He couldn't be sure where this engagement was headed, but those same cop's instincts warned him the Don had marched out the troops to do more than ask him to kindly pick up the check for ruining the boss man's dinner.

Which meant four on one, which meant he would probably need his good buddies of Able Team, and something in the way of firepower a little heavier than the .357 Magnum Colt Python in shoulder rigging.

He was rounding the concrete pillar, caught them stepping fast and hard down the entrance ramp, when he plucked the mini-tac radio out of his pocket and spoke in a harsh whisper, "Guys, talk to me."

"Carl, you sound stressed," Schwarz replied. "More so than usual."

"We've got a problem headed our way—can the comedy. Four Russian shooters. Look alive."

"We're on level three. We had a close encounter of the hostile kind ourselves."

Lyons gave the parking slots a hard search on the run, gathering momentum, ears tuned in now as he heard hard-soled shoes rapping concrete. So far they were clear of noncombatants, but if he read the goons right, they didn't strike him as the kind to fret and stew over collateral damage.

Schwarz filled him in quickly. "Pol took a page from the Ironman book on civility in the guise of psychological warfare."

"Cut the shit, Gadgets. Spell it out."

And Schwarz did. Lyons whipped around the next pillar, descending for the labyrinth of more shadows, parked cars, digging out the .357.

"You guys," he muttered.

"Hey, I thought you might be proud of Pol."

"If we make it out of here, I'll plant a big kiss on his mouth myself. Lock and load. Slide the van out near the exit ramp where they'll run. I want an intercept—cut loose on these SOBs when they try to beat feet. Oh, one more thing."

"This doesn't sound good."

"Get my SPAS-12 ready."

Lyons stowed the tac unit and darted past an oncoming SUV, the driver laying on the horn, nearly clipping him on the knees.

He hunkered down between a Mercedes and a Honda, sighted down the Colt Python. Shadows spread out from the pillar, four goons now on the fly, packed tight, searching.

"Freeze it up, scumbags!"

Mistake one.

Lyons saw that giving them the benefit of the doubt nearly cost him.

The Russians already had the hardware out and flaming.

RANKIN WAS LEADING the charge down the stairwell, Walker on his heels, the Russian Don having a little difficulty keeping up, breathing ragged and wheezing in the tight confines. He had the tac radio to his ear, ringing up Hopewell, when he heard the sound of weapons fire over the line. It wasn't on top of them, judging the rattling echo, which meant something had gone wrong on another level.

Which meant cops up top, shooting it out, most likely, with Russo's boys.

"Hopewell, we're on the way."

"We had a Justice Department flunky flexing some muscle few minutes ago."

"Where is he now?"

"Split. But I hear gunfire…."

"Yeah, so do I."

Walker suddenly snatched the unit out of Rankin's hand, and it was all the ex-cop could do to hold back his anger. It was crunch time, and Walker still wanted to throw out attitude.

"Listen up," Walker yelled. "You lead the way out of here. We follow. If possible, don't stop, but if anyone gets in your way shoot them, run them down, I don't care, but we're gone. We're heading for Bearhouse," he said, Rankin knowing the code name for the Don's posh beachfront digs north on Puget Sound. "Here!"

Rankin plucked the unit back, scowling, his Glock 17 out as he barreled through the door, sprinting for their sedan, Hopewell already in gear as the Lexus squealed on smoking rubber out of its slot.

LYONS WAS NEVER ONE to kick himself for thinking maybe he'd bitten off more than he could chew or maybe his ass had written a check his mouth couldn't cash.

Of course, there was a first time for everything, only he hoped that first time wasn't now.

The .357 was booming out the first of two hollow-points, Lyons crouched beside the back fender, aware if he didn't score four quick ones he was in danger of get-ting pinned down. Goons Number One and Two were poleaxed, slugs tunneling open their chests, blood and cloth flying, pistols cracking wild rounds into the ceiling.

He was sighting on Number Three when Four cut loose with a machine pistol, drumming the fender with a leadstorm that made Lyons flinch, pull back as hot steel sliced off metal. He was a warrior, but he wasn't suicidal. He got the speedloader ready, wished they were out in open real estate so he could measure down the direction from which the weapons fire came. Locked in under the roof and walls of the garage, the din was trapped, sounding as if it came from any and all directions. He went low, slugs rapping into the chassis and whining off concrete, and fired wild around the corner of the tire, squeezing the trigger until he ran dry.

Once in a while, a guy got lucky.

Lyons caught the sharp cry and burst of Russian cursing, knew he'd scored flesh. Whether or not another one had bit the dust...

Speedloader dumping six live ones home, he popped up, saw Number Three dragging Four for cover behind an SUV. By the time he locked in there was nothing but a thrashing leg, Number Three vanishing and hauling his comrade for cover when Lyons pumped one hollowpoint into the exposed leg.

If the goon was in pain before, he was in mindless agony now, nothing but wailing and gnashing of teeth, the garage nothing but some vault in the darkest corner of hell, hurling his screams back in his face.

A screech of rubber drew Lyons' attention, the Able Team leader looking back to the far end of the garage just as the van shot up over the lip of the ramp.

Pol, he saw, was at the wheel, barreling ahead, the cavalry to the rescue, with Gadgets hanging between the door frame, ready to cowboy the action with an M-16 M-203 combo.

Lyons got back into the act, rising, drilling slugs into the SUV, sidling out into the open, winging wild rounds off the floor in hopes a ricochet would chop the bastard off at the ankle.

The van went into a sliding halt, screeching out

smoking rubber as it came in for a landing behind Lyons just as Number Three thrust out the machine pistol and went back to work.

"Take him out!" Lyons roared at Schwarz.

Schwarz knew what to do, didn't even blink, nod or acknowledge the order with a sharp word or some smart remark as he caressed the trigger of the M-203. The 40 mm missile chugged on, the Russian shooter still going berserk, holding his ground, then he was lost inside a thundering fireball as Schwarz became some insurance agent's worst nightmare. Wreckage winged out, banging off concrete, slabs slamming into other vehicles, bashing in windshields.

Lyons hopped aboard the van through the sliding side door just as a gas tank ignited ahead, hurling out more debris and raging fire.

"Pedal to the metal, Pol!" Lyons shouted. "Reverse it back to the exit ramp! Where the hell's my SPAS?"

"You're almost sitting on it!" Gadgets yelled back.

RANKIN DIDN'T KNOW what in the hell had just happened, but he knew it wasn't good. For one thing, to keep the ball of fear rolling, the Don was plopped in the back seat, screaming into his own tac unit, with Walker riding shotgun, wanting to know the situation, damn near in panic again. Only the porky gangster, stained in au jus from chest to crotch, started the report with a flurry of oaths, creative cursing that even Rankin begrudged some admiration.

"No response from my men! I assume they are all dead, Max!"

Rankin glanced into the rearview mirror, catching the Don now giving him the evil eye. He wondered what horror could possible hit them in the face next when— lo and behold—the next horror show came barging up the ramp, dead ahead.

His fists wrapped tight around the wheel, Rankin had opted to keep some distance, roughly seven or so car lengths, behind his own shooters, at least until he found out what all the shooting was about, could judge the score for himself and figure out his moves to clear Dodge.

Then he found the truth was worse than he could have imagined.

It was a big black van, antennae sprouting all over the rig, the kind of surveillance ride he knew the FBI and the Justice Department used. Only usually they weren't so obvious about tracking bad guys like that.

Nor did they barge out into the open, shoot first with automatic weapons, forget the questions, no cuffs needed.

Miranda who?

He hit the brakes, as for some ungodly reason Hopewell went into a screaming slide, both his guys bursting out the doors, Glocks up, just about set to go for broke.

That was about as far as they got.

It was only a glimpse, but Rankin saw it was the big guy calling himself Chet Lemon who came out first and loudest. The sliding door was open, a riot shotgun that looked as if it belonged more in some Arnold flick than the real world, was flaming and thundering away like the combined wrath of hell.

"Floor it! Slam past these bastards!"

Walker was bellowing out the rage when the big guy and two of his pals, donning the same street black, popped into view. Before his eyes, he actually saw Hopewell vanish into a misty crimson cloud, sawed in two by the futuristic shotgun, nothing but shredded flying innards, blasted to so much gory flesh with such hellacious ferocity, Rankin found the windshield getting splashed with whatever was left of that poor bastard.

The problem was, Mr. Chet Lemon was suddenly swinging that mammoth piece their way, his pals—who the hell were these guys, anyway?—pounding out the lead, one with an M-16 with a fixed grenade launcher, another darker, banker-looking type swinging around the port-side rear and adding to the hellstorm, chewing Wheeler all to bits and pieces not even fit for a baby croc to feed on.

"Go, dammit!"

There was just enough room, if he bulled his way ahead, to plow through the back end, clipping the wall in a rending of metal, then they could be on their way.

What choice did he have? These guys were playing for keeps, and if anyone had any doubts before that they were legit law-enforcement officers, they were all but trashed before their eyes.

These guys had declared total war, Rankin knew.

Rankin stomped the glass. No one had to shout to hit the deck, since all hands out there turned the storm their way and started blasting out the windshield.

Rankin flung himself beneath the steering wheel as the glass hurricane mingled with greasy flesh blew overhead. He was flying blind, doing his damnedest to try to remember how close to shave it through the narrowest of windows, when he hammered into the back end of the metallic barrier.

LYONS KEPT pouring out the thunder of hell, Schwarz and Blancanales eating up the sedan even as the runaway rig bored ahead.

Standing in the door frame, Lyons heard Blancanales shout a curse, Schwarz still tracking with autofire, blasting in the windows, hammering the doors, gouging out big holes in the frame, then he jumped out for solid footing, aware what was coming.

Sudden impact.

Rankin got lucky, Lyons knew, driving blind, as he bulldozed into the back end, flinging the van halfway around. There was a rending of metal getting crumpled on impact, as the sedan bounced off the wall, tires screaming again, signaling Rankin was flooring it.

Lyons was racing for the back end, shouting, "Pol!"

Blancanales came back with an answer to Ironman's concern with subgun fire from his mini-Uzi. Schwarz on his rear, Lyons wheeled around the corner, stood beside Blancanales and thundered on with the SPAS. The chatter of Schwarz's M-16 was drowned somewhere in the deafening cacophany of weapons fire. One last barrage blew in the back window.

"Save it!" Lyons shouted, watching as Schwarz dropped a 40 mm hellbomb down the M-203's gullet.

The sedan was a speeding dark blur, tires clawing at concrete as it was quickly swallowed up between two pillars.

Able Team piled into the van, Lyons in the back with Schwarz, wondering how long it would take to catch up to the sedan, or how much blood would run in the streets of Seattle. The problem was, he knew, that this time of day, the workforce would be heading home, clogging up the streets, God only knew how many traffic jams....

Then there was the not so little problem of dealing with local Seattle PD.

The war had started, and Lyons knew in their world there was no point on dwelling on fatalistic thoughts of encounters unknown and not yet happening.

Blancanales had backed the van into the exit ramp, Lyons urging speed, but critical seconds were lost before he finally had them turned, charging ahead.

"Get that tracking monitor on, Gadgets!"

"I'm already on it," Schwarz said, hitting knobs and handles and buttons on the control panel, bringing to life three screens with grid maps of the city, what looked like a radar monitor. "No way we'll lose them, Carl!"

"Fall back some if we catch up, Pol. Let them think

they're home free. The night's young, and we've got our butcher's work cut out for us. Gadgets, get that police scanner going while you're at it!"

"I'm already on it, Carl."

Lyons, feeding his SPAS-12 live ones, flashed his teammate a grim smile, bobbed his head.

RANKIN FOUND another war zone waiting as he blasted around the corner for the next level. A wall of fire was blocking the way, Walker bellowing for him to keep going, no matter what.

Two bodies, Rankin saw, were stretched out and getting the scorched-earth sizzle as they baked in the spreading fire. These bastards had brought firepower enough to the party to take out a city block. Rankin sure as hell hoped Walker or Russo's people had something just as heavy, or none of them were going to live through the night.

He jounced the tires over the burning dead, burst through the firewall.

"Any questions, guys?" Rankin shouted. "Any doubts any longer these are cops or Feds?"

"Just drive, don't stop!" Walker roared. "Don't talk, either! Give me your radio!"

Rankin checked the rearview and side mirrors. All clear, but for how long? He knew the city streets, the quickest way north to Bearhouse. Ruskavka was already on the blower, bleating out orders in Russian to his guys as Rankin handed over the tac unit to Walker.

The final stretch saw the attendant coming down the ramp, the guy flapping his arms, a face of frenzy framed in Rankin's grim death sights. The ex-cop gave the engine more thrust, the attendant leaping out of the way at the last possible second before he was roadkill. One last burst of speed, and Rankin crashed through the lowered arm of the barrier.

CHAPTER FIVE

Max Walker had never been in a full-blown shoot-out, or any war for that matter, live combat where men were shooting one another all to hell and gone, screaming and dying in horrific pain, their blood running in great washes before their fallen bodies, while life faded out of their twitching limbs.

He had been a karate champ, a martial-arts master, using hands and feet, covered with pads in the ring so the devastating kicks and punches weren't lethal. That had been a different arena of combat, though, worlds apart from what he'd just seen, the square ring where men displayed—or showed off—their martial skills, some hoping for glory, trophies, money, female adulation, whatever. All of it, back then, he thought, pretty much done with the utmost of vanity and self-promotion.

And it paled in comparison to what he'd seen back in the garage, night and day. That was death being dispensed, total war declared on his empire, the Ruskavka Family, their dreams, and he could be sure, after one look in the eyes of those three men in black, they weren't in it for the money or the glory or medals of honor.

He shuddered, staring into the black night before his eyes as Rankin turned off onto the main trail. Back there, he had seen guys blown to crimson smithereens before his eyes, wasted by men who looked carved from death—seasoned warriors—who wielded weapons, stood their ground and mowed down the enemy as if they'd done it a thousand times before. Unflinching, unyielding, unmerciful. There in Seattle, no less, wielding right by might on their sides, separating the bad guys from the good guys.

The real deal. The real thing.

Us and them.

And clearly they had come for him, and to tear down Ruskavka's organization in the process of some scorched-earth policy. Somehow they knew the score, or some of it, which left him wondering if, no matter where he went, they'd hunt him down. No place to run, nowhere to hide. Who were they? he wondered. Well, as Rankin had said, they weren't cops, but that went without saying, as if there had ever been some doubt after the big guy's menacing antics in the restaurant, standing there, balls the size of grapefruits, damn near daring one of them to try to take him on. NSA? CIA? Some Delta or Special Forces black ops? The stuff of spook legend, these new warriors splashed by word of mouth all over cable by the talking heads? Those shadow warriors over there, rooting out the terrorists in Afghanistan and the Middle East? Who could say, but he damn sure cared. They weren't on any recon or scouting mission. They were headhunting.

Well, Max Walker wanted to live. There was too much to do, too many worlds to conquer. And he didn't want to see that threesome of death again, but his churning gut warned him he would. They were on the way. They would be there again, to mop it up.

Mop them up.

Worst of all, he wasn't so sure anymore of his manhood. That much he knew, and it bothered him greatly, even as he tried to rationalize his feelings—that he'd been taken by surprise on his home turf, that he'd been careless in his dealings, damn near holding hands with a well-known, notorious Russian mobster in public view, the brazen nonsense having finally caught up to him, three bastards come to call in his marker. If they were that skilled with guns, combat tactics, then he could be sure they were trained in the lethal delivery of blows using empty hands. How would they match up against him, if he could get one of them without a pistol or a machine gun? A part of him wanted to know; then again, another part of him believed he might be outmatched this time around. These guys were no street punks with more mouth and attitude than balls and guts.

The real deal. Spooky.

Still, he couldn't let it go, wanted one more shot at

them, hoping for a hand-to-hand engagement, all or nothing.

He shoved the images of death and mayhem out of his mind. Rankin led them down a long winding road, through wooded hill country, another quarter mile or so they'd make Bearhouse. Somehow they had made it out of downtown Seattle, no cops flying up on their sedan, and he thought that was a good sign. Maybe the night could be saved, hope for the future. Somehow he had made the calls to his security detail, got them all in one place at his shooting ranch, ordered them to be waiting at Bearhouse. A force of fifteen, including Rankin, and he had to wonder if it would be enough, even if they were bringing dozens of automatic weapons. Of course, Ruskavka could field an additional eighteen shooters, with more on tap in Alaska, but still…

Ahead, he saw the massive, weird-looking, glass-domed split-level estate. The back end was perched on beams, the deck edging out over the cliff. The blackness hanging over Puget Sound was infiltrated, here and there, by lights of distant boats, or homes planted in isolated pockets across the way on Whidbey Island. He felt his confidence bolstered some as he counted up the luxury vehicles, the SUVs staggered around the front of the house, figured thirty shooters inside, judging by the size of the motor pool.

The silence held during the long trek unnerved Walker suddenly, more than ever as they approached the Russian stronghold.

"How long, comrade?" he asked Ruskavka over his shoulder.

"As long as it takes."

"These documents…"

"We will discuss the future once we are inside."

The future, he thought bitterly. Was there a future? He was finished in Seattle; that much he was sure of. Where did he go from Alaska? He needed to get his hands on some chem, bio or nuke packages he knew the Don could deliver to get the program jump-started, and that meant a trip to Russia. For the deal to get done, he needed money, more soldiers, combat vets who would help him put the torch to a number of oil fields he hoped to hold hostage. But if the opposition already suspected what he was up to, they might start freezing assets, bank accounts, stocks and bonds. Without question, they were hunting him.

It was time to fight back, up the ante, turn up the heat.

He wasn't about to stand around and take it on the chin.

Or catch a bullet through the brain.

Rankin was strangely quiet, and Walker wondered if the ex-cop was on the point of bailing. With that in mind, he put together a game plan, just in case the three warriors came crashing down the doors here. Three men had him running scared. A mere three guys in black.

Unbelievable.

He saw the armed shadows stepping out onto the porch, shuffling about. He stepped out into the night, shivered as the chilly breeze blew in off the water. He searched the hills, the patches of trees and shrubs reaching out for the cliffs.

"Yeah, Max, bet your ass, they'll be coming."

Rankin sounding, what? Pleased? He turned and looked at the ex-cop from across the hood. "Then I suggest we get ready."

"I thought we were running to your airport."

At least that was a short boat ride down the coast, just in case they needed a quick exit for the jets to ride out of the country. Running? He felt contempt—Rankin staring him down—and for himself.

"Inside," Ruskavka growled, brushing past Walker.

One last search of the black heart of night, images of three men on the hunt somewhere out there in the woods, and Max Walker wondered if he'd even make it out of Bearhouse.

If only to keep on running.

"SOUNDS LIKE you've got the show out there jumpstarted with a real bang, Carl."

Lyons was at the control bank beside Schwarz, Blancanales driving them west now past the quaint little towns and farmland that made up this stretch of Puget Sound enclaves. He was on the satlink with Brognola, having updated the Farm on the long haul up I-5. Schwarz was watching the screens, their target blipping, holding fast, heading due west, then stopping. The Farm had faxed the latest batch of Justice Department surveillance photos of the stronghold where Lyons believed their quarry was headed next. The beachfront compound belonged to Ruskavka, which meant a force of God only knew how many Russian shooters was on-site.

If Lyons didn't know any better he would have sworn Brognola sounded a trifle annoyed they had already started shooting up Seattle.

"We didn't shoot at anybody who didn't shoot at us first, Hal. And we always shoot the right people—collateral damage, other than a few citizens' automobiles got in the line of fire, isn't part of our vocabulary."

"I'm not criticizing, Carl, but where does it all go from here? And you've gotten lucky not getting snagged by Seattle PD."

"Maybe the gods of war are simply on our side again," Lyons said gruffly into the mike. "Hey, I didn't come out here for a simple P.I. stakeout, swilling coffee all night and eating stale doughnuts. I thought we had an understanding. I thought you said the Man wanted any and all traitors and terrorists and saboteurs of the American Way brought to justice. Our brand of justice, which means taking justice to them."

"He did, and what the hell's wrong with you, Carl? I've never heard that tone before."

"I'm not trying to sound shitty or insubordinate, Hal, I'm just cranked up. Adrenalized. These bastards are dirty—we both know that. All I'm asking is if they somehow make it out of Seattle, you guys find a satellite and put them back in our gun sights. I've already got your people out here watching Walker's airport. It's a shout away from where we are, and I'm thinking he's here with Ruskavka to pick up reinforcements, maybe a suitcase of money to keep their dirty dreams going. I also told your Special Agent Turlison he is under no circumstances to approach or engage the opposition. It's our show to bring the curtain down. The enemy started it, we finish it."

"I agree. Okay, so where do you think Walker and his Russian Mafia comrades will run next if they slip through the noose in Seattle?"

"Alaska. Maybe Russia. Both of them are cooked, well done here in the States. If they're behind what happened to that oil reserve, I'm thinking maybe they're somehow in touch with the commander of those subs. I'm thinking they'll fly, set down, radio for a pickup, try to catch a ride on one of those subs. Where will they end up? The North Pole, this Chukchi Peninsula, hell, in Moscow for all I know. But I want to be there at the finish line, wherever it ends."

"Do it your way, Carl. I'll fill in the Man on progress. If this operation is as big as we fear, meaning navy Spetsnaz, with a black-ops Russian sub base in the North Pole, you might need a little assistance to nail it down."

"Special Forces to aid and assist? SEALs?"

"Could be."

"No sweat. As long as it's understood we're the point men."

"I can only twist some arms. Okay, we've got our work cut out for us here. Stay in touch."

"I'll keep you posted," Lyons said, and Brognola signed off with a good-luck.

"Okay, Pol, pull it over somewhere. We peruse these pics, then it's lock and load, guys. We're going for broke this time."

"You know, Carl," Blancanales said, "I think the gist of what Hal was saying is maybe, just maybe, he'd like us to put a live one or two in the net for questioning."

"I'll take that under advisement."

THE BULK of any top Russian Mafia Family, Walker knew, was made up of former KGB agents or Spetsnaz commandos, tough men who had fallen on hard times after the Wall came down, out of work, down on their luck and in search of a better tomorrow any way they could find it. Since crime did pay and handsomely, he thought, where only a few had it all in any revolutionary society, most of the former backbone of the motherland's intelligence and military community gravitated toward the fat, corrupt paws still able to feed and use their martial talents and former connections to military installations, missile silos, all manner of weapons they told the West were dismantled but were really just stashed away for a rainy tomorrow. These former castaways of the old guard of communism were suddenly employed, a golden road paved before them in terms of monetary reward they had never dreamed of before, and they became the muscle behind the crime juggernaut, men of vision who had seen the future after the Berlin

Wall collapsed, clearly knew there was no place for the peasant even in a so-called democratic Russia.

The Ruskavka Family was no different. And what he found in the sprawling living room fit for royalty—with its sunken marble floor, horseshoe couches, whirlpool spa, wall-to-wall bar, two giant-screen TVs, chandeliers the size of cars—fit the bill. They were all lean, chiseled, in shape like Olympic athletes, mean and wary in the eyes. Black turtlenecks and matching khakis for the most part, a few sport shirts, wingtips and rubber-soled combat boots here and there, but all tough guys in caps, carrying themselves in the way only a man who had walked through the fires of hell and survived could.

They were the flip side, he thought, of the three men in black.

He was following Ruskavka toward the bar, taking in the well-armed contingent with an admiring eye. The Russians appeared almost aloof, smoking, talking in quiet tones among themselves, assault rifles and machine guns within easy grasp. Out on the balcony, he spotted a trio of armed shadows, near the rail, watching the cliffs, the black waters of Puget Sound for any invaders. To the untrained eye, they appeared almost arrogant in their quiet confidence, glancing now and then at his own security force, content to sit at the bar, smoke and pretend to be watching TV.

Walker could tell his salty crew was hardly up to any East-West mingling of the guard, judging the scowls and tight-lipped masks, and it bugged him for a second these guys couldn't seem to get past their own bigoted ideas. He figured cut them some slack, some of them had been to the joint, and he could only imagine what they had seen, done and endured. To their credit, none of his troops was swilling booze, edgy, though, almost to the point of looking as if they wished they were somewhere else. All of his men were armed with pistols in shoulder holsters, big nylon bags opened at the foot of the stools to reveal an assortment of assault rifles and machine guns.

"In my study," Ruskavka said.

"Give me a minute with my men," Walker told the Don.

"A minute, no more."

Walker turned and told Rankin, "Get these guys off their asses. Get those weapons out and ready. I want half of them out front. Tell them to lose the cigarettes, and they'd better not be bullshitting when I come to check. You're in charge. Don't let me down. If you're right, it's going to hit the fan. One more thing."

Rankin's gaze narrowed, eyes glinting, as if he was dying to share the joke. "Just one thing?"

"How come—?" Walker bit down his anger, realizing an outburst might reveal his jumpy nerves. "Pass the word. If we get hit, the men who stand their ground and show me victory each will receive a half-million-dollar bonus. In cash."

Rankin bobbed his head. "That should be motivation enough. I'll spread the news of your generous offer."

Walker found himself more and more wanting to slash a backhand hammer-fist off that smirking mug. But he needed Rankin, and he was counting on their greed to steer him clear if they were hit. He knew Ruskavka kept a seventy-foot cabin cruiser docked at the foot of the cliffs, the two of them having conducted business while tooling about Puget Sound.

Should the sky fall once more, he knew they'd need that boat ride out of there.

COM LINK WITH THROAT MIKE in place, Lyons was advancing on the stronghold, HK MP-5 subgun leading the way. Swift and silent, he kept low, skirting past thin stands of trees but cutting his course around brush that might rattle and sound the alarm to nervous ears tuned in to the night. The SPAS-12 was hung across a shoulder, combat vest stuffed with spare clips, grenades hung from his webbing, shells for the mammoth man-eater riotgun in a pouch. NVD goggles in place, he searched the grounds, the high points of all trees for any sensors, motion detectors, the compass on all points for roving sentries, anything out of the ordinary. So far, so good.

They had gone over the layout, strategy before leaving the van up the road in a dense thicket of shrubs. Lyons had laid out the attack plan, and he was keeping it simple, as usual.

Bring down the house and, if possible, drop the net over a prisoner or two for interrogation. If not…

Kill them all.

Lyons had taken the north side for the penetration. Blancanales was the heart of the advance, Little Bulldozer poised to get the fireworks started once Lyons gave the green light. With his M-16/M-203 combo, Schwarz was at the far southern end, right then, Lyons hoped, paralleling his own approach.

According to the Farm's sat imagery and Justice Department intel, there was a boathouse and dock at the bottom of the cliffs, with a cabin cruiser, large enough to hold a small army, anchored down there. Once they dropped the hammer, Lyons expected some of the harder combat types to stand and fight, while others would bolt for the concrete stairs leading for the boathouse.

No problem.

It was Schwarz's task to make his way around back, move in from the south, cut off any escape. Well, Lyons knew battle plans always looked and sounded good when they were on the table. In reality it was quite different when bullets were flying, bad guys were taking their venomous dreams to hell, holding tough and willing to fight it out to the last bitter breath.

In short, anything could happen, some of it unexpected, all of it bad when death came calling.

Through a break in the tree line he saw the shadows, six, no, seven in all, spread around the motor pool, watching, unmoving. No smokers, talkers or loungers— they were on high alert.

He crouched, keyed his com link when—

There it was. The small black box was at the base of

a tree, no beam or red eye, but in this high-tech age he could be sure it was meant to be cloaked by the night. There was no way past it without letting the hardforce know they were coming in.

Lyons shed his goggles, hung them from his webbing as he adjusted his eyes, focusing on the light shining behind the wall of glass that ran all the way down the front of the house.

"I just hit a snag, guys," Lyons told Schwarz and Blancanales. "Motion sensor or some other toy Gadgets might know better about, but where there's one...here it is. You in position?"

They copied.

"Check your watches. Sixty seconds and counting—starting now."

Lyons lifted his MP-5, watched the standing guard. They were holding their turf, no one running from the house, which meant he hadn't stumbled through any sensors along the way.

Lyons watched the doomsday numbers ticking down.

CHAPTER SIX

After a brief discussion between them, Walker was feeling they were back on track, colleagues in conspiracy again, all that mutual cooperation Ruskavka had mentioned when the Russian boss had given the order to one of his own soldiers to go start the cabin cruiser.

Anchors away. There was hope yet.

If nothing else they were in agreement that driving to Vertigo's private airfield would be too dangerous. A short boat ride, and Walker knew they could practically walk to the airport from shore.

Beyond that one concession, Walker didn't have a clue where it all went from there. He was getting more edged out the longer they stalled around the stronghold, certain their hunters were closing in, about to drop a net of bullets and bombs. How many would they bring this time? Twenty? Fifty? As good as those three men in black were, he couldn't believe a mere three men would even dare dream in their wildest masturbatory macho fantasy of tackling thirty-plus hardmen. If it came down to a shooting match, he could only hope the combined members of the American-Russian security force proved up to their billing, earned all the cash they'd been lining their pockets with so long for pretty much doing nothing but driving the bosses around town, eating like kings on the plastic fantastic of their lords and masters, shining their guns and watching dirty movies.

This, Walker feared, would prove a night soon enough where somebody needed to earn his keep.

At the moment, sitting in a rolling chair beside the Russian boss, Walker watched as Ruskavka juggled the vodka and cigar, while tapping the keyboards on two computers. They were in the Russian boss's study, nothing ornate or fancy, just a fax, a big teak desk and, of course, the two computers, the wall safe open now, emptied of whatever valuables Ruskavka had brought to America. Two aluminum briefcases and one huge suitcase didn't escape Walker's eye. He had already seen one of the Don's soldiers stacking hundred-dollar bills into the suitcase when they entered the room. Judging the size of the suitcase, he figured Ruskavka was taking somewhere in the neighborhood of twenty to thirty million, U.S., either walking-around or grease money or both.

The monitors showed what Walker believed were grids with detailed routes of transport or weapons depots in the breakaway republics of Uzbekistan, Turkmenistan and Tajikistan, outlined all the way to Moscow.

A list of what appeared to be numbers and codes and encryptions scrolled up as Ruskavka copied the disks.

"You want your weapons of wholesale destruction, comrade," Ruskavka said, sipping his vodka, blowing smoke, "it will cost you."

"How much?"

"Depends."

"On what?"

"What and how much you want. You will also need soldiers, Spetsnaz, I have on my payroll, to assist, if you wish to enlist their services to further your agenda. In that case, you want their services, you pay them out of pocket, for whatever your endgame. I'm sure you figured out that what you saw were—how shall I say? Established safe windows. We use military convoys to go to the border of Uzbekistan now to pick up heroin from the Taliban. We used to fly straight to Kandahar, but considering what is happening in that part of the world, it is too dangerous. However, the right amount of money you can purchase just about any man's allegiance. It never hurts to have a little help from the CIA. I can get you chemical, biological, nuclear weapons. Delivery systems for intermediate missiles likewise. I can hand over suitcase nukes, conventional explosives packed with radioactive waste or a chem or bioagent. Very nasty stuff. The oil fields I wish to develop are in Siberia, to answer one of your earlier questions. Like you, I intend to own and monopolize petroleum production in Russia. The area in question is rich in mineral, fossil fuel, among coal, gold and silver, virgin untapped land that is just waiting for the right person to come along and begin exploring—and exploiting. I know you have done business with the Saudis, but how you intend to conquer that part of the world, blackmail them…I hope you understand I consider that madness, it could very well begin World War III."

"That's my concern. Just get me the merchandise."

"You realize that your bank accounts, all assets will probably be frozen by the Feds in light of what has happened."

"I have enough spread around, especially in Moscow, to make it happen my way. I can get my hands on five hundred million tomorrow. More, if necessary."

Ruskavka nodded, began saving the files, extracting the hard drives and placing them in a lockbox. "You realize you will probably become, as the Taliban is fond of saying of bin Laden, my guest of honor in Russia."

"Not a problem. I need a vacation until I sort through this mess we're leaving behind. I'm thinking we get to Alaska first, round up some reinforcements you told me you have there."

"And I call in the commander of the attack sub for a ride back to Russia. It can be done, with timing, luck, provided they can safely avoid American antisubmarine warfare, but we could be delayed for a day or more in Alaska. They have docked by now at a base in the North Pole."

"As long as you can make it happen, comrade."

Walker was feeling his confidence rising. Despite the earlier near fatal encounter, they were still in business, a future to salvage. He nearly felt the smile taking to his lips, Ruskavka killing his drink, placing the lockbox in one of the aluminum suitcases beside other documents when—

The first of several blasts sounded as if it came from out front, followed by a thunderous barrage that sent shock waves rippling beneath Walker's feet, his throat squeezing off the air as terror shot through every limb. The walls seemed to shake next as the roaring sounded closer, and Walker felt his heart lurch straight for his throat. Ruskavka looked shocked and angry, then he loosed a terrible outburst of cursing, grabbing up the briefcases.

They were here.

It was all Max Walker could do to keep from screaming his outrage.

RANKIN COULDN'T BELIEVE what was going on, wondering just how professional his Russkie counterparts were. The Russians acted as if life were just one big party, nothing to worry about, everything under control. Disgusted with something he couldn't quite put his finger on, he shook his head at the sight of the Russians. They were actually lounging around the couches, half of them watching porn, cool as a fall breeze, chuckling quietly among themselves. The only visible sign of true macho excitement, he found, came from a group glued to the documentary they had obviously taped off the Discovery channel for repeated viewing, something called *Air Jaws*. Even Rankin found himself staring at the screen, as some monster sixteen- or eighteen-foot white shark burst out the water, some poor seal exploding in bloody spray, the giant fish actually spinning in the air with its catch in its mouth, high above the water, as if it was showing off a trophy for any other seals fortunate enough to make it back to the shores of Seal Island. The Russians pointed at the screen, laughing, smoking up a storm as a tremendous pool of bloody froth spread over the water when the beast splashed down after what seemed like five seconds of hang time in the air.

He wondered how those clowns would feel if they'd been hunted for extinction as he had been a few hours earlier. Three bastards in black, he thought, were the white sharks, and he had been their frigging seal—almost. Shaking his head, he went to the bar, firing up a cigarette, screw Max's order, and built himself a whiskey. The offer of a cool half mil if they stood their ground and routed any raiders didn't impress Rankin, though he'd do his damnedest to try to collect on that bill if and when the time came to kick ass. What bothered him about that sudden show of generosity was the nagging suspicion he and his guys were supposed to become sacrificial lambs, given up for the slaughter while Walker and the Russians bolted out the back door.

He had a Colt Commando assault rifle slung across a shoulder, had gone and picked one up, in fact, after his first mesmerized viewing of one of those acrobatic beasts breaching the surface with prey clamped in its jaws. Something about being turned into a grisly meal by a predator he couldn't see, much less defend against, inflamed visions of his own demise at the hands of the three bastards, put him on edge, as if the blackness of the woods beyond the motor pool was actually that triangle of death where the white sharks patrolled for seals off the Cape of Good Hope.

He was sipping the drink, stepping around the corner of the bar, glimpsed another seal goner chomped into bloody spray in midair when the first of several tremendous explosions rocked the night, ripping through the motor pool. Scarecrow figures, what were the cream of his guys, he saw, were riding the fires, a mangled shape blasting through that damnable long running window that would allow the enemy to see them as clear as day from their firepoint. The glass slipped from his fingers, the assault rifle off his shoulder.

Three white sharks, he knew, had just breached the surface.

Rankin heard the commotion from the sunken living room, the Russians shouting and grabbing up arms, when the whole front section of the house, nothing but glass, was blown like a hurricane, coming to blind and carve them up into shrieking crimson sacks. Rankin shielded his face from the flying glass, the shrapnel storm blowing over the Russians, guys who had seconds ago been chuckling and watching skin flicks, crying out in pain.

Then whatever chunks of the foyer were wood and marble came winging his way next, banging him in the arms and legs, a piece of something burrowing into his guts, kicking him off his feet, the lights doused when a hunk of rubble slammed off his skull.

LITTLE BULLDOZER GOT the rain started. Blancanales peppered the motor pool with a 40 mm barrage. Explosions tore through the heart of man and machine, bodies, severed limbs and giant sheets of metal puking through the running front window, showering and bowling down the enemy in the living room.

The newest addition by Kissinger to the multiround projectile launcher was a thumb-sized digital readout that counted off the rounds fired in red. That way, Blancanales didn't have to keep track of how close he was to burning through the ten missiles. In a large nylon pouch, he had three more cylinders as backup. They were much like a speedloader on a revolver. All he had to do was thumb down the latch on the back of the housing, hold the cylinder over the chambers, hit the release button.

It saved time, not having to load each individual round by hand.

And he could tell time would be critical on this hit.

One look at the readout showed he had six bombs left to fire away. Lyons was hollering over the com link, "Dump a few into the living room, Pol!"

Blancanales copied with action, moving out, hitting the exposed foyer with a blast, chugging another hellbomb for the bar, all but vaporizing a few hardmen too slow off the stools and all the party favors in a giant saffron cloud. One more for good measure, and he managed to score a chandelier, bringing down a giant chunk of the ceiling, crushing a few goons under the massive torrent of wood, glass and crystal.

Charging out of the woods, Lyons was already hard at work, hosing down a few survivors who came staggering out of the flaming beds of debris with his subgun, kicking them back into the fiery shells, screams lost to the constant burping of the HK MP-5 as he hit the front porch, searching for fresh targets.

Blancanales slipped his arm through the strap, hanging Little Bulldozer across a shoulder, taking up the Uzi submachine gun.

There would be survivors, wounded hardmen ferociously clinging to life and looking to even the score. They were already rising from the smoking rubble inside the stronghold.

From there on, Blancanales knew it would be hand to hand, eye to eye.

No problem. He could live, or die, with that.

WALKER WAS BEING LED by Ruskavka onto the balcony, after having followed him out of the study and down a hall that ran behind the warzone that was the living room. He couldn't resist staring into the ruins of the living room, out of horror or fear, he wasn't sure, when two guys were mowed down before his eyes, toppling over, howling, weapons firing for whatever was left of the ceiling in impotent death. Judging all the smoke and dust raining down, he figured half the house had been blown to hell. From the jagged maws of glass and bits and hanging pieces of decorum, he balked at the sight of two shooters pounding out the lead, made out the face of the bastard from the restaurant.

Why wasn't he surprised?

From the other end of the balcony, he spotted three of Ruskavka's shooters at the rail, blazing away with AK-47s. He could be sure the third bastard of the tandem was homing in from that direction.

"Come on!"

It galled Walker to leave behind his men to fight a losing battle, seeing more than a few of the Russians had opted to cut and run to join the exodus, spilling out onto the balcony.

He was turning, following Ruskavka down the steps, maybe six or seven of the Don's shooters thundering in descent behind him, when the whole deck behind him seemed to crumble, a rolling wave of shards uprooted and hurled his way from a massive explosion.

"GADGETS, WHAT THE HELL are you waiting for? Bring that goddamn deck down!"

Schwarz was taking serious return fire, bark from three or four trees flaying his face as a trio of shooters hugged the corner of the deck, firing away and burning through clip after clip, pinning him down. They had

spotted his approach, call it luck or instinct, and cut
loose right away in a lightning triburst of autofire. It
didn't matter now; he wasn't going anywhere soon.

Lyons bellowed for him one more time to get his act
together, and never one to disappoint his teammates, he
hit the ground on his belly, drew a quick bead on the
edge of the deck, a line of slugs shearing off more bark
just above his head and rapidly coming down to burst
his skull apart, and let fly a 40 mm missile from his M-
203, whipping back for cover a microsecond before he
was nailed.

The blast that sheared off half the deck at least, he
saw, looking around the other side of the tree cover,
eliminating his own problem in the process, should keep
Lyons quiet for at least thirty seconds or so while he got
it together and checked the situation out back.

IT WAS HARDLY a wrap. At least Schwarz, Lyons saw, had
finally taken out the balcony or most of it.

The Able Team leader rolled over the lip of the jagged teeth of the window, sighted on two mangled hardmen rising from the smoke and ruins. From somewhere
in whatever was left of the foyer, he heard Blancanales
turning on the Uzi heat. Together, their converging
lines of fire nailed the goons, flinging them through
clouds of stuffing still being blown all around like a
snow blizzard.

He cursed next, aware six or seven Russians had
just made the balcony, clearing the blast eye blinks be-

fore Gadgets did his demolition duty. Whether or not they made it...

Lyons, boots crunching over glass and wood shards, cautiously stepped into the hellzone. Something was rattling around in debris, twelve o'clock. That something had eyes fiery with pain and hatred, and even with his face shrouded in blood, Lyons recognized Rankin.

The dirty ex-cop nearly made it, rage and agony oiling the limbs as he clambered quickly to his feet, hauling up an assault rifle.

Blancanales was a heartbeat quicker on the trigger, but Lyons jumped in, his subgun chattering out a long burst, stitching Rankin, crotch to throat. He twitched, wild dance steps carrying him up a pile of rubble, the rotten ex-cop holding on, absorbing rounds, gouting blood, his assault rifle leaping before he toppled.

Lyons checked the debris pile. One poor bastard had ridden a blast, a headfirst impaling through one of the giant-screen TVs, legs still kicking in death spasms.

Out back Lyons heard the sudden din of weapons fire.

He keyed his com link. "Gadgets! Talk to me!"

"I've got seven, maybe eight heading down the stairs for the boathouse. Walker and Ruskavka in the lead. One shooter hugging the top of the steps."

Lyons was bulling ahead, stomping hard over beds of rubble, when a possum decided to rise up from the matchsticks of the bar. The guy opened up with an assault rifle, but opted for cover, somersaulting over a section of the bar still miraculously intact before Lyons or Blancanales could nail him.

Lyons cursed. Schwarz was pinned down while the big game fled. Now they'd have to root out the gunner, waste precious time on one lousy shooter.

The guy popped up, firing, driving Lyons to cover, a flying leap behind a shredded portion of couch. "Pol! Little Bulldoze that sucker!"

A moment later, Lyons hugging the floor, he heard the deafening crunch of the blast.

WALKER WAS RIGHT BEHIND Ruskavka as they hit the bottom of the stairs, his shoes drumming hard on the concrete of the dock. Ruskavka began lagging behind, wheezing and sucking wind from years of self-indulgent piggery, when two of his comrades took him by the arms and hauled him for the boat, which, Walker heard, had the guns blessedly chugging away, two armed shadows waiting in the stern. Walker turned, looked back up the steps, tuned in to the incessant rattle of autofire beyond the cliff top. One Russian had gone beyond the call of duty, kneeling beneath the lip of the top step, firing away, holding back the wolves.

He gave that comrade a mental salute, then felt the bitter sting of defeat, worse, the idea they were being chased like a whelp kicked in the ass—by three men, no less.

He had to believe Rankin and the rest of his security force had been eighty-sixed. He was a man who had all the money in the world, but a whispered thought danced through the back of his mind. At least he wouldn't have to shell out any bonus.

AGAIN LYONS SAW one shooter was holding back the charge, willing to commit suicide so the main quarry could boat it on out of there. He was leading Blancanales out onto what remained of the balcony, wood groaning beneath his boots where remaining floorboards hung precariously together, when he made out the familiar chug of an M-203 round. Hats off, he thought, to Gadgets, for not wasting any more time with that guy.

Only Lyons thought he saw the shadow tumble back down the stairs, out of sight, right before the missile blew, a fireball touching off just in front of the top step.

Lyons keyed his com link. "Gadgets, we're clear up top! We're coming down, a south-side slide."

"Gotcha."

The blown deck had dropped at an angle, boards still pieced together, and Lyons hit the man-made sliding board on the seat of his pants, figuring the worst he'd get was a few splinters in his ass from the rough ride of twenty or so feet. He touched down on his boots, lurched up and tumbled head over heels, Blancanales right beside, rolling up in the same acrobatic act.

Schwarz was rising from his crouch beside a splintered beam when autofire chattered again from the stairs.

Through the smoke cloud, Lyons spotted the guy, had to believe it was the same shooter, having seen the missile flaming away and taken a tumble to clear ground zero. One gutsy bastard, if that's who it was, a shame to waste that kind of talent, Lyons thought, but it was time to nail it down.

"This guy's really starting to piss me off!" Lyons growled. "Gadgets, hit him again!"

Schwarz sent another zigzagging rocket flying for the shooter, only the guy, it looked to Lyons, fell back again, in commando anticipation. Lyons, a fresh clip slapped home into his subgun, charged ahead. As he peered into the thick smoke, the shadow came back seconds later. He got two or three rounds ripped off, but Lyons was already zipping him with a long burst of subgun fire, flinging the hardman from sight. Gone for good, or so he hoped.

Into the smoke, Lyons bulled, spotted the shadow bouncing down the steps, flopping like a broken rag doll. He cursed, moving down the steps as he stared out to the black waters of Puget Sound. The cabin cruiser was already a quarter mile out into the sound, full throttle, well out of range for any attempt to blow it out of the water.

Southbound for the Vertigo airfield.

"Let's hit it," Lyons told his teammates on the bound back up the steps. "We hit that airfield and we get the chance, I want them blown off the runway or out of the sky. Hal's just going to have to burn my ear if he wanted us to snap up a live one."

Schwarz sported a grim smile as he fell in with Lyons and Blancanales. "Shouldn't be too severe a dressing-down, Carl. I mean he did tell you to do it your way."

"If I catch hell from Hal, Gadgets, I'll be sure to pass it on to you guys, word for word, same angry, jacked-up tone, with a little embellishment Ironman style, you can be sure."

"I can hardly wait."

THEY MADE record time, Schwarz dictating the quickest route to the Vertigo airfield using the sat grid map of Seattle.

The problem was, Turlison had just informed Lyons the catch of the day had just boarded a Gulfstream, rolling now down the runway, the SAC wanting to know just what hell was going on, why they were being ordered to hold back.

"Sit tight, Turlison, that's an order. Our way isn't your way."

"Whatever that means!"

"It means stay put!" Lyons barked, and cut the radio.

He told Blancanales to floor it as they cleared the gate, blowing past the armada of unmarked sedans, Turlison's scowl lost to view in the side glass as their van shot parallel down the runway. The Gulfstream was gathering speed, gaining distance, Lyons figuring a hundred yards or more, getting worse as the van roared ahead.

The Gulfstream went wheels up, Lyons shouting at Blancanales to brake it. They were coming to a hard skid when Lyons burst out the door. His subgun was up and chattering, Blancanales on the other side, chugging out four, then five quick 40 mm rounds as Schwarz added to the furious salvo with an M-203 round, then held back on the trigger of his M-16. Lyons and Schwarz charged down the runway, firing on. Whether the opposition was watching the ground show through the cabin windows, someone had to have been bellowing at the pilot to cut the bird into evasive maneuvers. The starboard wing dipped, then the Gulfstream banked to port, straightened out, seemed to shoot off for the sky on a sudden thrust of speed.

And Lyons knew their grim effort was in vain as missiles and dozens of spent rounds flew out to Puget Sound.

Lyons let the subgun fall by his side, glanced at the angry disappointment framing the faces of his teammates. One more look, and the Gulfstream was swallowed up by the black sky.

"We'll find them—we'll see them again," Lyons vowed, then turned and saw the sedans racing for the runway.

Now this, he thought. Slapped in the face by Walker and Ruskavka, now he'd have to pull rank and probably get Brognola dragged into the act.

CHAPTER SEVEN

"You might say I'm pretty much on my own. Nothing new, really, only this time it could prove a little stickier to finesse and feel it out."

Brognola had been called to the Computer Room minutes earlier, Price telling him Striker was checking in. Heart racing, he had done the closest to a full-bore sprint he could conjur up in distant memory. He was jacked up on yet another cup of Bear's coffee, a fresh unlit stogie in place, staring at the situation map, where Striker had faxed a computer printout of the CIA's base in the Punjab where they were allegedly working up a strike against the pharmaceutical plant. Only the ISI didn't want any part of the proposed surgical strike against their own on home turf, even if the compound was run lock, stock and barrel by Pakistani collaborators sympathetic to the Taliban "plight." Politics mingled with religion, Brognola knew, the Pakistanis still nervous about upsetting their Arab neighbors or getting knocked asunder and called out by any Taliban or al-Qaeda conspirators watching the Pakistani hierarchy within its borders, or ready to light the fuse to ignite internal strife or launch terror attacks. The Taliban had already infiltrated terror squads into Pakistan—that much they knew, and Bolan's short update so far said enough. Pakistan could explode from within any day, unless he took out the plant in the Punjab. Brognola wanted to fire off any number of questions for Bolan, but he could tell by the guarded tone of his old friend's voice that all was not well.

And in short order it was all going to get only worse.

When Mack Bolan, also known as the Executioner, got the war ball rolling, he knew an avalanche was just a few strewed bodies away.

"I guess you can just let us read between the lines, Striker," Brognola said into the intercom. "You're trying to feel out who your friends really are."

"You could say that. I'm in a Company safehouse in the heart of Karachi. I've got some positive leads on some Taliban hideouts. Breaking news, you could say. It took some work, but the ISI gave me the green light to do it my way. Pretty much, if you want to read between the lines again, this is an American problem. They've also got their hands full, with the riots, military bases choked already with political prisoners. I can tell you, from what I've heard, the ISI interrogators would give Marquis de Sade a lesson or two in torture techniques."

Brognola felt the grim smile forming around his stogie. He could read between the lines, all right. Bolan was about to go hunting, and Price, the soldier's sometime lover, but always the professional, voiced her concern.

"Any backup, Striker? You know the city is a hotbed for riots, demonstrations. You start shooting up Karachi, you could get stomped in the street before you get off the first shot on an angry mob. We're not even sure where the Company's ISI man, this Colonel Mujhan, really stands. Can he be trusted."

"The good colonel is my ride in and out of here, but I hear you, I'll watch my own back."

"We've got another pressing item, besides a bunch of extremists burning effigies of the President in the streets of Karachi, Striker," Kurtzman said.

"Such as?"

"Phoenix's mission. You haven't forgotten a major incursion into Afghanistan was the primary goal. David," he said, referring to David McCarter, the former SAS commando who was the leader of Phoenix Force, "checked in and was wondering when you'd make the Eagle Base."

"David," Price added, "says they can't wait much longer, that intelligence on known new camps and potential hideouts is rolling in by the droves."

"I understand. They want me on board. Tell him, or if I get the chance, I'll tell him to go without me. I can catch up later."

Brognola nodded. "Do what you have to do first in

Karachi. If you're on to something, go for it—we trust your instincts. But do me a favor? I don't want to turn on CNN and see you getting dragged through the streets of Karachi."

"If you see that, I'll already be dead before the stomping starts. I'll keep you posted."

There was a moment of quiet concern when Striker signed off, then Brognola asked no one in particular, "What are the particulars on Phoenix's strike into Afghanistan?"

"Air strike to soften up the targets," Tokaido said. "Basic saturation bombing. Here," he added, handing Brognola a printout with areas marked in red where the hits would go down. "According to David, two B-52s will get the bombs launched. They'll be flying down from an American base in Uzbekistan. Our team—known to our CIA and special ops in place as X Force instead of Phoenix, for purposes of keeping their cover—will be in touch with the B-52 pilots, coordinating their own ground insertion, B-52s first, then their death from above coming in from the south, across the Khyber."

"We're looking at the mother of all surgical strikes, Hal," Kurtzman said. "If this part of Afghanistan was prehistoric before, it will be preprehistoric by the time our people get finished and bail. No stone unturned, smoking craterland, the dark side of the moon, when it's over. The CIA believes two to three thousand fanatics of the Taliban have regrouped in the AIQ. They will be pounded to red pulp, then our people go in, smoke them out of their holes in the mountains. The bulk of the strike force will be Special Forces and Delta, four platoons, flying ahead of Phoenix Force, going in by ground to the north of the targets, while our guys hit the ground from the south, the Predators circling to cover our people after they do their part in the carpet bombing. Lock them in."

"We hope," Brognola grunted.

Price joined in. "Intelligence has added three major heroin labs and warehousing for what they think could be a combined twenty metric tons of heroin, ready for delivery to you know who."

"The Russian Mob," Brognola said.

"Specifically the Ruskavka Family," Wethers said. "A CIA source inside Uzbekistan states emphatically that the Russian military gets the heroin shipments from Taliban sympathizers inside that country. They then either fly or truck the dope loads to Moscow."

"Everyone getting a piece of the action," Brognola grumbled. "This thing makes me angry, damn near sick to my stomach. Drugs, Taliban insurgents getting enough money to buy, what we believe, are weapons, small and large arms from Pakistani sympathizers. Worse, we're hearing reports how this so-called pharmaceutical company may be ready to ship chem, bio, even nukes to the Taliban."

"If that turns out to be the case," Price said, "we have no choice but to cut Striker and the CIA black ops loose and raze the place. CIA HAZMAT teams are prepared to go in and seize any of the real nasty stuff."

"What's the story on our friend Mr. Rutgen up in Alaska?"

"Former NSA," Tokaido told Brognola. "Worked in something called the Energy Sabotage and Terrorism Division, a lot of overseas, classified stuff with the Saudis, whole chunks of his record blacked out. The scuttlebutt is he has good buddies at State and the Federal Energy Regulatory Commission. Way I hear it, they practically threw him at the Man on bended knee to get the job as head of security at Spectron."

"Thinking some unholy bastards are working behind the scenes in Wonderland," Brognola said. "Rotten sons of bitches."

"We're following the money now," Kurtzman said. "And we're getting a very dark and sordid picture."

"Keep on it. I've got the FBI sitting on Rutgen now. By the way, I just talked to Carl. It went to hell, sort of, in Seattle. Walker flew on."

"We picked them up on satellite," Kurtzman said.

"I also managed to find and scramble an AWACS," Price said, "from California. They were in the air before Walker's jet would have even left the ground. We'll know when and where they touch down."

"Walker's Vertigo International is finished," Brognola informed the group. "FBI is already freezing his assets. I've got my own people storming his office palace as we speak. There's going to be a lot of unhappy employees at Vertigo tomorrow when they go to that office. Least of my woes is, unfortunately, unwitting participants joining the unemployment line."

"Question is, Hal," Kurtzman said, "if he blew up part of the oil reserve he put together, again why? And where does Ruskavka really fit into the puzzle?"

"Well, Able didn't seem real eager to take a prisoner. For some reason, Carl is wound tight, taking no prisoners. I'm thinking the guys are on their own version of a holy war, a mission from God, but I'm cutting them some slack, letting them do it their way, no punches pulled. If they're headed for Alaska, I'm hoping we'll get some answers then."

"Another major item, Hal," Kurtzman said. "We found the trio of Shark hunter-killers."

Brognola felt his eyes light up. "Where?"

"An arrow-straight run, straight across the Beaufort from Point Barrow, on the 160 degree latitude. I've got the sat imagery for you. We're looking at a fairly large base. Sat dishes, major compound of corrugated structures, what look like APCs custom-made for deep snow, complete with mounted machine guns, antiaircraft battery."

"Give it to me, Bear. The Man needs some good news for a change."

IT CAME BACK TO HIM at times like this, the mental image of some murderous extremist flunky of the Taliban standing and clapping and laughing at the film footage of those plane bombs plowing into the WTC. The image still knotted Mack Bolan's gut with a cold rage unlike anything he'd felt and even nurtured for a long, long time. Not that Bolan ever needed motivation to go kick in doors and start waxing the terrorist scum. But this time it felt a little different, a little angrier, more urgent than ever, especially if what he'd heard through the intelligence grapevine was true. He tried, but couldn't at times wipe out the faces of the innocents in his mind and thoughts, even though he'd never laid eyes on any of those victims. He could only imagine the horror of their final moments as they realized what was actually happening, their doomsday planes aimed and hurtling at hundreds of miles per hour at the WTC, the Pentagon. And God bless those heroes, he thought, who took on the terrorists and somehow sent the fourth plane plunging to earth, sacrificing their own lives in the process, but saving God only knew how many other lives, whatever that plane's final destination. Women and children, whole families, in fact, he knew, wiped out in the blink of an eye, while some evil bastards in the cockpits were most likely shouting in triumphant glee, "God is great," right before impact.

He could be sure the monsters who perpetrated those atrocities weren't basking in the glory of God.

Small comfort, but he'd take what he could get, even if it came from the other side, where cosmic justice waited and prevailed with the final answer.

Well, the U.S. had been at war since then, a war that

was nothing new to Bolan, and he was in Karachi to do his part to bring justice of the ultimate kind to her enemies. Beyond whatever would happen in the coming days, Bolan, no doomsayer, always believing the good fight could be won, was grimly and even a trifle sadly aware the world was headed into a dark and perilous time. One more calamity, and the human race could be thrust to the edge of Armageddon. He was there in some of the most hostile, virulent anti-West real estate to make sure the free, the proud, the good people and the innocent and the brave remained that way, kept on living, free of the murderous terrorist scourge.

It had been a hard sell for hours, getting Colonel Mujhan to cut him loose. The CIA-ISI connection seemed on the surface to be an honest effort to weed out any and all Taliban and al-Qaeda extremists holed up and ready to fan the flames of jihad in Karachi and beyond the city proper. It was time to root them out, as well as those Pakistani sympathizers who aided them.

It was already well into the morning in the Old City, the armies of hawkers out en force at Boulton Market, the noise up and down Bundar Road deafening, even as Bolan began his jaunt away from the heart of souks, stalls and squawkers, slipping into the first maze of alleyways too tight for even a donkey cart. The soldier had three nests of human cobras to track down and burn. He was on the colonel's clock, a bad blind date with the pharmaceutical plant in the wings. His primary source of intel while pulling double duty as taxi service was a CIA black op, known to Bolan as Commander Alpha, who was hanging around the general vicinity, a radio call away as he tooled around Chakiwara Road in a rattletrap VW van, waiting to scoop up Colonel Brandon Stone, the soldier's cover name. In a city the size and sprawl and congestion of Karachi, just moving about would prove a tall order. And with anti-American riots and demonstrations all over the city, part of the daily scenery, the warrior knew it could go to hell at any moment.

Bolan was never one to shy away from the craps table of combat.

The Executioner checked the grimy two- and three-story apartment buildings, turbaned men skirting past, glancing at the tall, dark man in the loose-fitting tunic, but moving on. At a passing glimpse, Bolan, with his dark hair and swarthy complexion, burnished even deeper by the harsh sun of Pakistan in recent days, could hopefully pass as being of partial Arab descent. The false beard helped, he hoped, give him some edge in the ruse.

If all else failed, and someone wished to push the issue, he was cocked and locked beneath the tunic. The AK-47 hung from a strap beneath the tunic. Likewise he had the tried and true Beretta 93-R, already snug with sound suppressor in shoulder holster, and the monster head blaster, the .44 Magnum Desert Eagle, was riding on his hip. The combat vest was chocked with spare clips, flash-stun, frag, thermite and tear-gas grenades, the latter for any unruly mobs who might take exception to a Westerner shooting up what a lot of Pakistanis viewed as holy warriors, and right under their fanatical watch.

Bolan followed the silent signal of the GPS module, flashing brighter now, pointing the way to several alleys. At the end of one was a cul-de-sac and a Taliban headquarters. Two offshooting alleys, and Bolan veered off in the right direction.

He stopped at the edge at the end of another narrow passageway, braced against the alley wall, checked his six. All clear. Just one warrior, ready to start dropping the hammer.

A look around the corner, and HUMINT—or human intelligence—was on the money. One black-turbaned fanatic with the four-fingers of scraggly beard, was reported to stand watch outside the front door at all times. He was also armed with an AK-47. For this setup to go unmolested by the ISI and Pakistani military signaled Bolan someone was turning a blind eye.

No more.

It was high time to strike back.

He had been told ten to twelve terrorists were inside this Taliban apartment, heavily armed, perhaps with vital intel on present and future operations, whether in documents or disks. Commander Alpha had asked Colonel Stone to try to come back with more than blood on his hands.

It was time to start making the bad guys feel the pain of the innocents their associates had so wantonly murdered.

The Executioner slid closer to the edge of the wall, palmed the Beretta 93-R.

The GPS module, courtesy of a CIA hookup to outer space, had landed him on the doorstep of the first target, and he stowed the supertech instrument in his combat vest. However, good old-fashioned human intelligence had nailed down, eyeball confirmation yesterday, the three Taliban and al-Qaeda dens.

The legwork done, it was time to start burning the enemy down.

The Executioner took aim.

CHAPTER EIGHT

Hnammi Jhadanal wasn't afraid to die, but he wasn't willing to go to God just yet.

Martyrdom was still down the road, weeks or maybe even days off, when he seized the chance to strike back at the infidels, assured that his own name would go down in Islamic legend, on his way to Paradise eventually when he drove that suitcase nuke, at best, or the radioactive or anthrax-laden conventional truck bomb onto one of the many large U.S. bases he knew were in either Pakistan, Uzbekistan, even Saudi Arabia, at the very worst.

Numbers of dead infidels was important. The more the better, the greater his glory. If he couldn't obtain suitcase nukes from the plant in the Punjab or SCUDs with the promised ten-kiloton warheads, he would take whatever he could get. Bio or chem weapons, anything that could wipe out hordes of infidels would work.

Just as long as there were big numbers of dead.

Once again, he thought, sitting at the operations table in his office, staring at the maps and routes and computer monitors and numbers for contacts in Pakistan and Afganistan, America had invaded the Middle East, declaring war against sovereign Muslim nations. How many times, he wondered, did the Great Satan have to trample Islam in this part of the world, bombing cities, killing women and children, housing whole armies on Arab soil once they had razed an entire country, before the rest of his people woke up, took up arms and fought back? What was wrong with a lot of his fellow Muslims, he wondered, who would turn their backs on jihad, look the other way and allow infidels to take up residence in their own country, like Pakistan, from which to launch military operations against their own?

An abomination.

It disgusted him without end, this knowledge there were traitors among his own people, but he was there, in Karachi, to make sure the ones who were sleeping or straddling the fence got up and saw that all of Islam was at war with America, no matter how much money and so-called foreign aid they received from the infidels. Perhaps now was the time, once and for all, and he would be the sword who garnered a united faithful Islam that would finally drive, not only the Americans out the land of Mohammed, but also thrust the Israelis out of Palestine and into the sea.

There was no other way. Peace would come by the sword.

He had that one regret, still, as he penciled in the new route for the transport trucks through the Khyber Pass, the word having just come through on e-mail via his ISI contact about when and where he could expect pickup and safe passage for the promised weapons of mass destruction. A long time had passed since he had trucked in with the hundreds of thousands of Afghan refugees, when word the Americans would soon start bombing, even landing shock troops on the ground to, as their President called, "smoke the terrorists out of their holes." Even with all their sophisticated technology, that so-called real-time intelligence, believing they were superior to any and all Muslims, they hadn't unearthed the ones they so desperately wished to martyr. Thanks to the Soviet invasion, resistance fighters had spent years digging out entire mountains to create a vast labyrinth of tunnels and bunkers, most of which were so heavily mined and booby-trapped even some of the Taliban mullahs had to radio two days ahead before they gained an audience with the man, freedom fighters forced to defuse certain mines before the clerics arrived for a conference.

Yes, he would die someday soon, he knew, and his great pain was that he would never see his family again, at least not in this world.

Regret. So be it.

He picked up his AK-47. It was time to round up the others, pray as a group in the main room. The jihad could wait a few minutes; God couldn't. Besides, all he had to do was pass the word along to his contacts in the Punjab, and the shipment of heroin could proceed, disguised, of course, as food and medicine bound for the refugee camps.

It was an extraordinary but very simple scheme. There were many Pakistanis in positions of power who told the Americans what they wanted to hear, but did something else entirely. Lying wasn't a bad thing, as long as one was lying to the devil.

Stepping out of his office, he called out down the hallway that it was time to pray. Moments later, they came out of their rooms, bearded faces fashioned by war beneath the black turbans, warriors all, carrying their weapons, even to pray.

Despite protection by certain factions in Pakistan, none of them could ever be too careful.

THE TALIBAN THUG WAS blown off behind a thick spray of blood. A quick check of the curtained balconies before the fatal shot, and the Executioner determined there were no nosy neighbors.

Now the tough part.

How many inside? He didn't know, but he was going in, full-bore, no prisoners.

At the door, he listened, heard the low singsong chanting of the faithful from some point inside. He tried the doorknob, found it unlocked. Snicking it open, leathering the Beretta, he pulled the Kalashnikov free. To keep his tracks covered from any passersby, he quietly dragged the corpse through the doorway, the sounds of praying growing louder now, muting his quiet penetration.

He closed the door, homed in on the prayer session. Twenty or so feet ahead, he saw the first row of turbaned heads, bowing for the prayer rugs, facing east. With a basic understanding of Arabic, he heard them praying for the deaths of the infidels, that the faithful would prevail, God would direct them for the final victory over their enemies.

Strange words, he decided, praying for murder, even more peculiar for the prayer session was the fact they had laid AK-47s beside the prayer rugs.

It was time to send them on their way.

He pulled a frag grenade, armed it, then sent it rolling in a bowling-ball toss. He hugged a niche in the wall, glimpsed the steel egg rolling up right beneath the belly of the first gunner in the first row. A second later, their prayers went to hell in a deafening blast. Screams were lancing the air, but the soldier was already charging ahead, AK-47 up and chattering, cutting off their prayers in a long roaring of autofire. Figure twelve Taliban thugs tops, at least half that many already blown away, and he went to work, hosing down the mangled and the mauled with autofire. Three were grabbing their eyes where shrapnel had all but sheared away flesh to expose gleaming bone, but holding on to assault rifles, bellowing in Arabic as the Executioner drilled them, left to right, sent them flying from the boiling smoke.

Two got lucky, the farthest from the blast, last row, bouncing off the wall, AKs flaming when the Executioner locked on and zipped them, crotch to throat, everything that was flesh and cloth blown to crimson showers.

It was over in about the time it took to say, "God is great."

The Executioner walked into the room. He pulled the colored computer printout of an al-Qaeda leader with Wanted Dead Or Alive on top.

Or Alive he'd already penned an *X* through.

A statement, damn right. He let it flutter down to come to rest on a dead Taliban gunner. Of course, if any Pakistani who wandered into this death zone saw the calling card they would put two and two together, but Bolan was rolling, and if they weren't with him, they were against him.

No other way.

Swift but cautious, slapping home a fresh mag, he came to their war room.

Bingo.

One look at the table, and he figured Commander Alpha would offer to buy him a drink. A quick perusing, and he was sure he was looking at the mother lode of hot intel.

Routes to and from the Punjab lab, contacts and numbers. Careless, boys, he thought, very confident and careless.

Which told Bolan the Pakistanis weren't playing it straight with the Americans. What a surprise.

He found a satchel, emptied everything from the table, extracting hard drives. Mujhan, or better yet, Commander Alpha could sort through this later.

Next stop—an al-Qaeda nest.

The Executioner fastened the AK-47 in its special rigging, stepped outside and made hard time for the edge of the alley.

PANJAHL MOHAMMED THOUGHT he heard shooting from across the courtyard, but couldn't be sure. There was lots of shooting these days in the streets of Karachi, his fellow Muslims taking to the streets, burning effigies and American flags, firing assault rifles into the air.

He knew a faction of the Taliban had claimed a headquarters across the courtyard, and his initial fear was that traitorous elements of the Pakistani military had raided the apartment.

He hoped not. He sympathized with the Taliban, their country in ruins, American invaders all over the place, wishing to impose their will once again on Muslims.

He hated America. He prayed daily, staying at home more often these days, sending his family to the souk to sell their rugs and jewerly, while he fasted and feverishly implored God to aid the Taliban in their mighty struggle against the great oppressors, that they could regain their power base in Afghanistan.

He was through the beaded curtain, stepping onto the balcony when he spotted the tall, dark man in the brown tunic. The stranger was practically running, a swarthy man, but there was something about him, the features...

That was an American, he was positive. Even from across the courtyard he smelled the blood and the smoke, fearing the worst.

Heart pounding, he raced from the apartment, running across the courtyard. As soon as he spotted the first body, he knew what he would find inside. He felt sick, stepping toward the strewed bodies.

They had been slaughtered right where they had been praying.

No Muslim would dare commit this sort of sacrilege.

The man he'd seen leaving this apartment could only be an American.

The indignity, the blasphemy of it all!

And then his suspicions were confirmed when he spotted the picture of his al-Qaeda hero, the edges soaking up the blood of a holy warrior.

Alive Or...

Mohammed felt his blood boil. He knew what had to be done. These days, he had many like-minded Pakistanis in Karachi. They demonstrated on a daily basis, hot with anger to take out their frustration on anything American, trying to turn the tide against the infidel forces in his country, or even aid the Taliban in their armed struggle.

He took up an AK-47.

He would call his fellow Muslims, those Taliban sympathizers first, alert them an infidel murderer was running amok in Karachi.

They would find this blasphemer, and crush his body to broken, bloody ruins in the streets of Karachi.

CHAPTER NINE

Colonel Abdullah Mujhan wasn't quite sure what to make of the American called Brandon Stone, if that was even his real name, since all the CIA and Special Forces ops came to him with an assortment of martial-sounding aliases. And, no, he didn't know what branch of the U.S. military or intelligence agency he actually worked for, but that was the least of the grim mystery. There was something a little different, even more deadly about Stone than any black operatives he had seen inside Pakistan, a look of death about the man, as if he had walked through the fires of hell to slay all manner of demons. Behind the ice-blue eyes, there was also some other look, as hard as diamonds, that made him wonder if Stone was on some sort of crusade to single-handedly rid this part of the world of terrorists, a fire that forever burned to slay what their President called the "evildoers."

As if one man actually could.

Pakistan was a seething hotbed for extremist activity these days, and the violence had already spilled across the border into India. Not only that, but Mujhan knew the Taliban and al-Qaeda extremists had been plotting a huge operation to strike inside India, car bombs and rampant shooting attacks in the streets and such, attempting, for one thing, to point the fingers of blame toward Pakistan, fan the flames of hostility even more between the two countries, perhaps drag India, full scale and flaming out the missiles, into the war. At the moment, Mujhan believed he and his other ISI agents had that explosive situation contained, although the Taliban–al-Qaeda contingent in Pakistan was hardly shut down. Where there were twenty terrorists, he knew there would be twice, three times that many spread around the city and the wild frontier country to the north. It was simply a question of math, given the current state of fanaticism, the intelligence gathering coming up with numbers of extremists that began to make him wonder if Pakistan had been invaded by a shadow army of wild-eyed suicide bombers. If they didn't beat back the odds now, he feared Karachi would make the worst day in Beirut or Tel Aviv…

Well, a stroll in the park by comparison.

The refugee problem was a colossal nightmare in and of itself. While many had returned to their country, legions remained. Feeding one million starving mouths strained Pakistan's own dwindling resources. Even worse, as it turned out, many of the terrorists had infiltrated Pakistan, hiding in the teeming squalor of the camps, biding their time, waiting to slip out to carry on the terror torch. To get as far as they had, Mujhan knew they had to have had inside help. He would get to the bottom of it, root out any conspirators, and they would be executed on the spot, but only after they literally spilled their guts and implicated any other traitors.

Then there was the problem of the Bahadun plant in the Punjab. He had done some inquiring already about this classified facility run by a faction of the Pakistani military, tapping his own sources north, and what he was hearing was the worst of all possible news.

Yes, they were building and shipping not only the latest in high-tech radar, countersurveillance and communications to the Taliban, but weapons of mass destruction.

It would have to be shut down. Permanently. He could be sure in the near future an all-out assault on the Bahadun plant was in Stone's plans. If the plant was allowed to continue to operate, he knew the Americans would accuse his country of stabbing them in the back, or worse. The horror of American reprisal would go far beyond slapping that twenty-five-billion-dollar debt back in their faces.

What could he do except cooperate with Stone and the CIA black op he knew as Commander Alpha, even if that meant the streets of Karachi ran with rivers of blood? Mujhan had been ordered, in fact, by the president of Pakistan, to aid and assist the CIA and Special

Forces, allow them free rein inside the borders, hand off any intelligence he had on current terrorist operations in Karachi and beyond.

And cut them loose, to, as the American saying went, do their own thing.

There was something disturbing, he thought, about the dark man's manner that he couldn't let go of, put out of mind. Stone didn't strike him as any ordinary foot soldier, much less the standard special or black op he'd seen in his country these days, grim soldiers who had erected roving bases to the north, seasoned professionals prepared to go into Afghanistan, weed out the terrorists where they hid in their holes. Stone had fairly insisted Mujhan point him in the right direction, following the interrogation of the Taliban and al-Qaeda prisoners currently under the roof of the Pakistani Military Defence quarters. It was strange, if he thought about it hard enough, how Stone, who had the look of a blooded combat vet—something he could clearly see in those glacier-blue eyes—but seemed to find the methods they used on the terrorists distasteful. He would watch as an al-Qaeda terrorist was hung upside down, naked, and exposed wires sparking with electricity were applied to the genitals, ears, anus, nose. Death, Mujhan knew, was something the fanatic hungered for, craving to go out of the world as a martyr, instant paradise, or so they thought.

Pain was something else entirely. There was no glory in pain, not when a man was screaming his lungs out, thrashing about in chains, soiling himself. In the eyes of the fanatic this was dishonor.

Well, Mujhan was in the midst of his own jihad, attempting to stem the floodtide of hatred and rage and violence that was sweeping Pakistan. He would help Stone, if just to see the man crush as many terrorists as he could. But how? He had struck out on his own, Commander Alpha assisting, but riots were spreading across the city again. Two Westerners, even with their thin disguises, attempting to pass themselves off as Arab, were prime targets for the howling mobs teeming in the streets if they were made. Most of the trouble was confined to the Old City, centered near Memom Mosque. Just east of the mosque was where the ISI-CIA intelligence had pinned down the locations of three terrorist hideouts.

Stone was right in the heart of anarchy.

And so the man had marched out to slay the evildoers. He couldn't be sure that was the intention, but Mujhan already had a house full of prisoners, his cells choked with dozens of Taliban and al-Qaeda extremists already rounded up, and a body count of more terrorists in the city would certainly alleviate the problem of finding space to house more fanatics. He had plenty enough prisoners to grill, as it stood, top Taliban and al-Qaeda terrorists, in fact. The interrogations went on around the clock, the shower stall the Q-and-A room to facilitate cleanup. Slowly but surely, they were whipping, electrifying and skinning the answers out of the terrorists. If they didn't survive the interrogation, there was a furnace out back, east of the helipad, where the bodies were quickly disposed of. War, he knew, always called for extreme measures, and always brought out the savage worst in men anywhere. It was simply the nature of the beast. Terrorism would not be tolerated on his watch.

He checked the situation map, the red areas pinning down the locations of the cells in question. By now, Stone had either shut down one, maybe two, or...

What?

He was dead?

Mujhan didn't think so, hoped not. At some point, when the Americans were finished smoking out the terrorists, destroying the Taliban, his own country would need their help, financial, even military perhaps. The bad blood between Taliban supporters in Pakistan and the Americans could find its way to his doorstep, anarchy unleashed, the country going up in flames, retaliatory strikes against Pakistanis who had helped the Americans.

The future looked dark, he feared. They needed the Americans.

"Colonel, you need to come with me. You need to hear this."

Special Agent Ghazri was in the doorway, eyes wild, his dark, bearded face frozen in an expression of intense excitement or terror, Mujhan couldn't decide.

With long strides, he followed Ghazri down the narrow corridor, passing the barred cages where anger and hate-filled stares of extremists bored into him. A few muttered obscenities, but he ignored the outbursts. The stench of their filthy bodies was bad enough, but when he entered the shower stall, the stink of pure misery and terror nearly bowled him off his feet.

"Tell the colonel, you son of a whore!"

The interrogator, Agent Zirat, placed the wires on the al-Qaeda prisoner. He screamed, thrashing, straining against the manacles, jumping about like a fish out of water.

And the prisoner spewed out a list of names, Pakistani collaborators, the whole rotten bunch, most of whom, he claimed, were operating out of the Bahadun plant.

"Colonel!"

Pivoting, Mujhan found Captain Pekashan in the doorway.

"We have a situation erupting in the Old City. Our informants on the street tell me the demonstrators were informed an American is murdering Pakistani citizens. There is shooting, a full-scale riot breaking out."

Colonel Mujhan bolted out the door, barking for his men to follow. He knew what to be done, but didn't like it. It was dangerous to the point of madness, all things considered, but there was no other course of action, not if he wanted to save Stone's neck.

THE STINKING FUMES of burning gasoline, as the fires consumed the American flags and the effigies of the American President, swelled Panjahl Mohammed with great pride and determination. This was Islam at its best, he thought, brothers in blood and arms, hoping the world beyond their borders saw how much and how great their love of Islam was, unbending and unyielding in the face of naked American imperialistic aggression.

With his AK-47 by his side, he searched the packed mob, their chants of "Death to America" rising in feverish pitch. He was looking for Bhujtar or Abdul, aware they would know where other freedom fighters were housed, and where he believed the murdering American would go next to attempt to butcher more holy warriors.

It was a maddening surge, shoving his way through the howling throngs, fighting his way through the walls of flesh, bounced around, but he knew Bhujtar and Abdul were somewhere in the demonstration, which seemed to sprawl all over and beyond Boulton Market.

They never missed a demonstration, and he had to find them, enlist their help to hunt down the murdering American, perhaps get the crowds all over the streets or hanging from balconies in nearby apartment buildings to join them in their righteous wrath.

Call it divine intervention, he thought, but he found them, standing on top of a Toyota pickup, inciting the mob to even greater heights of hatred toward America, waving both Pakistani and Afghan flags.

"Bhujtar! Abdul!"

He made the side of the truck, his fellow Muslims not appearing to notice he was there until he bellowed their names again.

"Where are any other freedom fighters in the Old City?"

"What?" Bhujtar shouted over the din.

Mohammed climbed onto the Toyota, forced to practically shout into their faces as someone in the mob began firing off an AK-47 toward the sky. "There is an American—I saw him with my own eyes. I just came from a Taliban headquarters. He murdered them all, and as they were praying! He can only be an American to commit such an atrocity!"

Mohammed saw their faces wilt into shock, then rage blew up the storm in their eyes.

Abdul plucked up an AK-47. "I know where! Grab some of these men and follow me! I will tell this crowd on the way out!"

"YOU'D BETTER WRAP this up quick, Stone. I've got a situation, looks headed your way, pal, a whole sea of raving fanatics. Something has got scads of these folks worked up into a frenzy. And they're surging your way. Something tells me you were fingered after the first hit."

The Executioner was on the handheld radio with Commander Alpha. The GPS had locked on to the second target, guiding him east of Boulton Market. It was another apartment building, just off an alley, a stone structure, drab and cracked in the walls, balconies lined with laundry and colorful rugs. Second floor, midway down, and the al-Qaeda nest was writhing with human snakes he wanted to trample before moving on. But

Bolan was reading between the lines, and knew the pot of anti-West hatred was boiling over. A riot was breaking out, surging his way, and he figured someone had spotted him on the way out of the slaughter zone, investigated, hit the streets in search of the shooter.

He was marked.

Silently he cursed. If the mob got hold of him, they would tear him to pieces, and no amount of bullets and grenades would hold back the howling jackals. He checked the corner of the module where Alpha's position was marked.

"You're on Nishtar," Bolan said. "I'm in the neighborhood."

"I know where you are. I've got you homed in on my unit, but I'm telling you, if we get hemmed in here, we might as well say a Hail Mary, friend."

"Give me ten minutes, then I'll make my way toward you."

"Step lively, and I think you can scratch number three."

Bolan stowed the unit and the GPS module. Somewhere up the alley he heard the roaring of a vast mob coming his way.

If someone recognized him…

The Executioner had slugged, shot and blasted his way out of many tight corners where the heat was past scorching and his back was pinned to the wall.

This time, he wasn't so sure. It was a strange and fearful place to be, but he wasn't about to give up hope, not by a long shot.

As long as he was breathing there was fight left.

Make no mistake, the soldier determined he would go out with a roar, if this was the end.

CHAPTER TEN

The demonstrations in the streets of Karachi against the Great Satan, in living color on the television set in the main room, all those American flags and their leader burning in effigy from the swarming pockets of holy protesters, brought a wide smile to the lips of Mussam Mahlad. He sipped tea, sitting on the divan with six other al-Qaeda freedom fighters, his holy warriors scattered about the room, enjoying the show.

It was a beautiful sight to behold, he thought, Islam raging on against its oppressors, and the only thing that would have made it more holy was if living, breathing infidels were suddenly found and dragged and beaten to death in the streets of his new home away from the camps. Barring that, he would have settled for some Pakistani collaborator, a whore of his own people, strung up in the square or hanged from the front of a mosque, a warning to any Arabs who would defile and betray their own bloodline by helping the hated Americans.

Mahlad joined in the chuckling as someone began stomping on the burning remains of an American flag on-screen. "God is great."

They echoed his sentiments, embellishing with a few choice words about the American President and the barbarian hordes he knew were hunkered down in Pakistan, Special Forces and Delta commandos who continued to make forays into hallowed Afghan ground. He had been astounded when the Americans had moved into Afghanistan, enraged that they still hunted al-Qaeda fighters.

Mahlad hoped to make a statement, unleashing attacks throughout Karachi, even two incursions into India planned that would bring the Muslim faithful in that country on board, a rallying point, for sure, where more of the devout would follow, aware it was indeed the West against Islam, new armies of holy warriors taking up arms, willing to march out on suicide missions wherever the devils could be found for slaughter.

He was at present a long way from home, in a land that had American sympathizers, worst of all, but his training in the camps of Afghanistan would soon pay off. He knew how to shoot almost every sort of weapon in that part of the world, how to blend in with locals of any race or religion, maintain a low profile, obey the laws of the land, never call attention to himself. It never hurt to have forged passports and visas, either, or enough money to buy off border guards, politicians, policemen and soldiers.

He could arm C-4, set plastique to go off by radio remote or timer. He knew dynamite, even how to plant land mines in hotels or airports in certain places where the untrained and unsuspecting eye would never look. Trash cans were good for explosives, the underside of dining-room tables could also be rigged with plastique, even toilet seats could be fixed, slender wires trailing into the tanks, a weary traveler just stepping off an international flight, too tired to notice until he sat down and it was too late and half the terminal was blown away in a fireball. With enough explosives, he could get a hotel suite, check out during the night when the place was at full or even near capacity, say Paris or London, and take down the whole building.

Then there was the comforting knowledge the Taliban and al-Qaeda had gone high-tech, keeping up to or ahead of the FBI, CIA. They had sophisticated cell phones with scramblers with which to stay in touch with the other members of the Taliban and al-Qaeda in the city proper and beyond, no Pakistani authorities or CIA able to intercept messages when the word came down to proceed. Secured e-mail, faxes, cutouts who would use encryption learned in the camps. It was a brave new world out there, Islam on the march, and Mahlad wanted to be a large part of the coming triumph.

The big catch, though, was just a few days off, when the special shipment was slated to go north, through the

Khyber Pass. Again he wasn't in the loop about precisely what the merchandise was, but he had been told it would be grand, big and powerful enough to show the West that Islam could and would fight back, and win.

The plan was still up in the air, though, Mahlad not privy to all the details, just in case there was a leak by way of capture of one of their own, and already he knew that had happened. The Taliban, though, had anticipated that sort of trouble, aware that eventually the Pakistanis collaborating with the Americans would arrest a few of their own. Enough heroin money, courtesy of the hated Russians, had been spread around so that hopefully any loose tongues behind bars would somehow be silenced.

These days, he could never be too careful. He could only trust his own warriors, and only if they were in sight.

He was about to turn up the sound, wondering why the demonstrators suddenly looked more incensed than ever, a tidal wave of Islamic fervor surging down a boulevard that looked very familiar when—

The door crashed open, a sound of thunder that jolted Mahlan off the divan. He was grabbing up his AK-47, wishing he had posted guards outside but figuring that would be too obvious if collaborators happened by, when something like a baseball bounced into the main room.

"Grenade!" he heard one of the others shouting.

They were slamming into one another, the air knocked out of Mahlad's lungs from a flying elbow, bodies scrambling for the deeper cover of the hallway when the egg blew. There was a blinding flash of light, his ears pierced by a terrible noise, then he plunged for the floor, gagging on smoke, unable to see, hear or stand.

WHEN THE FLASH-BANG rocked their world, the Executioner gave it a full second, then barged into the apartment. It was the anticipated blind chaos, six or seven al-Qaeda savages, all of them flailing about, firing wild rounds at nothing at all.

To their credit, they held on with the tenacity of the damned who knew they were on their way out of the world, so why not take somebody along for the ride into oblivion. Several bullets snapped past Bolan, gouging the wall beside his head, but he was already raking the doomed with a long burst of AK-47 autofire.

A turkey shoot.

The warrior sent one al-Qaeda thug tumbling through the television, three other shadows flung over the divan, driven out of the smoke cloud by Bolan's barrage of autofire. He swept the Kalashnikov back and forth, hammering them this way and that, lamps crashing to the floor, bodies sailing, great smears of crimson splashing the stone walls.

HUMINT was on the money once again. The bitter hell of it was that Bolan knew he would be unable to make target number three.

It was time to bolt, indeed, bail Karachi.

Outside he heard the thunder of angry voices, rolling for the apartment building, a long crescendo of fury that seemed to grow louder by the second.

A lynch mob was just around the corner, he knew.

He hid the assault rifle beneath his tunic, but hefted a tear-gas grenade. He really didn't want to have to fire on a mob hell-bent on tearing him limb from limb, unarmed combatants, just the same, but if it came down to that...

And the first wave came rolling around the corner of the alley, a human flood of pure rage, and turning his direction.

"There he is! That's him! The murderer!"

PANJAHL MOHAMMED LED the frenzied charge up the steps, AK-47 up and tracking. It was him, a face he would never forget, had committed to memory the very first instant he had laid eyes on the dark man and instincts warned him something had gone terribly wrong in the Taliban safehouse. Now Mohammed was certain the killer had scored again, this time wiping out an apartment full of al-Qaeda freedom fighters.

It was an abomination.

Say this was some CIA killer, he thought, and say they dragged him through the streets, pummeling him to bloody pulp, eventually holding up his body before the cameras as a dire warning to the West, perhaps dousing him with gasoline and torching him finally. Vengeance would be served, and he would be a hero to the cause for setting the mob onto this killer.

It was a blind charge, nothing organized about it, his Islamic brothers bumping into him, and he began to regret the sudden haste with which they had arrived at the al-Qaeda headquarters. He realized he should have taken his time, organized the demonstrators, sealing off the various alleys that led to Nishtar Road, cornering the killer.

The infidel, he feared, might get away.

He was topping the stairs, when the acrid smoke cloud erupted, spewing noxious fumes into his face, stopping him blind in his tracks as the rush of bodies from behind bowled him down.

BOLAN HIT the opposite stairway, heard them hacking on the tear gas, but knew he was far from any finish line. Before he began his descent he looked back, saw the first wave of rabid demonstrators stumbling through the sizzling cloud, even trampling their own in the murderous charge to get their hands on him. Two AK-47s opened up, but the soldier was already lost to any lethal spray, as bullets gouged up the landing above his head in a flying sheet of splinters.

He hit the alley running, veering in a northerly direction, where he hoped Commander Alpha had somehow closed in, ready to scoop him up. There was no time to radio an SOS, since three fanatics, either part of the mob or looking for a way to vent frustration and rage, came charging, snarling.

The Executioner broke into a sprint, left his feet, angling his body sideways. He hammered the trio on the fly, two of them sailing back to bring down a shelf of pots and pans hung in a market stall. By now the mob was swinging his way in the bazaar, Hindu women in bright skirts flapping their hands and shrieking. Another would-be hero rushed the soldier, the shouts of "Stop the American murderer!" boiling from the alley he'd just left behind. A turbaned Pakistani raised his arm, a balled fist craning for Bolan's skull when the Executioner planted a toe in the family jewels, thrust a forearm up and through jawbone like lava suddenly erupting from a volcano. The woof was all but lost to the resounding crack of bone as the flying body was swallowed up by a kaleidoscope of hanging carpets before it crashed into shelves of hookahs.

Two more wanna-be heroes tried to take on the stranger fleeing the mob, which, Bolan saw over his shoulder, was rushing around the corner, a tsunami of human fury bowling down any- and everything in its path, cries of fear and outrage lancing the air. The Executioner did another acrobatic launch, flinging himself sideways again, this time driving his mass through both sets of legs, sent them flying on in a tangle of arms and legs.

He was up and running, no idea where in hell he was going when autofire rattled the air behind him, hot lead tugging at his scalp, peppering the stone wall beside his charge.

A wide boulevard, choked with countless Pakistanis, donkey carts, buses and pickups, fanned away from the mouth of the alley. Figure Nishtar Road, and where the hell was Commander Alpha?

Behind him Bolan heard the shouts and screams and

voices raging on how someone should grab the American murderer.

He was dashing between the choked traffic, horns blaring, angry faces behind windshields shaking fists, when he heard a familiar sound, which descended straight from the blue sky.

Looking up, he saw the brown-camoued Huey gunship swooping down over the high-rise apartments, rotor wash whipping into his face. It lowered, the mob streaming out into traffic now, Pakistani hyenas jumping over the hoods of cars. Bolan jumped up on the hood of a battered pickup truck, the driver craning his head out, shrieking obscenities as the soldier bounded onto the roof of the cab.

A rope ladder, like manna from heaven, unfurled out the side door. The Executioner grabbed the first rung, began hauling himself up for freedom when he heard the din of rage converge on the truck, a maelstrom of raw, unbridled fury that told him the mob was not about to give it up. Above, tails of smoke began curling away from the gunship, the sounds of choking and gagging below signaling some wise soul was going to bat again, attempting to hold back the throng with a tear-gas-and-smoke bomb shelling.

Then something hard clawed into Bolan's lower pants leg. The grab and lunge forced him to twist around on the ladder, his grasp slipping against the sudden impact, the rage and force behind the digging nearly tearing him from the rung. Looking down, he saw the fanatic's face, teeth bared as he used Bolan's leg, an improvised step ladder, to get higher, a clawed hand appearing as if it wanted to talon its way into his crotch. The soldier raised one leg, then smashed his boot heel repeatedly off that swarthy demonic visage, mashing a hawkish nose to crimson froth, shattering jawbone until the bloodied human hyena plunged and hammered into the roof of the truck's cab, rolling off, taking a few mounted jackals to the street in a heap.

"Go! Go!" Bolan heard someone shouting from the belly of the Huey.

The gunship lifted, Bolan clawing his way up, finally grasping the edge of the doorway. Two sets of strong hands dug into his shoulders, hauling him aboard. He took a second to catch his breath, the muzzle of the Kalashnikov digging into his side. Standing, he found himself face to face with Colonel Mujhan and Commander Alpha.

The Executioner peeled off his false beard and flung it out the doorway. "Glad you could make it."

"I'll bet you are," Commander Alpha said.

CHAPTER ELEVEN

Brognola cursed, rubbing his face, unable to watch, but since he already knew the outcome he looked on. The big Fed was in the War Room with Barbara Price, both of them watching the CNN footage piped in on the wall monitor. It was a close shave for the big guy. Brognola chomped down on his stogie, digging out the antacid tablets next and popping four, washing them down with coffee, the acid volcano in his belly feeling as if it were eating a hole through his intestines with shooting lava. Even watching it with the knowledge their man made it out set Brognola's nerves on fire.

The worst-case scenario damn near happened. In the streets of Karachi they were watching the taped version of the riots earlier in the day. Teeming mobs were chasing a tall, dark man in a black beard and brown tunic into traffic, a Pakistani gunship coming out of nowhere over the rooftops of the apartment buildings, rope ladder flung down. The blond female reporter was bleating on in frantic tones, head swiveling, hair flying in her face, damn near railing, it sounded to Brognola, about a Taliban–al-Qaeda connection getting violently severed in Karachi by an unknown gunman—presumably American—who had gone on a rampage before a Pakistani mob began chasing him down in retribution for the attacks. If he didn't know any better, he would have sworn this little snip, probably fresh out of journalism school and just off the casting couch, was commiserating with the Taliban and al-Qaeda. He caught himself, wondering for a second why he was feeling a trifle mean and angry, thinking unusually cynical thoughts, directing his silent ire at some kid who really didn't know any better and was probably just scared to death to be anywhere close to that kind of action.

Brognola was damn grateful the cameraman was too scared to venture deeper into the thrashing mob. Whatever the reasoning, there was no close-up of the gunman in question. The gunman had some problems when he hit the ladder, fanatics now swarming the truck, a jackal grabbing onto a leg only to find his face smashed in by repeated blows from a boot, falling next, bowling four or five of his fellow demonstrators off the truck. The gunman was hauled aboard the gunship, then they were up, up and away.

The gunman, of course, had already checked in with the Farm, updating Brognola and the others.

"He's damn lucky, Hal."

"Tell me about it. What a mess."

"No, it's the Pakistanis' problem to cover up. They're either with us or against us, and so far they're toeing the line."

"Can you imagine what would have…?"

Brognola let the morbid line of thought trail off. The Executioner was used to feeling the heat in the killing fields, finding a way out to the other side to live to fight another day. Still, sitting on the sidelines and watching their man nearly get stomped…

"Okay, so we know there's a definite connection between the Russian Mob, the Taliban," Price said, "and some ISI traitors. The Bahadun plant in the Punjab is on Striker's list of things to do."

"Straight from a torture session with an al-Qaeda extremist," Brognola said. "This General Abed Muammar. How in the hell could he have gotten away with actually building weapons of mass destruction right under the noses of the Pakistani government and military?"

"Military government," Price gently corrected.

"Right, the country is run by the military, I almost forgot. How many others are involved, we can't say."

"Striker, Commander Alpha and his CIA black-ops team are set to go, twenty hundred, local time. This connection to the Taliban has to be severed. Whatever other dominoes topple in the process…"

"I hear you. Okay, as for Able's situation, the Man asked to put them on hold. Carl grumbled, but I ordered him to hold off. They won't set down at the Spectron

Reserve until the Man has called up a Special Forces team to assist in the North Pole assault, or until he gives me the thumbs-up for Able to finish hammering down on Walker and Ruskavka. We're looking at a war, Barbara."

"I thought we always were."

"Yeah, but where this all ends is anybody's guess. Unless the legitimate Russian powers shrug it off as a renegade operation, we could be setting back our relations with that country...well, Stalin's worst days would be preferable."

"We know where Walker's jet landed. We have a firm fix on numbers. We have the lodge under satellite surveillance. It looks like they're content to hole up and figure out their next move."

"I'm thinking they already have it figured. I'm thinking those subs will move out anytime and attempt to finish blowing up the reserve and picking up our bad guys...stay on it. If those subs move out, I'm going to have to light a fire under the Man."

He saw Price watching the action on the screen for another moment until the chopper was soaring off over the Karachi skyline, swallowed up by the distance. He saw the concern, then the relief in her eyes. He understood, since he felt the same damn way, but not quite the way in which she cared about Mack Bolan.

"Go get some rest, Barbara."

"Maybe. I'll see."

"I'll be in the Computer Room in a while."

She nodded again, stood and left.

Brognola sat there, massaging his tired face, grimacing against the rumbling bile in his gut. He chomped down another antacid tablet, sipped some coffee and chewed on the end of his stogie.

He felt strangely alone, even though he was under the same roof with what he considered his family—or most of them.

The world was going crazy, he thought. Were they looking at the beginning of the end times? he wondered. Was the Apocalypse one more riot in Karachi, one more WTC-type bombing away? All the dire missions his people had undertaken, the close calls where calamity could have struck down entire nations if not for the Stony Man warriors, and he couldn't ever remember feeling this heavy, so grim, so troubled.

Where did it all go from there?

He couldn't say, but at least he had the best of the best out there, willing to go the distance to keep the fuse of Armageddon from lighting the whole damn planet on fire.

If they weren't enough...

Well, he thought, God help them all.

God save the human race.

"YOU WANT TO TELL me, Colonel Mujhan, how in the hell this so-called pharmaceutical plant that turns out to be not only building weapons of mass destruction, but also has Taliban gorillas right under that roof went unnoticed for what it was up until now? Look at 'em, right there, on sat imagery, walking around, armed to the teeth, doing everything but shooting our eyes in the sky the middle-finger salute. You want to tell me how the hell we've already picked up on sat imagery and unmanned recon birds a whole convoy of trucks now heading for the Afghan border with what we believe are warheads, stuffed with bio and chem agents, intermediate missiles, to boot, these upgraded SCUD-44s, which can land as far away as the heart of Tel Aviv? You want to tell me who the hell we—meaning myself, my men and Stone—can trust from here on out?"

"I can only say it has just come to my attention. I can only say we must act promptly. I can only tell you, as a soldier and a man of honor, that I have no involvement whatsoever with this plant, or any extremist traitors in my country. If I was a terrorist collaborator, would I have risked my life, my helicopter to fly into the middle of the madness we put behind to pull you and Colonel Stone out of the fire?"

Point taken, Bolan thought.

The Executioner was in the deep corner of the command tent, listening to the exchange between Colonel Mujhan and Commander Alpha, the former keeping his cool, the latter hot as a desert sun, but backed off some as he mulled over the ISI man's words. The CIA commander was jacked up on righteous anger; the Executioner could understand that, and even Bolan had to wonder how far the Pakistani connection reached. Even if Mujhan was clean, a small army of rats had been flushed out of the dark, thanks to the ISI's bloody magic touch on Islamic extremist prisoners hung up by their ankles.

Bolan moved to his radio unit, glancing back as Commander Alpha shook his massive head. The commander was a Yeti of a man, the M-16/M-203 combo slung across his shoulder dwarfed by his size. He had to have been six-seven, in the neighborhood of 270 pounds, all of it solid muscle, Bolan figured. A thick black wooly nap of hair, arms bared to show more matting of hair that reached all the way to his knuckles, a face like a Neanderthal, with eyebrows that were knitted together, and the commander could probably get the enemy to lay down their weapons by just showing up and presenting his menacing self. Of course, that would never happen, Bolan knew, and from there on, he could be damn sure they weren't taking any prisoners, Taliban or Pakistani soldiers or officers who had secretly sworn allegiance to America's enemies, an unspoken rule of engagement, he sensed between himself and Commander Alpha, which was to mow down anything that was armed and angry. It was the only viable way to do business. It happened that way all the time in Bolan's world, allegiances shifting behind his back, whether for warped ideology, money or outright extortion by the opposition, armed with the other guy's sins, threatening to go to his family or public....

Deal with it, Bolan told himself.

He looked away. Let them have it at. He was dialing

up David McCarter to let Phoenix X Force know where he stood. The CIA mobile base had been planted several hours ago in the Cholistan Desert, which was at the very deepest southern edge of the Punjab. The two squads of black ops had flown in from another U.S. base just inside the Indian border in the assembly-line Predator gunships. Like any other American bases in Pakistan, they were thrown up in a matter of hours, away from populated areas, bearing in mind the greater the distance from any tribal regions the better. No sense in stirring up the hornet's nest of armed natives.

To keep the heat off the Pakistani military government, no clandestine U.S. base remained in one spot for more than two days tops, tents rolled up before any locals grew wise, warbird lifting off in two shakes, nothing but a mystery and a memory for native speculation. Security for the special ops first and foremost, since some extremist sympathetic to the Taliban could charge in with a truck stuffed to the gills with explosives. Naturally, armed guards were always on alert, radar and heat-seeking sensors always searching out the terrain for any encroaching bodies. Punjab, the "Land of Five Rivers," was the richest, most fertile and the most heavily populated of the Pakistani provinces, Bolan knew, something like seventy million folks, most of them to the north. The Cholistan had been selected, the way Bolan read the intel flying over from Karachi, for this CIA base for both its close proximity to the Bahadun plant and because the only human eyes out here were the nomadic tribes who might wander by in a camel caravan. Not much by way of human traffic in this desolate corner, but the Cholistan, Bolan knew, was a land of forts, all of them abandoned now except for the tourist trade, which had dwindled to next to nothing, since foreigners were pretty much and understandably nervous about putting Pakistan on their vacation spots these days. He heard Mujhan attempt a feeble explanation of how such a thing could have happened, tossing in widespread support for the Taliban among too many of his countrymen, then saying how the Punjab was the industrial heart of his country, producing steel, textiles, fertilizer, chemicals, with cotton being the cash crop, and so on. It made some sort of warped sense, Mujhan said, for a plant the size they were looking at on intel pics to be out there, even if they were producing weapons.

Commander Alpha grumbled something, then lit a cigarette, scowling at the intelligence spread out on the metal table, blowing smoke rings in angry puffs big enough to clear out a yuppie lunch crowd.

Bolan rang up McCarter, got right to it. "X-Mac," he said, using McCarter's cover, "Striker here. What's your status?"

"Holding," the Briton said, "but for how long, I couldn't tell you. The mates are getting antsy, both my men and our fellow shooters. In other words, we're all itchy to strike up the band. Real-time intel is coming in as fast as you can burn through a 30-round clip. We're set to go, presumably the big birds will be coming down on this Ramadan camp, wheels up at 240 hours. We'll watch the fireworks over real-time sat surveillance while flying in, coordinating our own gig with the big bang from above. Into the smoke, then smoke them out of their holes in the mountainside. Our own people back home," he said, referring to the Farm, "can likewise catch the Apocalypse."

"I've got a situation that needs my immediate attention. I have two of those prototype Predator gunships parked outside where I'm located. We've tagged this Bahadun plant as a major supplier of some very nasty stuff for the Taliban and al-Qaeda."

"Eighty-six it."

"That's the general idea."

"You telling me you might not make the party with us?"

"If you have to, go without me. I can catch a ride with the troops down here. We fly on, I'll touch base, arrange a DZ. We'll need to refuel at your base. Is that a problem?"

"I'll inform the good colonel. He's leaving behind a standing guard. Re-upping on fuel and hardware shouldn't be a problem. I have to tell you, Striker, we could use all available hands on this one. We're looking at a massive camp, old Soviet T-72 tanks, APCs, bunkers, antiaircraft batteries, the works. We figure anywhere from two to three thousand fanatics. The plan's on the table, the irons are in the fire, the good Delta colonel is set to give us a final brief, then we could be gone anytime."

Bolan wanted to be there, would do his damnedest to go in with Phoenix Force when the fireworks began to blow. It was going to be the toughest, ugliest foray, he suspected, for the warriors of Phoenix to date. Forget that Afghanistan was number one when it came to rugged, inhospitable terrain that would make a stroll around the dark side of the moon or Mars pleasant by comparison. Three thousand fanatics? he thought. It would be quite a major coup if they nailed them all. Bolan wished them luck, even if he couldn't be there. The key to success, he knew, would be how much damage the air strike could pull off.

"You'll be hearing from me, X-Mac," Bolan said, and signed off.

The soldier walked back to situation table.

"The colonel here," Commander Alpha said, "tells me there's anywhere from twenty to thirty Pakistani soldiers and officers on the premises. On top of that, they're baby-sitting another twenty or so Taliban and al-Qaeda gunners. Then you've got the legit workforce, fifty-plus civilians…here's the pictures, Stone."

Bolan looked it over. The compound was marked off by the meter, by four quads. It was the size of any large American factory, built of stone, a squat rectangular structure running the length of a city block, wrapped around by razor-topped cyclone fencing. There were six canvas-covered trucks out back in bays, on the north side, with steel containers scattered about, forklifts, other heavy machinery, a complete picture of a warehouse in the desert. Sat imagery detailed the armed guard, the crates scattered near the rolling doors, and more than a few black turbans milling about with AK-47s.

"We think the convoy left three hours ago," Alpha said. "I can't spare the HAZMAT team I'm taking, since we agreed to hit the plant first, then go for the convoy. No telling what we'll turn up once we blast our way inside."

"I will fly with you," Mujhan said, "but I cannot be seen openly engaging in combat."

Alpha waved him off. "Yeah, yeah, I gotcha. But I want you to understand everyone there is fair game."

Mujhan nodded. "I understand. It is—how would you say?—your show."

"That's how we say it," Alpha growled. "Okay, it'll be dark in an hour or so. Let's hammer out the finer details, Stone. My guys are already on board those Predators and I didn't bring them or those warbirds in from India for show and tell. I can have them briefed in fifteen minutes, then we're gone."

Bolan felt the sense of urgency rising inside as Commander Alpha began laying out the plan of attack.

Alpha stabbed a sausage-sized finger at a sat picture. "See that concrete dome? You know what I'm thinking, Stone?"

"Antiaircraft battery."

"You got it. We'll have to blow that off the roof first."

CHAPTER TWELVE

"You're going to be hit."

General Abed Muammar wasn't sure he'd heard his ISI connection in Karachi correctly, the trundling of a tracked carrier passing his windowed office, carrying the new SS-40 SCUDs for the loading bays, muting the voice on the other end of the phone. The general asked Agent Hibal to repeat himself when the noise faded. This time he heard him right, terribly loud and crystal clear, and the phone became a great weight in his pudgy hand. He pulled back, staring at the phone as if it were a viper poised to bite.

"How do you know this? When? Who? Americans?"

"The interrogations have proved successful for Colonel Mujhan. It would appear as if our vaunted freedom fighters, so feared in the American media, plastered all over their cable news shows in black kaffiyehs covering their entire faces like hoods as they perform commando exercises in the camps of Afghanistan, couldn't stomach a little bit of pain. They talked. Mujhan knows about the plant. They named names."

"And myself?"

"You were one of the first conspirators mentioned."

Muammer felt his near three-hundred-pound bulk heaving as he waddled around his office, his heart thundering, the blubber of his triple-deckered chin quivering, sweat breaking out beneath the bill of his cap. This was incredible, he thought. No, it was a nightmare beyond comprehension.

The world suddenly felt strangely out of kilter, the room spinning as fear turned to panic and churned bile in his stomach. Beyond his window, he stared at the space-suited workforce in the quarantined bays beyond the decon chambers, his soldiers strolling about, barking orders, his black-turbaned honored guests helping to load the canvas-covered trucks with the containers of anthrax shells, the sarin nerve gas, rolling up the delivery systems for missiles on their tracks into other beds.

"I do not know precisely when they will attack, but Colonel Mujhan has already contacted the president and informed him of the situation. CIA black ops, Delta Force, I do not know. But the raid was approved by the president. It could happen anytime. I suggest you conclude whatever business with Mullah al-Wahbin and his men as soon as possible. We have already received millions in payoffs."

"But the intermediate missiles they want are not all—"

"I understand. It takes time to reprocess plutonium and uranium waste into weapons grade. However, they must take what they have, and I understand at least one convoy has already left for the border, so they will have to be patient until we can rebuild another facility."

"Rebuild!" Muammar nearly screamed, his voice rife with horror. "What are you saying? They are coming here to blast us off the face of the desert?"

"That would be a good assumption. I would prepare yourself accordingly."

When Hibal hung up, Muammar slammed down the receiver. Prepare himself accordingly? he bitterly thought. And do what? Flee the country? Throw himself at the mercy of the American commandos? Denying any personal involvement was impossible. He had openly invited the Taliban and al-Qaeda into Pakistan, arranging for them set up cells in Karachi, or arrive at the factory to pick up merchandise already paid for. If he had been fingered, he would be branded a Taliban collaborator, marched out to the nearest square and hung.

He trudged across the office, knew what had to be done. Their antiaircraft battery would have to be raised on the roof, for starters, then he would have to order the Taliban and their al-Qaeda brothers-in-arms to vacate the premises. Or would they choose to stay and fight? Either way, Muammar knew he was in deep trouble. These days, treason was punishable by death, considering the current state of tension between his country, the Americans and the Afghans, and the Americans would surely scream for his head on a pike, assuming, of course, he survived the coming attack.

It galled him, just the same, to know his own countrymen, men of high military rank and power within the government, were supporting the covert war against the Taliban. Couldn't they see that the entire Islamic world was watching Pakistan, judging them in accordance to what they did or didn't do to help the Americans? Pakistan would be held accountable, perhaps become a free-fire zone for extremists who wanted to punish the country for its cooperation. Someday the shadow war would be over, the Americans would be gone and his country could well become another Beirut but on a massive holocaust scale.

Then what?

It was insanity, all of it, but Muammar had made his decision from the very beginning. Take the Taliban's drug money and arm them with weapons of mass destruction, since he despised the Americans himself, hating them for invading sovereign Muslim countries wherever and whenever they pleased, declaring war on his brother and sister Arabs, leveling their cities, leaving behind entire nations in utter shambles.

Not this time. The plant had been his to run for almost four years, operating under the guise of a pharmaceutical factory so as to not alert the Americans to the real purpose here. He had never believed it possible for the Americans to be so crazy or brazen as to launch cruise missiles on the plant as they had in Sudan and on the Afghan camps several years back.

Only now they were coming for a face-to-face engagement.

Muammar rolled his great bulk out into the warehouse area, sounding the alarm, telling his soldiers to man the antiaircraft battery, seal off a perimeter around the building.

They were running for their battle stations when Muammar spotted Mullah al-Wahbin coming his way.

"What is happening?"

"I regret to inform you we are about to be attacked."

The Afghan cleric slipped the AK-47 off his shoulder, barking over his shoulder at his holy warriors to go and board the trucks.

Muammar looked up toward the ceiling as the platform with the multibarreled cannon rose, the concrete bunker parting to reveal a velvet sky.

The cleric was firing off a slew of questions, none of which Muammar could answer, then al-Wahbin raged, "Are you listening to me? Do you have any answers? When?"

Muammar was lowering his eyes from the ceiling, was about to tell the mullah he had no idea when frantic shouting erupted from the antiaircraft battery. He looked back toward the sky, just in time find the answer to all questions come blasting out of nowhere. The fireball vaporized the antiaircraft battery, hot slabs of metal and grisly chunks of what used to be human beings, raining down, pelting him in the face.

STICKING TO THE PLAN to let the gunship take out the antiaircraft nest first before hitting the roof, Bolan waited while the lead Predator gunship veered east, swinging wide, then straightened and vectored in from the north. Standing next to Commander Alpha, M-16 with attached M-203 grenade launcher in hand, the soldier watched as the multibarreled cannon, similar to a Russian ZSU-23-4, was blasted, along with its crew, off the roof by a single Hellfire missile.

"They knew we were coming!"

Commander Alpha was directing his wrath at Colonel Mujhan, but the ISI man shook his head vehemently. "It was not by me."

"Drop it down!" Alpha roared through the cockpit hatch.

Bolan watched as the other Predator lowered below the north face of the factory. In the distance, he heard the heavy rolling thunder of a chain gun and a Vulcan Gatling eating up whoever was fool enough to attempt to hold their ground and fight.

"Let's hit it, Stone!"

Bolan jumped out the doorway, landing beside the big bear of a CIA black op, six more shooters on their heels, fanning out in a skirmish line.

Rising from the middle of the roof, Bolan took in the cooling tower. The hot zone, he knew, a plant building nuclear weapons, was directly below. The HAZMAT team was aboard the lead Predator, and Bolan knew Alpha would give them the go once the factory was cleared. Still, they would need assistance getting inside if they came under enemy fire from the north.

It didn't take long for the Pakistani soldiers to attempt to intercept their charge. Six, seven, then ten Pakistani soldiers with assault rifles came rushing out the concrete housing of the stairwell.

Bolan let a 40 mm frag grenade fly from his M-203 as Alpha and his shooters chopped up a few uniforms with autofire. The big bang flung the remaining soldiers in all directions, the housing blasted to concrete fangs.

Running beside Alpha, Bolan heard the autofire beyond the north lip of the roof. The Predator was taking hits, and judging all the racket of return fire, he figured a dozen to two dozen soldiers or Taliban extremists were raising hell.

"I'll catch up to you!" Bolan said. "The trucks! I don't want to see anyone leaving the party too early! HAZMAT might need me to clear the path!"

Alpha looked set to object but nodded, obviously aware the Predator and his HAZMAT crew could probably use a little help from above.

"START THE TRUCKS! We will cover! Go!"

He had been sent by the exiled Grand Islamic Council, to secure whatever weapons their heroin money could buy. Mullah al-Wahbin wasn't about to let the other holy men down. If they were to crush the Americans and regain their seat of power in Afghanistan, they would need to deliver a powerful blow, and since they had friends in high places in Pakistan, they had been assured they would receive a variety of new and potent weapons of wholesale destruction, including backpack nuclear devices. They had already been trucking an assortment of high-tech equipment through the Khyber Pass, soldiers on both sides of the border receiving ample monetary reward to let them go their way. Radar, satellite jammers, cell phones and radios and faxes, all of them with secured lines, were necessary in order to detect the enemy and not only communicate with the front-line troops in his own country but also reach other freedom fighters in Pakistan, India, Yemen, just to name a few countries where jihad was due to launch across the Middle East and middle Asia soon.

All the money handed over to the Pakistanis to help the Taliban seize back the initiative in the war against the infidels, and now his hated enemies had come to attempt to rob him of his dream of conquest. It was an abomination. Why was it, he wondered, the Americans couldn't or wouldn't understand that without the Taliban Afghanistan couldn't survive, or at least remain stalwart and true to the tenets of the Koran under their God-fearing leadership? Sure, they had executed common criminals, or the adulteress or disobedient female in public. Sure, they had shot teenage boys who refused to join the army and fight the Great Satan. But what were they supposed to do? Become some nation of god-less heathens like the Americans? Too often, he thought, those who were weak of faith need some coaxing, or an example, if they were to submit to the will of God. The Taliban, he knew, originally created by students and priests, had to defeat the Americans and overthrow the current puppet Afghani government, retake control of the masses if Islam was to flourish in that country. There was no other way. It was God's will that the Taliban rule Afghanistan.

The mullah raced across the warehouse floor, his fellow holy warriors boarding the cargo holds of the trucks, others charging up the side to fling open doors and fire up the engines. Later, when they were safely on their way, he would raise the UN flags. It would have helped, of course, if they'd had time to bury the lead containers and the sleek tubes beneath the sacks of wheat and grain stamped with U.S.A., hide them from prying eyes, some American recon plane that was always patrolling the skies anymore.

Al-Wahbin heard the terrible racket of some hellish thunder out in the loading bays suddenly, felt the rotor wash of the helicopter sweeping through the wide doorway. He offered up a silent prayer that they all be spared so that they could be the instruments with which to stave off the Western invasion, retain control of their country, carry on God's work.

For some reason, as he watched his Taliban followers toppling, chopped up to bloody rags, death falling from out of the sky, out of nowhere, the firing seeming to come from two directions, hemming them in a scissoring of bullets, faces began flashing through his mind's eye.

He balked, shuddered, became aware of whose faces he was recalling.

How many boys, many of whom were not much more than ten, had he shot in the head by his own hand for refusing to enlist in the army? Too many to count, certainly, and he wondered why he was suddenly disturbed by the memory. How many homes of Afghanis who spoke out against the Taliban had he ordered burned down, or put the torch to begin the flames himself? Forty, fifty? How many fatherless children, women without husbands had his own actions condemned to the refugee camps? Four, five hundred, a thousand or more? How many women who were caught without the *burqa* in public, or who were found in secret schools teaching young girls to read and write had he personally marched out onto the goal line of the football stadium, forced them to kneel, then placed the muzzle of his Kalashnikov at the base of their skull and blown their brains out? Ten? Twenty? And how many young girls had he likewise executed?

What was this voice and where was it coming from all of a sudden? What was he feeling? Guilt? Fear? He had fought the Russians hand to hand in the mountains and the caves for ten years, and he had never once flinched at the idea of his own death.

Now he felt a cold, nagging dread, frozen near the doorway, watching as his holy warriors were mowed down. He wanted to be sick at the sight of his small army getting cut to ribbons, but told himself to be strong, that God was with him.

Still, he knew he would never make it to the trucks, pivoted at the latest round of autofire sounding from behind, and saw black-clad commandos with M-16s running across the catwalks, firing down into the warehouse proper, dropping Pakistani soldiers where they stood.

Mullah al-Wahbin knew he was trapped in a vise of certain death. This wasn't the glory he sought. Still, if he died on his feet, there was a chance he would still fly straight to Paradise.

"Allah akhbar!" he bellowed.

And ran outside, twisting and firing skyward, instantly locking in on the lone shadow up there who was cutting down his holy warriors with an assault rifle. He nearly had a bead on the lone shooter, his AK-47 tracking, concrete chips gouged off the edge of the roof, when the lone gunman reacted with lightning speed. Another nanosecond was all he needed to nail the infidel, but he was denied victory, as he felt hot lead coring into his chest.

CHAPTER THIRTEEN

All the blood of the innocent on their hands, and it never ceased to amaze Mack Bolan how the militant Islamic fanatic—whose beliefs and ways were anathema to anything in the Koran—believed he was going straight to Paradise, and with a bevy of beautiful nymphs waiting to roll and flutter around with him in the clouds, no less. How they believed murder fit into the big scheme of the universal deity...

Well, there was only one way Bolan knew how to react to that sort of mindless savagery. And that was to fight fire with his own hammer-down of conflagration.

The Executioner kept on lowering judgment day on the swarm of gunners in the loading bay. One Taliban goon came rushing outside, bellowing the fanatic's suicide war cry, his assault rifle blazing, when Bolan drilled him with a long burst to the chest, a slice and dice that rose up and blew off the turban along with a portion of his skull.

Another fanatic down, but at least a dozen were still in play.

The Predator was having a field day, the soldier saw, hovering forty or so feet north of the line of canvas-covered trucks, chain gun and Vulcan Gatling hammering out twin songs of doom. The line of heavy slugs tore through the cabs, blasting out windshields, screams swept away by the infernal racket, engine housings sheared away like flimsy tin, then the explosions began peppering the convoy as fuel caught and ignited in saffron balls.

A few gunners began pouring out of the beds of the trucks, and Bolan waxed them off their feet, sweeping his autofire down the back ends while the Predator's nose began a wide swing and the chain gun kept on rocking and rolling. More militants came charging out of their temporary hiding holes, and the Executioner chopped them off at the legs, scored a few gut shots, his aim thrown off some as he was forced to shuffle away from return fire.

Bolan spied a ladder to his side, checked the hellgrounds, a few moaners crawling through their blood and leaking guts. Screams raked the air, more militants dropping as they burst apart by Predator's big guns. Slapping home a fresh clip, the warrior, training the assault rifle one-handed on the bed of mangled and mauled, quickly descended the ladder to mop it up.

Fire was now blazing from several pulped vehicles, the stink of spreading gasoline digging into his senses, among other noxious smells. He checked the mini-Geiger counter, which doubled as a sensor for leaking toxins, and took a reading of the slaughter zone.

The dial fluttered up, indicating the zone was hotter with more than angry fire.

Quickly he palmed the tac radio, raised Commander Alpha. "It's hot back here, guy. I think it's time the HAZMAT boys earned their keep."

"Yeah, well, if you'd like to join us, I could use a little help in here, Stone."

"Give me a few seconds to clear it out back, then I'm on the way."

Bolan heard the incessant rattle of autofire from beyond the open bay doors, knew Alpha and company were locked into a serious shooting war. Marching, he counted eight shot-up but still very much alive and angry Taliban flunkies. Some crawled, some attempted to shove their guts back into the gaping holes of their stomachs, some staggered to their feet, clutching assault rifles, turbans askew.

All of them were sent on their way for final judgment as the Executioner stitched them on the move, sparing none. He pulled the mammoth .44 Magnum Desert Eagle when his clip burned out, advancing for the first lake of fire, and cannoned three quick rounds at mauled shadows reeling about on the other side of the flames. One militant was left, crabbing through a pile of smoking trash to his three o'clock, blubbering something incoherent.

The Desert Eagle silenced the militant for good.

HIS REAL NAME WAS Bill Tobin, and he had been reactivated after his brief retirement from the CIA's Special Operations Division for this shadow war. His specialty was infiltration and termination.

He hated terrorist scum, considered them nothing but cowardly butchers of the innocent, and anyone who financed, supported or armed said scum could expect the same rough justice. So he got busy dishing it back, in remembrance, he thought, for all those who had perished in terrorist attacks over the years.

He was off the ramp, hosing down a half-dozen Pakistani soldiers, pinning them to large wooden crates when a fat man came waddling his way.

"General Muammar, I presume?"

"Yes, yes," he cried, and hit his knees. "Please, there has been a terrible mistake."

"You're right there's been a mistake. Yours."

He lifted the assault rifle, Muammar shrieking, and capped off a half-dozen rounds, stripping away a few of the medals on the blouse under the long barrage.

By now, Pakistani soldiers seemed to think flight was better than fight. He had already ordered in the HAZMAT teams, wondering when Colonel Stone would grace them with his presence when the big guy in black came wheeling through the open bay door and began dropping the runners in their tracks. A few Pakistani soldiers managed to fire off a few wild shots, but Stone had them dead to rights, holding his ground, drilling them with precision autofire, then slowly advancing, checking his compass on all points. It was a pleasure to watch the man in action. It took a pair, after all, to have even ventured off on his lonesome and wax two of the three terrorist nests, then fight his way out of a mob bent on ripping him to pieces.

Stone was all right, as far as Tobin was concerned.

At the far corner of the warehouse, leading his Alpha shooters, he saw a dozen or more space suits behind the thick, hermetically sealed glass of their workrooms. They held up their arms.

"Blast them the hell out of there!" he ordered his men.

They emptied a salvo of 40 mm frag grenades at the chambers, glass caving and blowing over the space suits. To insure some sort of sterilization against toxins, he ordered, "Thermite, gentlemen! Burn, baby burn!"

THE EXECUTIONER WATCHED, unsure how he felt about the slaughter of unarmed civilians right then. They had been, after all, creating horror that could easily have wiped out an entire country, willingly going along to arm the Taliban with weapons that, if used, would unleash a nightmare unlike anything in human history—worse, or so the experts warned, than any plague that had nearly wiped out Europe centuries back. There was no telling how far they had come to landing the Taliban a cache of chem or bioweapons, but Pakistan was a nuclear power, and he had been around long enough to know that the right amount of money could buy anything from the wrong people. If the Taliban or al-Qaeda got their hands on nukes, they would use them. If that happened, worst case, the soldier grimly suspected Afghanistan would be turned into a glowing cinder on sat imagery, the entire Muslim world then taking up arms in outrage over a tactical nuclear strike by the United States...

Well, it hadn't happened—yet.

He let Alpha and his fire team have at it, space suits flailing about now as waves of white phosphorous rolled through the chambers. The air became ripe with roasting flesh, as Bolan wandered the factory, toeing the dead to make sure there was no Pakistani version of Lazarus among the bunch.

All done, he knew, as Commander Alpha rolled his way.

"Let's saddle up, Stone. We've got that convoy on deck."

"ABANDON HOPE, all ye who enter Afghanistan."

David McCarter had his hands planted on the war table in the tent the Colonel had given them as their personal quarters. Not that they were being granted special treatment or getting the snub, but McCarter read the Delta colonel—known only to them as the Colonel—as a soldier's soldier. He also understood the need for this covert five-man commando team to maintain its cover as black ops, hinting as much, and guaranteeing his cooperation, when they had first choppered in from India to land at Eagle Base. Of course, the Colonel didn't know who they really were, or where they came from, but he had his orders, and they reached him straight from the President. X Force was on board the surgical strike, one of the biggest forays yet into Afghanistan. It was going to be nasty, messy, McCarter knew, nothing none of them had never seen and tasted in the killing fields before, but this time out brought special problems to their attention.

Land mines, for one thing.

Beyond the camps, McCarter knew their own personal mission was to fly on, deeper into Afghanistan, and burn down the heroin labs and warehouses. Logic dictated that no matter how many bank accounts of the terrorists were frozen around the globe, they could still finance their war by selling heroin to the Russian Mafia.

The final brief was wrapped up, twenty minutes ago, and word had come down that the B-52s had left the U.S. base in Uzbekistan, en route to start bombing the Ramadan camp off the map, pave the way for the ground forces to go in and start smoking whatever was left standing or reeling about. The ex-SAS commando and leader of Phoenix Force was giving the sat imagery and recon photos from the unmanned spy birds, Predator and Global Hawk, a final scouring.

And he knew the task before all of them was daunting to say the least.

Which was why he was suddenly hearing those ominous words the Colonel had muttered after he'd dismissed the troops.

"Abandon hope…"

Afghanistan was a living hell on earth, home to the Four Horsemen, if ever a country was. Disease, pestilence, famine, war, and even the UN—which McCarter as a realist and soldier had never put much stock in—called Afghanistan the most evil country on the planet. The horror stories had been coming out of Afghanistan for years—torture, public executions, forced starvation of rival ethnic tribes—and McCarter was once again staring down some of that evil. Two pictures detailed a trench piled with the bodies of young boys who had been executed at the camp, obviously deciding the Taliban wasn't worth fighting for. In recent months the refugee situation alone had gotten worse, with disease spreading through the camps, militant infiltrators moved out by Pakistani collaborators into Karachi, Peshawar, human time bombs that were going off all over the country and over in India….

Afghanistan was the devil's playground, he thought.

And it appeared the Taliban and al-Qaeda militants were staging a major counteroffensive, maybe three thousand militants holed up in a camp that sprawled through valleys and gorges and up the mountains of southeastern Afghanistan encompassing an area the size of a small city. Okay, they knew the enemy numbers, everything marked off and staked out on the pictures, all of it having been gone over for hours on end by the Colonel. It would be a pincers attack, McCarter knew, X-Force jumping from the Predator from five hundred feet, and moving on the camp from the south while the combined Delta and Special Forces commandos hit them from the north, fanning out, east to west. After, of course, the sky had fallen on the camp, an aerial barrage by B-52s, Stealths and F-15Es that was supposed to last for an hour or more, one wave of strafing and bombs-away after another.

McCarter looked up, peering at the other members of X Force as they perused the intel.

"The land-mine problem alone could stop us in our tracks before we even get the first round off."

Down the line, around the table, they were Gary Manning, T. J. Hawkins, Calvin James and Rafael Encizo. Jack Grimaldi, Stony Man's pilot extraordinaire, had joined them after giving his warbird a last-minute preflight check. Their weapons, combat vests, harnesses were on board their Predator ride. Donning skintight blacksuits, they were ready to go just as soon as the Colonel gave the green light. To the rest of the combined Delta and Special Forces team they were known only by their cover names, beginning with X, followed by the first initial of their names.

It was Encizo—X-R—who had voiced the concern.

"Well, when we land we won't have time for any minesweeping detail, Rafe," McCarter said. "Despite the air show, there will be survivors, plenty of them, firing on us from their holes in the mountainside, gullies, trenches, bunkers."

"The Colonel's suggestion and his statement about

that potential land-mine disaster made sense," Gary Manning said.

"Right," Calvin James said. "Carpet bomb the hell out of the camp, and we march right into the smoke, hoping everything that was cratered got the land mines in the process."

"You have blast, shrapnel, trips, antitank," Hawkins said. "Then when we hit the caves…"

McCarter understood the nerves jangling before him. They were all seasoned combat vets, but there was really no defense against a land mine, not when the soldier was under fire.

"We spray a path," Grimaldi said, "from the gunships, you guys just follow the bullet-riddled trail. That's one option already laid out."

"Or we burn up a few clips going up the mountainside on rock and scrub," Manning said.

"Nothing we can do about the land-mine situation, mates," McCarter said. "We take our chances, keep our eyes peeled, fingers crossed. Everybody is in the same predicament."

"What's the latest on Striker?" Grimaldi wanted to know.

"They were in the process of burning down that plant in the Cholistan," McCarter said. "Just called in, said there was some delay. The CIA commander was busy interrogating a few prisoners about what they might expect to find on that convoy now on its way through the Khyber Pass. The convoy is Striker's show. He'll raise me once they cross into Afghan airspace. The Colonel already cleared Striker's play to link up with us. Seems he also has some prior experience with this Commander Alpha."

"That good or bad?" Encizo said.

McCarter shrugged. "I didn't go into any specifics about the man's character or lack thereof, Rafe. The way I read it, the CIA black ops are about as good and tough as they come. Besides, something tells me we'll need all hands once we hit that camp."

McCarter was checking his chronometer, mentally gauging the time it would take them to make the DZ on the camp's perimeter in coordination with the air strike, when the Colonel walked into the tent.

He was a tall, lean man, salt-and-pepper bristles tinging the sides of his flattop. The guy was hard in the eyes, and McCarter knew a no-nonsense officer, a man who led from the trenches, when he saw one.

"I presume it's time to go, Colonel?" McCarter said.

The Colonel nodded. "Let's rock and roll, gentlemen. I just stopped by to wish you good luck, godspeed and good hunting."

X Force was on its feet and trailing the Colonel and McCarter out of the tent, into the night.

The Predator gunships, McCarter saw, were already kicking up rotor wash, the Delta–Special Forces contingent marching from their tent, hopping into the fuselage.

Ready to fly, time to go.

Into Afghanistan.

Into the belly and the crucible of hell on earth.

He didn't want to, but for some reason the Colonel's dark words echoed through his thoughts once again.

"Abandon hope, all ye…"

CHAPTER FOURTEEN

"Word is, they'll stop somewhere along the way before they hit their border, and pay their tribute to their Pathan or Pashtun cousins in cash or weapons."

Bolan listened to Alpha, watching the monitors as the convoy, seven trucks in all, wended its way through the towering black mountains of the Khyber Pass. Whether the view was piped in by satellite or unmanned recon birds, the soldier didn't know, nor really cared to inquire from Commander Alpha, but they were looking at real-time intel. It was happening, they knew when and where, and how many.

They were in the Predator's belly, half of the CIA black-ops shooters crammed up the fuselage, sitting on metal benches, the other half of the strike force in the second gunship. Saddle up, Bolan recalled, hadn't come as quickly as he would have liked. A few bleating CBW scientists had crawled out of the woodwork back at the plant, coming to them on bended knee. Alpha had spent a good thirty minutes grilling them about the load that was on its way to Afghanistan, kneecapping two of the scientists with a couple 5.56 mm tongue looseners, slapping around a few more when they prattled on in Urdu, the CIA black op cursing them all to hell and back, railing at them to speak English or start praying.

They all began speaking English, fluently.

And the convoy, as it turned out, was stuffed with some of the most virulent toxins known to man. To say they were faced with a potential nightmare was an understatement. The new so-called shadow war had taken a turn left into another corner of hell.

"Okay, Stone, here it is, see what you think. We refuel, re-up the hardware at Eagle Base, and I want it done twenty minutes ago, then we're gone. I already talked to the Delta colonel in charge of the ground forces. They're already wheels up and going for the throat of this Ramadan camp. It's our job to take out this convoy. I hope my flyboys will only blast up the cabs, engines, cut down any runners, because I sure as hell don't want to fall down, gagging on leaking nerve gas. Bad way to go, I'd rather have my gnarly ass chewed up by a white shark. I'll worry about a HAZMAT detail later on. Taliban, al-Qaeda, Pashtun assholes, they're all dead meat, no prisoners, no exceptions. Also, we don't have any gas masks, no anthrax antidotes, antibiotics, whatever, and space suits are never an option in my playbook. Too confining, and dead is dead, I'd rather have freedom of movement to keep on waxing the bad guys than lumber around. Anyway, they've got dirty shells, stuffed with radioactive waste, nerve gas, bio shit not even I've heard of, a few of those intermediate missiles on board, assholes think they can fly the UN flag and fool this old warhorse. Those CBW Pakistani bastards back there informed me they were in the process, a week away from putting the finishing touches on a few suitcase nukes. This convoy goes up in flames. What I'm saying is, are you game for that? You willing to give it up—your life—take a whiff of leaking nerve gas if it means we have to go beyond full-bore to shut down these assholes?"

There was no other way but to go in, take their chances, hope some shell didn't crack or get blown all over the Khyber Pass and drop them all in their tracks. Bolan told Alpha as much.

"I figured you for a guy that will go the distance, no matter what the odds or the potential horror. One more thing. The Russian Mafia, namely a bunch of goons from the Ruskavka Family. What they do, and are about ready to do, is fly down from Uzbekistan. They drop off supplies for the northern tribes, who are destitute, carrying favor with the Afghan government. They fly on to a village called Dharwhar, smack-dab in the desert, center city, heart of this shithole on earth. Taliban goons hand off the heroin to the Russians, grab the cash. We've known about this for some time. Word is I've got a few shitbags in the Company who've been aiding and abetting the goons. I'll deal with them in time. You in Nam?"

"Yeah."

"I had a feeling. Maybe you know the score…"

"A few snakes on the home team always slither out of the hole and try to line their pockets during wartime."

"Well, that bullshit stops. I've got a line on that Russian transport. We'll be there when they land."

Bolan was thinking about Phoenix Force. "The Ramadan camp?"

"We'll help them out first, unless I get word the goons are moving."

"Good enough."

Bolan held Alpha's stare. His methods were efficient, if not brutal to the point of sadistic, but he got results, and this was, so the media had coined, a new war, after all. Extreme measures, which normally went against Bolan's grain, were being employed. The soldier read Alpha as a straight shooter.

"Coffee up front, or maybe you want to grab a quick combat nap, Stone?"

Bolan shook his head.

"No rest for the weary, I got ya."

The Executioner almost told Alpha he could say that again, but rest was the least of his concerns.

The war was on, heating up as the bodies kept piling up, and the soldier knew the only sleep anyone there might catch would be the big one.

WABIN ZAHIT BELIEVED in jihad. It was an insult to all Muslims that the Americans had once again bombed sacred Islamic soil, Iraq, but the organization he belonged to had plans to teach them the worst of all possible lessons for the defilement. As a top lieutenant in al-Qaeda he had pledged his life to jihad, having trained in the Afghanistan camps. And in a few more hours, once they crossed the border into Afghanistan, he would be the instrument, an angel in the holy war, no less, who could deliver what they needed to strike back at the infidels. It was God's will, he thought, that the ranking mullahs of the Taliban were still alive, hiding in caves, he was sure, but not even he was privy to their exact location. He nearly laughed out loud, thinking that the Americans and the British could send over their journalists and camera crews, interview the man they sought above all others, but the infidels, even with all their sophisticated spy planes and satellites, couldn't find him.

God's will.

With Muhbal at the wheel, Shareej beside him, Zahit checked the rugged foothills. The road that ran through the Khyber Pass on this stretch was just wide enough to allow their truck convoy to keep rumbling ahead, wheels hugging the edge where the gorge dropped away for several hundred feet. They had the lead truck, stuffed with both the intermediate SCUD-44s packed with radioactive waste and bio and chem warheads that could wipe out an entire city, such as Tel Aviv or Karachi, if his fellow Arabs who were helping the infidels in their war didn't get their act together. There were also suitcases from God, only they were conventional explosives, a mere one kiloton, but likewise they could disperse viral or chemical horror. Two steamer trunks were topped out with rupees, and right then he was searching the hills to the west where they had agreed to meet the Pashtun rebels, unload the payment.

They were his cousins, brothers-in-arms who also needed money to buy bigger and better weapons if they were going to defeat the Americans who had so brazenly attacked Afghanistan. There were military installations already known to al-Qaeda in Pakistan and northern Afghanistan, infidel bases that were already tagged to be the first to taste a counterstrike. For days, Zahit had prayed to deem him worthy of being the one who drove a truck bomb into one of those bases, or find his way to America to detonate one of the suitcases. At twenty-five, he had no home, no family other than his al-Qaeda brothers, and he didn't plan on living much longer. Jihad was life. And he wanted nothing else but to ultimately sacrifice his life for the holy war, but only if he could take as many infidels with him as possible.

Just around the bend, he told Muhbal to slow down, as he saw the forty-plus armed shadows rise from the rocks. They stopped, Zahit anxious to conclude this business when something like a giant black bird came swooping down from the north. Zahit was grabbing up his AK-47, aware of what that winged bird was, watching the helicopter nearly skimming the road when—

The windshield blew in on his face, glass tearing at his cheeks, a sliver spearing into his eye. He heard himself shriek, tumbling for the door, hands grabbing his face when he saw Muhbal's head erupt into a dark cloud. He glimpsed Shareej a nanosecond before the arm was blasted off at the shoulder.

THE EXECUTIONER WATCHED from the fuselage doorway as the Predators got the next round of slaughter started. Alpha had laid out the air strike en route, and their own gunship had veered east, then come down over the mountains from the north. Predator Two had the rear of the convoy, both gunships hemming in the terrorists in what was now a scissoring blanket of death and destruction.

As messy, nasty and down-and-dirty as the fight had been up to then, the soldier knew it was about to sink to a new, bloodier and more savage level. Factor in the militant Pashtun rebels, skirting up the hillside but firing on the gunships, and the coming body count could fill up a quarter-mile stretch here.

The chain guns were eating up the cabs of the trucks, Predator Two now swinging out over the gorge, the door gunner with the 20 mm Gatling gun chewing up runners who were disgorging from the cargo holds, canvas sheared away, worrying Bolan a little that a round might punch a hole in a shell...

He was there, ready to go, and there was no sense in steaming over something he couldn't control.

"Let's hit it, people!"

The Executioner followed Commander Alpha out the door, hit the road and lifted his M-16 to start nailing targets. Bolan didn't have to wait long or walk far before he started waxing militants.

ZAHIT SPILLED OUT the door. Half-blind, blood filling his mouth, he felt hatred consuming him, washing away the pain, as he figured they were being attacked by Americans. No Pakistani, not even those who claimed to support the unjust American cause, he thought, would dare attack them in their own country.

The screaming of men dying in horrific pain was deafening, rising about the thunder that was pounding from the black helicopters. He stood, clutching his AK-47, then the engine of their truck erupted. The force of the blast knocked him off his feet, nearly flinging him off the road and down the gorge.

Feverishly, he implored God to spare him from death at the hands of his enemies, but as he heard the screaming down the line of trucks, he figured it was best to attempt to do something for himself.

He was staggering to his feet when a shadow seemed to materialize out of the night. Zahit nearly had him lined up with the AK-47, then the blackness was parted by a finger of flames. He felt the hot impact of bullets tearing into his chest, felt his legs being chopped up and down, then he was carried by the barrage over the edge. He was falling, then blackness blinded his one good eye.

BOLAN DRILLED the first one off the road with a quick hosing down of 5.56 mm rounds. Moving on as the Gatling gun in Predator one concentrated raking the Pashtun shadows up the hillside, the soldier marched into the chaos of armed militants trying to get it together, only they were locked in by a pincers assault as the other squad of CIA shooters began rolling them up from the rear.

Alpha had split up, as planned, leading another team down the port side of the convoy. On the other side, Bolan heard the racket of autofire, the sharp grunts of men absorbing lead.

A militant was jumping out of the cab of the third truck when Bolan zipped him up the front with a lightning burst, driving him into three other extremists who were running his way. The trio of militants took his weight and flying blood in their faces, their AKs chattering but their rounds skidding off the mark. Slugs whined off asphalt beside Bolan, but he held his ground, unflinching, and doused them with a left-to-right barrage of autofire.

It was slower going from there on, as he crept up to the bed of a truck, gunners shouting from behind the canvas. He could have fragged them, but it was too risky, since he couldn't be sure the dirty shells would withstand the blast. Wheeling around the corner, the warrior held back on the assault rifle's trigger. Spraying the interior, he counted up five militants, all of them dropping under his fusillade, AKs flaming skyward, ripping holes in the canvas.

Five more down, as their deadweight came to strew over U.S.A.-stamped sacks of grain, and Bolan heard Commander Alpha barking over his com link.

"Stone, I'm going after the Pashtun bunch. They're heading for the hills. According to intel, they come from a village that's in a gorge about a quarter-klick from here. If we lose them in some caves, we can forget it and pack it up. I'm leaving a few of my men behind to guard the store."

"I'll fall in, just as soon as it's nailed down here."

The check-in almost cost Bolan, as a shadow swung around the corner. Lurching away from the line of fire, bullets screaming off the gate of the truck, the Executioner returned fire. A few slugs tore past his shoulder, hot slipstreams against his ears, the militant howling, dancing a jig of death now as the warrior gutted him, the rising burst of 5.56 mm lead hammering into his chest, kicking him off his feet.

The Executioner moved out from between the trucks, racking a fresh mag into his assault rifle. He sighted down on more armed militants, and returned to the grim butcher's task of jihad payback.

CHAPTER FIFTEEN

Before the shadow war against the terrorist scum began in full savage earnest, Commander Alpha had long since taken the Man's words of war footing to angry and vengeful heart.

"We will not falter, we will not fail."

Good enough.

"We will smoke them out of their holes."

Better still.

And it was long overdue, as far as he was concerned, the terrorists having gotten away with murder for years while Uncle Sugar wrung his hands and stamped around in a snit, worrying about upsetting so-called moderate Arab countries like Jordan and Egypt if they went out and kicked some much-needed righteous ass.

Tobin had been around the dirty-deeds block long enough, though, to know that the CIA, among other U.S. intelligence agencies and special military black ops, had been trying to even the score, or keep one step ahead of the scumbags for decades, despite any restrictions and lack of funding on the part of Washington.

It was good, in the end analysis, to be here, laying it on the line, fighting for God and country, this time sanctioned up front and off the bat to lop heads and slam them on a stake.

Failure was never an option in his playbook, but he knew there would be great risks, danger and treachery cropping up at every turn in this shadow war against the terrorists. There would be casualties when they engaged the bastards hand to hand, planes shot down, even pilots or ground troops becoming POWs in some stone hellhole in what he considered the anus of the planet. But he was there, carte blanche, like Stone, to go the distance, do whatever was necessary to destroy the Taliban and crush al-Qaeda's network.

Part of the problem was the terrain. Caves pocked the mountainsides, where the terrorists could burrow in, hide in labyrinths that could go down hundreds of feet. Which meant rooting them out.

Which was why two of his shooters had flame-throwers.

Alpha Team took its first casualties as he led the advance up the hillside.

The Pashtun rebels were little more than grimy silhouettes, firing down from pockets of boulders and trenches cut into the hillside, either by dynamite, hand or Mother Nature. They were pouring on the AK-47 autofire, slugs buzzing all around Alpha, whining off stone, when he heard the sharp cries beside him. Turning, hunched behind a boulder, he witnessed two of his shooters toppling, blood spurting from holes in their chests.

They were history, judging the holes and the sudden end of bloodletting that signaled the hearts had stopped beating, but he ordered Alpha M to check just the same. They were his guys, most of them Special Forces loaners, and he wasn't giving up hope, nor would he leave them behind.

Thumbs-down, Alpha M shaking his head, and Alpha radioed Predator One to get their butts up there and lay down a blanket of fire—no, belay that, wing a Hellfire or two up the hill.

The storm of Pashtun autofire withered as the gunship vectored high up the hill, two Hellfires flaming away, eating up a chunk of real estate in a double whammy of earth-shaking blasts. The problem next was, even as bodies and amputated limbs were flying from the fireballs, signaling Alpha they had scythed through the crop, his flyboy informed him maybe a dozen rebels were right then lost to sight as they ran over the lip of a gully, sliding down the hillside, vanishing into caves.

Now they'd have to go dig out the rotten SOBs by hand. Not only a time-consuming chore, but probably the single most dangerous task in combat. The enemy knew their lair, probably had it mined out the wazoo, just for starters, and satellites weren't the eyes of God, able to peer through sheer rock and lay it out. He wanted to think back to all the VC over there he had to blow, blast and burn out of their holes, the infamous Tunnel Rats of Cong lore, how many guys had been lost... What the hell, he didn't like it, knew the coming chore was a monumental one to the bloodiest nth degree, but when in Pakistan and hopefully when in Afghanistan next...

There were wounded rebels up above, he found, trying their damnedest to hack out the smoke, firing wild rounds, but Alpha dumped them on their backs with an extended burst of autofire, thinking how lousy the next few minutes or hours of his life were going to be.

Leading the climb, Alpha told his firemen, "We hit the cave, it's your show but on my go."

A horror show, he knew, but there was no other way than to burn them out of their holes like the rats they were.

He hadn't come this far to play games or recite the rules of engagement as laid out by the Geneva Convention.

No, sir.

THE SLAUGHTER SHOW turned up a curtain call for the Executioner. A few of the less inclined to fight attempted to crawl out from under the trucks, lurching into a sprint for the edge of the road, as if they hoped the gorge could hide them and take them away to safety.

No such luck.

The Executioner sent them on their way, all right.

Bolan burned up a clip, raking eight militants down the line, front to back, spinning and flinging them in all directions, their cries of pain and terror lost to the sudden explosions up the mountainside. A fresh mag slapped home, the soldier watched as Alpha shooters hit each bed of the transport trucks, going in low, then lunging up, weapons out and sweeping. Sporadic bursts of autofire told the soldier a few extremists thought they could hide under sacks of grain.

The Executioner moved off the highway, spotted Alpha and his shooters scurrying up the hillside, giving chase to whatever Pashtun rebels hadn't been ripped to shreds by the Hellfire blasts. A look inside a truck, sliding away a sack or two of grain, and the soldier found 155 mm shells, stamped with the universal radiation and biohazard sign. It made his blood boil, thinking how the Pakistanis would have so readily aided the terrorists across the border, extending one hand to America while holding out the other to the terrorists. Going in, though, he already knew some of their so-called Pakistani friends would turn the other cheek—northward.

Bolan set off, aware that if they left even one rebel here to stand, it was potentially one more terrorist that could someday come back to haunt the innocent.

ALPHA CAUGHT one rebel in the back with a 3-round stitching up the spine, his blasted guts blown out the front of his diced tunic before the enemy fell on his face. He was vaulting over a boulder, ready to cut the M-203 loose, when a storm of autofire began peppering the mouth of the cave. The Predator, with its infrared and heat-seeking sensors, had turned up another cave where he hoped the soon-and-not-so-dearly departed had charged into.

One cave at a time.

Alpha wheeled around the corner, low, and sent a 40 mm frag charge flying into the cave. The light dancing around the rocky bend was probably shining from a torch—electricity, he knew, in this part of the world was about as rare as a good bottle of Scotch—but the fireball lit up the dark yawn in brilliant yellow flames a second later.

The screams were music to his ears.

The return fire wasn't.

He looked at his firemen, slipping a 40 mm thermite bomb down the M-203's chute, waving his other shooters on to take the next cave down. "I'll take the point. They're just around the corner, thirty yards or so, to your two o'clock. Let's hit it. Burn, bitch, burn. Give me a good show, gentlemen."

And he went in shooting. Shadows hollered from around the jagged wall of rock, a few of the braver rebels attempting a brief engagement, winging out the lead, ricochets skidding off the walls, then they retreated at the sight of a wild-eyed, rebel-yelling white abominable snowman rampaging their way. Alpha charged on, spraying the corner. He braked, peered around the edge and—

Bingo.

They were trapped, some sort of cul de sac, maybe five rebels right then jumping over a rocky ledge. There were blankets, canteens, other signs of meager creature comforts spread around that told Alpha they didn't mind holing up here like the rats he saw them as being.

Historically, the Khyber Pass, he knew, was home to bandits, marauders, murderers, rapists, kidnappers, and more recently drug runners and terrorists. The worst of the worst called this passageway to and from Afghanistan home, some of the most dangerous real estate on the planet without exception or equal. Not even the baddest SOB to ever walk through the valley of death, he knew, was safe here, unless he called in a B-52 for some serious carpet bombing. A man could, and did, he knew, get away with murder, all kinds of crimes and sins in the Khyber, and never had to worry about looking over his shoulder for justice if he was willing to hide his wrongdoing with more violence if someone came to call in his marker. He didn't know the track records of the rebels dead ahead, didn't much care, but it was time to exterminate some rats.

"Do it," he quietly told his firemen.

They did.

BOLAN FOLLOWED the familiar sickly sweet stink of toasting human flesh to the next kill site. He had called ahead, informing Alpha he was on the way into the gorge, the soldier homed in on the rotor wash of the Predator as it hovered over the black ravine, the gunship's position steering him to the battlezone. The Executioner was marching down the incline when Alpha rolled out of the hole in the side of the mountain. Two blacksuits with stainless-steel backpacks told Bolan everything he needed to know.

The heat was on for the enemy.

"Nice of you to join us, Stone. All neat and clean back on the highway?"

The Executioner fell in with the three-man hit team as they jogged for the next maw where autofire rattled through the ravine.

"Everything is beautiful," Bolan said.

"Outstanding. I lost a couple guys."

"I saw."

"So let's just say I'm in the mood to make somebody feel a whole lot of pain right now. Can you dig it?"

"Digged and dug. Let's shake and bake."

Bolan fell silent, combat radar on high alert, scanning the broken sloping sides of the gorge for hidden shooters. Alpha and his flamethrower duo were almost at the mouth of the cave when the soldier spotted a shadow popping up from behind a boulder. The Executioner's burst of autofire nailed the Pashtun rebel in the chest, a rising line of slugs that tore out his throat next, blasting away the jaw finally, rendering the corpse unrecognizable to even his own next of kin.

Alpha jerked his head in the direction of the falling shadow, throwing Bolan a thumbs-up over his shoulder.

"Keep up the good work, Stone!"

"No problem."

They made the cave entrance, Alpha squeezing through his troops, shouldering a few of them aside to have a quick peek around the corner.

"Screw this! How many?" Alpha barked at the squad of shooters, six to either side of the cave's entrance.

"Six, maybe seven, sir."

"Back off!"

He armed a grenade, Bolan on his back side, the Stony Man warrior watching as Alpha chucked the steel egg. The ensuing thunderclap sounded to produce all of two, maybe three screams. Alpha scowled, obviously infuriated they'd have to go inside to weed them out.

Bolan went in beside Alpha, M-16 up and ready. The cave reeked of blood and mold and things, human or otherwise, long since dead and rotting. Out of the boiling smoke cloud a trio of bats fluttered, zigzagging over Bolan's head. Unflinching, he advanced, the firemen on his six. Bursting through the hanging cloud of smoke, he anticipated the worst, gunmen rearing up beyond the pall, but he caught the voices, shrill and panicky, in the distance. Light danced from around a corner, outlining several shadows on the fly. Bolan looked up and down, searching the walls, the ground for trip wires, any sign of a booby trap.

"Hold up!"

It wasn't much, just a telltale hump in the floor, about twenty feet ahead. Alpha spotted it after Bolan's warning, cursing, falling back with the soldier. Then Bolan pumped a 3-round burst into the ground, the land mine erupting, shrapnel whining off the walls.

"Land mines! I hate land mines!" Alpha growled.

It was a sorry waste of ammo, but Bolan joined Alpha in a long wall-to-wall spray of the area around the smoking shroud, rolling on, and kept hitting the floor leading to the corner with autofire. No more land mines, but autofire began chipping off hunks of stone beside Bolan's head.

Alpha dropped to one knee. "Get ready, boys!" he snarled over his shoulder.

Then Alpha triggered his M-203. Downrange Bolan heard the crunching din of the confined blast. Adding to the horror were bone-chilling screams of men being burning alive by the thermite bomb.

The Executioner walked out into the open, hosing down the burning scarecrows with extended autofire.

Two pairs of legs were disappearing into a crack in the wall.

"Your turn, guys!" Alpha bellowed, waving on his firemen.

Bolan checked the stone cubicle for any more signs of life while the firemen cut loose a double brilliant tongue of leaping fire. It was an added dimension to this shadow war, the good guys forced to ratchet up the horror just to root out the terrorists.

And Afghanistan was just around the corner, a countryside choked with caves and bunkers. Bolan knew the worst was yet to come.

The Executioner listened to the wailing of men burning alive, his nose pinched with cooked flesh. Alpha sported a mean grin toward the ghastly sound, then looked at Bolan and said, "Let's get the hell outta here. I believe we have a date to keep across the border."

CHAPTER SIXTEEN

Rashid Waziri wondered if the glory of al-Qaeda would ever be realized in what had once been planned as the greatest jihad yet, the mother of all holy wars, no less, against their hated enemies. For the time being, the plans to ship out suicide bombers all over the Middle East and America had been scrapped. They were at war, chased and hunted all over the rugged countryside by infidels, had been ordered to stand their ground in this mountain valley of southeastern Afghanistan, fight to the death. A coming ground offensive was feared, but he knew the Americans would bomb the camp to a smoking crater before they dared land commandos on this soil.

And the Taliban, he believed, wasn't regrouping as quickly as they had expected, rival ethnic tribes from the north joining in the infidel cause, many of the mullahs already bombed out of their homes, on the run.

Which, he supposed, was one of several reasons why

seven of the mullahs had fled to the Ramadan camp, now hiding in the caves of the mountains. Once powerful holy men, bringing the iron and holy rule of the Koran to this country, they now struck him as little more than frightened criminals on the run.

It was a sad—no, he corrected, a disgraceful—day, the land of Afghanistan, which he called home away from Syria for so long, had been shattered by the infidels with their smart bombs, cruise missiles, the massive B-52 bombers laying waste to critical military installations with their indiscriminate carpet bombing. How did a holy warrior fight that kind of power? With only his AK-47 as his one weapon to bear and fight back, he felt hope fleeing, a wisp of smoke in his belly, up his throat, vanishing next as he heaved a breath.

From his position up the hillside, he watched the skies over the Ramadan camp. It was a clear, black sky, only the stars didn't seem to shine so bright, no twinkling he could see, or perhaps it was simply his imagination, inflamed by the sorrow of inevitable defeat by a technologically superior enemy. It was strangely quiet around and beyond the camp, even as he saw his fellow Muslims patrolling the grounds of the stone mock-ups, or warming themselves over the fires crackling from rusty barrels. A few of the old rust-bucket Soviet T-62 tanks scattered about, with antiaircraft batteries, a dozen ZSU-23-4 multibarreled cannons placed around the mountainside, through the valley, hardly enough if an armada of American warbirds swooped down. There were trucks, holding the multiple rocket launchers, all over the camp, perhaps a hundred of the freedom fighters wandering about with RPG-7s, a few Stingers, only he heard the batteries were low and those shoulder-mounted formidable surface-to-air bird killers may not fire.

He found it strange that so many of the mullahs, Taliban soldiers and his own al-Qaeda brothers-in-arms had been contacted over the months by top lieutenants close to Osama, ordered to make the dangerous trek from various parts of the country to erect this sprawling training camp, once abandoned, but rebuilt, rearmed and added on to with radar installations, bunkers, more antiaircraft batteries, courtesy of their Pakistani sympathizers. Surely the infidels knew it was here, what it was, their satellites and spy planes having long since detected the camp in their unholy quest to hunt down the mullahs and the Prince Osama. Unnerving, he thought, the silent heavens making him wonder when it would happen.

No "if"—the infidels were intent on destroying this country.

They would be coming. But when?

With this many freedom fighters he couldn't believe the infidels would mount a ground offensive. Or perhaps they would—who could say how the minds of devils worked? Still, it nagged him, putting so many in one place, easy pickings for their smart bombs and B-52s, even if they fled into the caves and dug in when the sky fell with bombs and missiles. He wanted to tell himself it was sacrilege to question his orders, but he couldn't help but wonder if they weren't in Ramadan as some sort of diversion, sacrificial lambs that would get hit, long and hard and bloody, while other leaders of the Taliban and al-Qaeda slipped out of the country.

Waziri stood. He was thinking about trudging down to one of the fire barrels when the first of several titanic explosions ripped through the camp. Freezing, he watched as tents, tanks and several antiaircraft batteries were obliterated in the crunching blasts, balls of fire hurling broken stick figures in all directions, screams riding the brilliant firestorms. They came scurrying and hollering out of the tents, the bunkers, the radar installation with its massive dish vaporized next as another silent missile slammed into the concrete structure.

The final war for freedom, and perhaps the personal survival of al-Qaeda, he knew, had only just begun.

McCARTER AND HIS Phoenix Force teammates stood, glued to the monitors, which had real-time air assault being piped in from a recon bird over the AIQ. They were airborne in a Predator, Grimaldi at the helm, having just informed the ex-SAS commando they were about to cross into Afghan airspace, to get ready.

None of them had to be told to lock and load. The hardware was basic, an M-16/M-203 combo to a man, commando daggers, Beretta 93-R as side arm, with C-4 blocks going with them in nylon satchels for rooting out tunnel or cave rats. Encizo would pull double duty with Little Bulldozer, and all of the commandos were laden with enough grenades and spare clips...

The ex-SAS commando hoped it was all enough.

The cruise missiles were already lighting up the camp, the screen flashing with countless explosions, a fireworks Apocalypse washing north to south, hill to hill, through the gorges. The saturation bombing came next, as the B-52s unloaded the five-hundred-pound gravity bombs from thirty thousand feet up, a rolling tidal wave of fire. McCarter could actually see the shock waves fanning out in rings, an amazing and fearsome sight to behold. Bunkers, tanks, men and antiaircraft batteries were getting the hammer-down, tasting the thunder of pure hell on earth. The problem was, McCarter knew, as eager as they were to move in on foot, the air bombardment would last for an hour or more. They would have to set down, ride it out, until the Delta colonel gave the green light.

The B-2s stepped up to the plate next, the digital readings on the monitor giving McCarter and his troops altitude and numbers of bombs and missiles unearthing the Ramadan camp. The bat-winged, futuristic-looking bombers had already cut loose the smart missiles from a little more than ten miles out. The barrage of J-DAMs, guided by GPS from a satellite, seemed to concentrate the bursts on the mountainsides where the Briton could barely make out figures manning ZSU-23-4s. One second they were cranking it up, aiming the barrels skyward, then they were gone, blasted off the mountain.

Just like that.

Then, a minute later, the gravity bombs fell again.

"If anything survives that holocaust, I'll be amazed," Hawkins said.

"They will, T.J. These hostiles have been digging into the mountains for years. Which means it's up to us," Calvin James said, "to go in there and wax them, up close and personal."

"Cave digging," Encizo grimly commented. "It's going to be ugly, guys."

"It's already ugly, and these bastards started the ugliness to begin with. The camp first," McCarter told them. "They may have tunnels in those bunkers. I know, mates, it's going to be down-and-dirty like we've never seen. If it moves, nail it. The enemy is on the ropes, and intel tells me the Taliban and al-Qaeda have forced teenagers into this camp. A twelve-year-old can wax your behind as easily as a salty old warhorse who went toe-to-toe with the Russians. Remember that."

He could tell the idea of blowing away children didn't sit well with them, but there was no choice. Hopefully that wouldn't be the case once they went in, nothing but the old guard left to take out.

McCarter walked to the cockpit, moving into the green glow of the instrument panel. "ETA?"

"Twenty-two minutes and counting," Grimaldi said, looking over at the monitors in front of the black-helmeted copilot.

"I'm changing the original game plan," McCarter told

Grimaldi. "Find a place, set us down, we're not jumping into that hell. No sense in some lucky shot blasting us out of the sky before we land. I'll dial up the Colonel, let him know the change. We can watch the show until they're finished bombing the hell out of the camp."

Grimaldi nodded. "I'll give you a shout."

The Briton returned to the monitors. If the bombing kept up much longer, the way the screen was lighting up in near blinding flashes, he thought he might have to don some sunglasses.

THE SATURATION BOMBING lit up the wall monitor in the War Room. They would never see this on CNN, Brognola knew, nor did he believe the newshounds even had an inkling the recon birds and satellites parked over the region could transmit the real-time killing show, an ongoing live war flick.

"The B-2s," Kurtzman said, checking his own monitor, "just brought down a part of the mountain to the north. If they're hunkered down in caves that way, they're buried alive."

Brognola felt disturbed about something. "Something's been bothering me about this camp."

All eyes turned toward the big Fed.

"Why put this many Taliban soldiers and al-Qaeda extremists right out in full view? Something doesn't feel right. All of them are little more now than fish in a barrel. If this is their last hurrah, some grandstand suicide play, I'm thinking they're expecting ground forces,

I'm thinking they want to take as many of our guys with them as they can."

"Or," Price said, "the leaders are using them to draw in our forces while they skate across the borders. We've heard reports about Iranian sympathizers willing to give haven anyone who wants it."

"Possible," Brognola groused. "I don't like it. Even with a sustained carpet bombing, I mean how many hostiles can we possibly take out?"

"The way it's shaping up... Whoa!" Tokaido whooped as a series of brilliant massive balls illuminated the monitor. "What in the world was that?"

"They hit some ordnance, munitions depot most likely," Price said.

Brognola wouldn't come right out and say it, but he would be damn relieved when Phoenix Force wrapped it up and got the hell out of Afghanistan.

"Remember, Hal," Kurtzman said, "beyond this camp, Phoenix is sanctioned to go on their own to take out the heroin labs to the north. If we're feeling our nerves now..."

"It's only begun—I hear you, Bear," Brognola said. "It's going to be a long day or more."

The longest of his life, he suspected, and watched the war go on.

MULLAH QAID HUZRAHBA believed he and the other mullahs were safe in the cave. God would surely protect them.

Still, he had his doubts, but surely, he reasoned, his faith was simply being tested. They were two-hundred-plus feet beneath the surface, but even still the terrible thunder could be heard as if it were almost right on top of them, shaking the walls, the endless bombardment raining down dust and pieces of stone on their heads. The other mullahs were kneeling on prayer rugs, feverishly praying for deliverance from their enemies.

Huzrahba had his tac radio, his top lieutenants contacted one by one. Unfortunately most of them were out on the mountainside, or in the camp itself, attempting to man the antiaircraft batteries. One by one he raised them, then, one by one, there was a deafening explosion, followed by static. Infuriated, he stared at his AK-47, wondering when he would be called to arms, march out there and confront any ground forces. There were bundles of dynamite that could be wrapped around the al-Qaeda soldiers who were hunkered down in this wide circular hole in the mountain's belly. If ordered, if the Americans sent in ground troops they would wrap the bundles around them, charge their enemies and attempt to take out as many infidels as possible as they blew themselves to Paradise. The way down was also mined. If the commandos raided the cave, they would lose many of their own in the process.

The orders had come down two months back, and Huzrahba now questioned the motives of the other clerics. Why march them here, in full scope of their spy planes and satellites, all of them aware military installations and camps all over the country were painted and being bombed? He had put that question to the Taliban leadership, and the answer chilled him now to the bone.

"It is your sacred duty, even to sacrifice your life for jihad, to slay the enemies of Islam. Our country will never again be the same, but there are those of us who will succeed, who will overthrow the new puppet government. The Taliban must prevail. It is God's will."

The walls shook around the mullah again, dust showering down, as he read the stark fear in all eyes, looking up, afraid the very mountain, shaking and rocking, would come down on their heads. He could only imagine the horrors beyond what he hoped were the safe confines of the cave.

The thunder rolled on above, the floor now trembling beneath him, and he decided to join the other mullahs in imploring God to spare their lives.

McCarter led the charge out of the Predator. Grimaldi's monitors had turned up a dozen live ones, heading up the gorge. The Predator had landed in a gully, hidden from the onrushing hostiles. In the distance, a mile away, McCarter glimpsed the world on fire. The F-15Es were now swooping down, adding more explosive fury to the conflagration raging for what the Briton suspected was close to two square miles. A halo of shimmering light hung over the holocaust, Sparrows and Sidewinders eating up whatever SAM batteries were painted on their screens. The wall of black smoke rising up the mountainside kept climbing, blotting out the stars.

"X-J to X-Mac, come in."

McCarter signaled the others to pull up as they moved deeper across the plateau, the Stony Man warriors stretching out on their bellies near the edge of the north lip. "X-Mac here. What do you have?"

"Twelve bad guys, coming up hard, to your twelve o'clock, forty meters and closing."

"Got it."

They waited, McCarter making out the frantic shouts of men on the run, fleeing for their lives. He drew up on a knee, the other Phoenix Force commandos, spread out in a line, imitating the combat crouch.

The Phoenix Force commandos raised their M-16s, holding. The firelight outlined the armed shadows, terror bugging eyes beneath the black turbans as they flew up over the rise. Several of the Taliban runners were looking back over their shoulders as explosions kept rocking the night behind them.

McCarter was first out of the gate, holding back on the trigger of his assault rifle, Encizo, Manning, James and Hawkins pouring it on. It was fast and furious, the terrible pounding of the combined autofire drilling them off their feet, dark waves of blood raining down on toppling corpses.

Twelve gone, and how many more left to take out? McCarter wondered.

The Briton was standing, weapon aimed at the twitching bodies when he heard the distant thunder. Looking up, as Encizo, James, Hawkins and Manning began toeing the bodies none too gently for signs of life, the Phoenix Force leader witnessed the two flying battleships soaring over the sea flames.

The two AC-130 Spectres began hosing down the earth with a tenacious hammering of howitzer, Vulcan Gatling cannon and Bofors combo. The way it looked at that point, the cleanup guns, McCarter figured, were simply getting the scraps.

The Briton was leading his men back over the plateau when the Delta colonel patched through on his com link. "Sir?"

"Move in. We'll meet in the middle at some juncture, X-Mac. Big Thunder is the encore. Keep me posted on progress."

"Roger. Game time, mates," McCarter told his team, picking up the pace as he led his men back down the gully.

CHAPTER SEVENTEEN

The air show wasn't quite over, not by a long shot, since Jack Grimaldi was good and jacked up on adrenaline overflow to begin performing, anxious to start chipping in to cut down anything that moved in the rolling sea of fire and mountains of debris. Ruins first, the hills next, stick to the plan, dumping Hellfires into the mouths of caves to pave the way for Phoenix Force.

Retribution time.

No amount of saturation bombing, he knew, ever nailed every last hostile, even if the sky rained nothing but a meteor shower of every type of missile and rocket and smart bomb in the whole U.S. arsenal, besides, of course, the conventional nuke payload being dropped off by a B-52.

Grimaldi had just touched down on the farthest southern and very much smoking and burning edge of the Ramadan camp, dumping off Phoenix Force so they could begin the grim and gruesome task of wading through a veritable valley of corpse-choked craters where the aerial bombardment had turned entire square miles of this corner of hell in Afghanistan into...

Well, he had never seen anything like it in his life. Imagine the dark side of the moon, he thought, only engulfed in flames and smoke with nothing but the dead, the mutilated and the mauled claiming damn near every square bloody yard of real estate.

He was up and away, checking the screens for live ones when he painted fourteen bogies on the IR. Friendly forces toted minitransmitters, and they showed up on his screen as blue blips while the bad guys were shaded in gray-green. Beyond the bulletproof Plexiglas, snugging himself in deeper in his Kevlar-armored seat, he grabbed the gunstick. His copilot, known only to him as Beavis, was giving him the coordinates, readings of hostiles all over the map, calm and collected, all pro, the guy sounding as if he knew his business. The Stony Man pilot, considering himself a better than average judge of character and even better when it came to assessing the flying skills of fellow aerial hotdogs, knew a highly skilled and experienced ace when he saw one. Beavis was no cartoon slouch in that cockpit, and Grimaldi was glad to have major-league talent on board.

Bonzo, the door gunner manning the Vulcan Gatling gun, was already hard at it as Grimaldi began his own strafe and spotted shadows tumbling in the ruins to his two o'clock.

The bunkers and training mock-ups of buildings that made up the terrorist compound had been reduced to smoldering rubble, with lakes of fire lapping out for as far as the eye could see. The problem would be some loose cannon out there with a Stinger, winging off a hope and a prayer and dropping them out of the sky. They would be flying nap of the earth, eating them up from tree-top level, so dropping flares out the hatch to throw off a Stinger wouldn't cut it.

Then there had to be a few terrorists on the prowl with RPGs, although the Predator's hull was similar to the Apache AH-64, boron armored skin that could absorb 12.7 mm rounds. Grimaldi wasn't up to finding out if the warbird could take a rocket on the snout.

He saw them, stumbling and trudging through whatever remained of the building mock-ups, some armed, some missing arms, then tapped the gunstick's button.

NOTHING IN Gary Manning's combat experience could have prepared him for what he found awaiting the team as it forged into the thick, choking swirls of smoke and grit, Predator flying on, the Vulcan door gunner already blazing away as the warbird rose into the sky. He was well beyond seasoned and bloodied, countless "deniable" black ops under the belt, but what he saw might have made the Devil himself shake his head and wince.

The big Canadian had taken the far left flank of the five-man skirmish line. McCarter was the point man, with Calvin James on the right flank. Everywhere Manning saw broken bodies strewed across rubble and stone, with so many severed limbs littering the march ahead, it would prove a chore alone just to keep from stumbling over some poor sap's amputated arm or leg. There were dark, stinking pools where limbs were entwined together in grotesquely misshapen webs, intestines running out like giant white snakes. Bodies were sawed in two or missing both legs, a few completely limbless torsos here and there in this hellish quagmire.

The face of war, in all its naked ugliness, he knew.

He couldn't even begin to count the dead, since the living enemy began posing a threat.

They were moving as one unit down the first of several craters when a group of armed shadows, hacking out smoke, slithered out of a hole in the ground. Manning held back on the M-16's trigger, hosing down the mauled extremists, his teammates adding to the cacophany, stitching up the wounded with such a ferocious, gut-spewing, head-blasting barrage they never knew what hit them.

They crossed the crater, climbing uphill, Manning hearing the brief stutters, swiveling his head. James, Encizo and Hawkins had pulled up, blasting away at militants who were crawling through the drifting shrouds of smoke.

Grimaldi was patching through on their one frequency tied into the Predator. "X Force, feel free to move on Target StoneHenge, now Target Stone Age. We've got bogies all up and down those hills, but I've turned up close to thirty hostiles still inside Stone-Henge," Grimaldi informed them, using the tag name for the terrorist compound proper. "I'm moving on, but I'll be in the neighborhood. Catch you on the flip side."

McCarter copied, said he'd call back if they got hung up in StoneHenge.

Manning topped the crater, dropping two hunched-over shadows as he marched for the next smoking hole in the earth. They were a little on the smallish side, but they were armed and had turned his way. He shoved down any sort of sentiment for any young men, or even boys, who had chosen to take up arms here, whether forced to serve the Taliban's last stand or not.

This was no time for pity.

RAFAEL ENCIZO HAD to figure there wasn't any need to start worrying about land mines yet, not until they made the mountainside and began their bloody excavation of the caves. There was no patch of ground that hadn't been hit by the air strike, everything pocked and dug up and smoking, from what he could see, and visibil-ity was a problem, with all the smoke hanging and holding in sheets that actually mirrored the firestorms. Factor in, too, all the bodies that had landed down in whatever turf wasn't cratered and land mines weren't an immediate concern.

Not that he would have balked. X Force never tippy-toed into combat.

McCarter, he saw, was leading the charge, the big

former SAS commando's M-16 flaming, pinning groaning wounded to the earth, angling his team toward the heaped mounds of rubble where bin Laden's boys had trained, all those black-hooded extremists who showed up on cable news, going through the obstacle course, kicking in the doors to building mock-ups.

Fanatic killers all, and he hoped a few of the Saudi's nutcases turned up in his death sights.

Encizo checked his six, instinct flaring up. A shadow was staggering to its feet behind Hawkins, who read the look in his eyes and wheeled just as Encizo cut loose with a long spray of lead.

Hawkins shot Encizo a thumbs-up. In this hell, he suspected there were more surprises ahead, and they would need each other like never before.

The snakes, he knew, had only just begun to crawl out of their holes.

No NVD GOGGLES WERE needed, since Calvin James could see clearly, thanks to the raging firestorms that blanketed the earth for as far as he could see. Smoke was a problem, able to conceal gunmen on the move, but he was pumped, senses electric, searching the compass on all points, ready to blast anything that moved.

It had been a fairly cold night, but there was scorching heat shooting from all directions, drawing sweat from his pores as he caught up to McCarter. They were forced to wend their way through a tortuous maze of rubble. Something slid down the trash pile, the black ex-

SEAL wheeling that way, but he found only a headless corpse rolling up at his feet.

"RPG, eleven o'clock!"

James dived, McCarter bellowing out the warning once again for the benefit of Encizo, Manning and Hawkins. They were bulling into whatever cover they could find, and there were plenty of hiding places to dig in and ride it out. The blast came a second later, rumbling from some point behind James. Fearing the worst, he hauled himself out of the rubble, glimpsed McCarter winging out a 40 mm hellbomb and dispensing the RPG boys downrange with a precision strike.

Encizo staggered out of the smoke cloud, eyes wild with anger at the close call.

"T.J.! Gary!" the Cuban barked into the ruins.

"Yeah, yeah!"

Hawkins slipped out of the ruins next, then Manning showed, growling curses.

McCarter was busy hosing down the rubble to their one o'clock, catching two more shadows on the fly. James joined him, tapped the trigger on his M-203 as he sighted down on a foursome of hardmen veering for the jagged teeth of a bunker. The blast cut through the heart of the group, a scream trailing off into the night as bodies sailed away.

Autofire rattled behind James. The black ex-SEAL spun, found Encizo and Manning flanking a break in a pile of rubble, firing through the crack, before the big Canadian primed a frag grenade and chucked it into the darkness. The thunderclap produced maybe three brief screams.

James pivoted, his M-16 fanning the sprawling ruins. He spotted another shadow charging out of the smoke, an AK-47 flaming before the former SEAL blew the shooter off his feet with a 3-round burst of autofire.

"The bunker!" James heard McCarter tell him over the com link, the ex-SAS commando pointing at a group of armed shadows climbing a mountain of broken stone, vanishing beyond the other side of the rubble heap.

THE VOMIT NEARLY CHOKED him to death, but Wazari somehow clawed his way through the pain and the mist, tasted the bile in his mouth and turned his head to the side, letting his stomach empty out. Moments ago—or was it an hour?—he had been knocked down the mountain side, hammered senseless by flying rock, until blackness took him away. How he had survived…

Did it matter? he wondered. Of course it did; it was a sign from God that maybe he was chosen to carry on, attempt at least a martyr's stand, a final strike at the infidels. He spit, shaking his head, somehow staggered to his feet and—

The entire valley appeared to be burning before his eyes. Beside him and above, he found bodies and limbs scattered everywhere, the warped teeth of cannons sticking up from the ground where the force of the blasts had impaled them through rock.

What could he do? he wondered.

Down there in the flaming Armageddon of the camp, he thought he spotted shadows charging whatever remained of the bunkers. Dazed, he searched for his assault rifle, but spotted a discarded RPG-7, its warhead still in place. With luck and daring and God willing, he might be able to strike one fatal blow before he went to Paradise.

And through the haze he found his mark.

It was a black gunship, swooping down for the south face of the mountain.

Wazari was raising the RPG-7, then realized he had waited a second too long as the nose of the gunship thundered and flamed, and the arm holding the grips of the rocket launcher was blasted off his shoulder. The last thing he heard was his voice, screaming daggers slicing through his brain.

GRIMALDI LET Beavis do the Hellfire honors. The RPG gunner was down and gone, a hurricane of 20 mm chain gun pounding all but vaporizing the shadow in a black mist.

Checking the screens, Beavis told Grimaldi they were running for the caves, holes, some large, while others were just wide enough to allow a man to squeeze through, filling up with shadows.

"Fire at will!" Grimaldi told him.

MCCARTER CAUGHT the mountainside going up in a rising wave of fire. The Predator was high up the slope, unleashing Hellfires, pumping them arrow straight into the maws of caves. Grimaldi knew his stuff, wouldn't waste that kind of firepower unless he had plenty of hostiles lined up and ready to burn.

Right then, the Briton knew X Force had concerns of its own.

It was slow and treacherous going, feeling their way down the slope of broken stone, watching the shadows for waiting gunmen.

They didn't have to wait long.

McCarter was nearly a split second too slow on the draw as a turbaned shooter lurched out of the shadows at the foot of the mound. The bellow of "Death to America!" helped McCarter haul it back together, the band of firelight shining down into the rubble zone lighting up his target. Autofire was already chattering from beside McCarter, his teammates a heartbeat faster ripping loose on the fanatic. Still, a line of AK-47 rounds tore up the stone, flinging stone chips into the Briton's face, but he held back on the trigger of his M-16 the bullet-riddled corpse flung from sight, chopped to bloody ribbons.

Descending, ears homed in for any scuffling sound, McCarter led his team into the trash dump. He was just in time to see the wooden door close on the floor between a mound of stone.

Leading the way, his troops searching the smoking ruins, McCarter crouched over the trapdoor.

Encizo made a hissing sound, drew a finger over his throat as McCarter met his eye.

The Briton nodded, understood. He held out his

hands, close together, signaling for a C-4 package. Encizo hauled out a block, primed it with a timer-detonator. Again Encizo mock-sliced his throat with his finger. McCarter scowled, mouthing, "What?"

Encizo handed him the block, unsheathed his commando dagger and gently dug the blade into the crack between the cover and the floor. Carefully, he lifted it up, exposing a slender wire. Manning stepped forward with a small pair of wirecutters, reached down and snipped the trip wire.

McCarter set the timer, indicating ten seconds, signaling Encizo to open it up and haul ass.

Encizo grabbed the rope handle, threw it up and back to a long burst of autofire that nearly scalped him. It was only a glimpse of maybe eight flaming fingers down below, but that was enough for McCarter, who counted off the doomsday numbers, taking a step back, then tossing the C-4 block into the hole.

X Force was hustling back, McCarter catching the frenzied shouts as the militants stopped shooting and their hole was blown to hell and gone.

CHAPTER EIGHTEEN

These "great" mullah-warriors of the Taliban didn't look so grand or remotely holy anymore, much less acting as if they were prepared to lead warriors straight into battle from out of the trenches. The sight of them, squawking about like frightened old women, spouting the Koran and ordering the al-Qaeda soldiers to turn themselves into human bombs, charge up top and confront the American commandos disgusted Ali Zhibariz. He stood his ground, guts knotted with cold anger, watching as men he had trained in the camps to the north began fastening the dynamite bundles around their torsos, preparing themselves to do the mullahs' dirty work while they rode it out down here, cowering in their hole. The rolling thunder of the air strike had finally stopped, only the mullahs were informed perhaps a hundred American commandos were on the ground. Most of them appeared confined to the north face of the mountains, bogged down in shooting engagements as they blasted their way into the caves. There were reports from the mullahs' faithful that the commandos were suffering casualties, setting off land mines as they stormed the mountainside, or were shot down as they surged into the caves.

Nothing would stop them, Zhibariz knew. The Americans had superior technology, air power, and that had proved, time and again, it could soften up a target area, men reeling about the pulverized earth, senses all but knocked out, before the ground killers came in to clean it up. His only regret was he suspected he would most likely die here. And before he could have been shipped out to the land of the infidels to strike a daring blow for jihad. A few more weeks, and the Pakistanis would have delivered—or were supposed to even be shipping right then—weapons of mass destruction. Armed with chemical, bio, even a suitcase from God, and he might have been able to take out an entire American city.

"Go! Go!"

Zhabiriz turned away from the cowardly mullahs, began leading his soldiers up the rocky trail, climbing hard and fast, listening when—

There was that terrible sound of rolling thunder, explosions cascading down the mountainside once more. He was sure the Americans were right then pounding the caves, looking to bury them all alive.

He ran, topped the rise, eyes watching the floor where he knew he had planted the mines. He held up his arm, the sounds of thunder coming closer, signaling his men they should follow his lead unless they wanted to blow themselves into a gory splatter all over the cave's walls.

He looked out the maw of the cave, focused on the wavering bands of firelight where the camp had been decimated. He was clearing the last mine when a gale force of wind and dust blasted him in the face. He peered into the storm, saw the giant gunship hovering just outside, heard his soldiers shouting in panic. He was about to tell them to go back, aware of what was coming next when he saw the missile flaming away from the pylon.

He stood there, knew it would be over in the next heartbeat, heard his mind cursing the mullahs, the fact that he wouldn't even have the chance to say one last prayer.

"THIS IS DELTA LEADER to X-Mac. Come in, X-Mac!"

It was one hell of a time to ring him up, McCarter thought, since they had just cleared the bunker killzone, the Briton's nose still filled with blood and smoke from the big bang in the hole. And all of them were coming under fire from al-Qaeda moles who had crawled out of the rubble, the standard white headgear betraying whom they served, but there was no mistaking the enemy was still in the game, fighting back with ferocity, pounding out the AK-47 autofire. Still, he needed to keep the Colonel posted, coordinate their effort since the mountain and its caves were next for X Force. There was a sense of urgency, even anger in the Colonel's tone, and

McCarter would have sworn he heard someone crying out in agony over the com link.

"X-Mac here! I'm a little busy right now, Colonel."

"I've got dead and wounded, mister, six down. These fucking land mines just cut both legs off one of my men!"

Not good, but they all knew the risks going in. Already X Force had sidestepped a few close shaves, and McCarter would take all the lucky breaks he could get, though he knew in combat a warrior made his own luck, but hoped the gods of war still smiled down on him. One of the Predators, McCarter knew, was a mobile hospital, filled with antibiotics, morphine, blood bags, medics on standby, and if the Colonel kept losing men that gunship would swell to capacity, and they might even be forced to abandon the mop-up stage. Still, McCarter could well appreciate the Colonel's ire, knew how he'd feel if he lost one of his own.

"Here's the story, X-Mac! These bastards are dug in but good in these caves. The Spectre and our Predators have thermal-heat imaging. They can pick out warm bodies from as far down as three hundred feet and more. And their screens are jammed to capacity with live ones. Every cave is a hornet's nest of armed extremists!"

So what was new? he thought. What was the big surprise? But he figured the Colonel was in no mood for smart-ass or callous wake-up remarks. McCarter slipped into a crack between jagged stone pilings of a downed bunker. His men were fanning out across what looked to be the training or PT area of the camp ruins, monkey bars warped and jutting out of the ground. X Force was firing on a group of shadows hunkered down in the mounds of debris to the east. Hard to tell how many al-Qaeda militants, but McCarter was figuring ten at least, maybe more. McCarter needed to get this situation under control fast.

"We've gone and smoked out close to a hundred already, but these caves are interlocked, interlaced, intertwined...."

"I have the picture, Colonel. It's a maze down there. We haven't even made our caves yet."

McCarter heard autofire rattle on the Colonel's end, the crunch of a grenade going off, followed by a brief scream.

"What? What the hell are you waiting for?"

"Seems the field we landed on is still crawling with live ones, Colonel. It's going to take a little time to clean it up. We're only five."

"That was your decision, mister!"

"I understand, Colonel, but this is going to take some time."

"Check your watch."

McCarter did, saw Encizo unsling Little Bulldozer as James, Manning and Hawkins began leapfrogging in the classic tactical advance of fire, run and cover, to shoving it right down the throats of the militants dug in and holding their turf.

"Sixty minutes and counting, X-Mac, then I call

back for another air strike. I'll drop this whole mountain on these bastards before I lose another soldier. And I'll tell you what…"

Suddenly the Colonel's tone took on a mean edge. McCarter sensed some sort of ugly punchline was on the way.

"I'm listening, Colonel."

"I have complete command and control over this operation, including our air fire support. That came down straight from the President."

"Other than C and C over your friendly X Force."

"You needn't remind me. What I'm saying, if I have to, and I'll clear it, by God, I'll dump a tactical nuke down one of these holes and turn this part of the world into a glowing dung heap."

Whoa, McCarter thought, wondering how serious the Colonel was, and decided he was deadly damn serious. Would he do it? Did he have that kind of clout?

"I hear I have your attention, X-Mac. You now have fifty-nine minutes."

"Be good enough to give me a heads-up before you blow this place off the sat imagery, Colonel."

"Count on it. Fifty-eight minutes, forty-six seconds and ticking."

"Keep me posted…."

The Delta colonel signed off. McCarter could well imagine the Pentagon and the White House had perhaps entertained the notion of hitting known but remote terrorist pockets with conventional nukes, something in the neighborhood of ten to twenty kilotons, just enough to let them know Uncle Sam hadn't forgotten about them out there, holed up in the boonies. Maybe discussed it or danced the horror through their minds, but just as quickly shelved it.

McCarter knew the F-15Es could be fitted with a laser-guided nuke, capable of flying by GPS to soar into a cave, even turn corners on a dime on its way down the labyrinth. Sometimes he wondered if the miracles—or the horrors—of this supertech age were better than the old-school way of doing business.

Right then, it was time to march back out there, he knew, and do things the old-fashioned and hard way.

Toe-to-toe, face-to-face, dish it out, fast and furious. Nothing but blood and thunder for the enemy.

Down their throats, in their face.

"WE COULD USE a little helping hand here, Striker."

Bolan was on the satlink with Grimaldi, glimpsed Alpha giving a hard perusal of the latest intel as he stood over the small metal war table amidships of the Predator.

"What's our ETA?" the soldier called out to Alpha, who checked his watch, then the monitors.

They had been stalled back at the Khyber Pass, but that was part and parcel, Bolan figured, for this kill-hunt. This whole part of the world had gone insane, and every Arab man who could hold a weapon was jumping into the fray at every corner. So another group of Pashtun rebels had cropped up, hell-bent on returning fire, the Executioner and the CIA black ops forced to hunt them down, more cave digging.

A critical time-eating task.

They had just put it behind, with Alpha calling in another CIA HAZMAT team on standby in India to fly in to secure the latest round of goods. The soldier was anxious to get to Afghanistan and help out X Force.

"Forty minutes, give or take."

Bolan relayed that to Grimaldi, wanted to know how the team was doing.

The sitrep was grim. McCarter and the others were forced to slog ahead through the rubble and smoke, gaining ground yard by bloody yard. Apparently the enemy had burrowed deep in the earth when the bombs rained down, crawling out now at every dark nook and cranny.

"I'm on the way, tell X-Mac! You'll have an extra bird by your side, X-J, so hold on and keep hammering."

"Roger, Striker. Gotta go, I'll keep the faith."

"Do that."

Bolan took off the headset, walked up to Alpha. "What do you have?"

"People, places and things. All bad news." Alpha stabbed the sat pictures. "This Dharwhar is a Taliban stronghold."

"The heroin warehouse."

"Labs in this valley, but word is the Russians have already gone wheels up from Uzbekistan. I know who and where my fellow Company snakes are. May they sleep well tonight, counting money in their dreams, because their ass will be grass soon enough. What we believe the Russians will do, they'll set down at this base in an Antonov transport. They unload food, supplies, weapons, cash to the resistance force."

"We're talking about Russian military?"

"Them, and more than a few goons from the Ruskavka Family. This won't bode well for relations between Washington and Moscow, but screw the press and the politics."

"I've got friends of mine at this camp who need our assistance."

"I understand, Stone. But understand, we make this short and bitter, then we're gone, soon as I get word that Russian envoy of cutthroats is closing in for their rendezvous with the Taliban."

"Part of the goal of the operation of my friends over here was to hit these labs and burn them down."

"Then we're all on the same page. Since I lost five shooters, I could use all the help I can get."

"The camps first?"

"Sure. We'll aid and assist. But it's still a seething hellzone out there. All you need to do is take one look at that screen. The Delta–Special Forces detail is bogged down in pockets already up their side of the mountain, and I've touched base with the Colonel. They're taking hits, and he's lost a few good men already."

"We already knew it wasn't going to be easy."

"Easy," Alpha grunted. "It would be easier to walk through the fires of hell."

"That's exactly what we'll do."

"I like your confidence, Stone, but—"

"No 'buts.' I've got friends who need me—us—and we'll help them nail it down before we move on."

The Executioner held Alpha's stare. The CIA black op nodded. They had an understanding, but Bolan knew that cooperation between the teams was only a first step.

This one, he knew, was set to blow from several corners of hell. And who would feel the fatal winds of war?

The Executioner would do everything in his power to see that X Force finished hammering the terrorists and left the hellgrounds in one piece.

HAWKINS RUSHED AHEAD, firing his M-16 at the shadows returning fire from their rubble roost, then darted into the next cover of debris. McCarter, he noted, was thirty yards directly across the way, cranking out the autofire on the fly. They needed to do something fast, he knew, since getting locked down in a long-running shooting war wouldn't cut it.

Encizo began blanketing the enemy's position with a barrage of 40 mm charges, chug, chug and crunch, crunch filling Hawkins's eardrums. Hawkins took the cue, as did James and Manning. Three missiles from their M-203s nearly converged in flight, streaking on, erupting behind the storm of fireballs marching down the enemy's hole. Bodies sailed on the crests of the blasts, but there was no sense in counting on that pulverizing blow to end it.

Hawkins knew they needed eyeball confirmation of

kills, which meant getting in close, up and over the rubble, take it inside.

He was out from cover and running in a skirmish line with Encizo, Manning and James, all of them slipping live charges down the chutes of their M-203s when he was momentarily distracted by the sudden bombardment as the Predator's chain guns unleashed a torrent of heavy-metal thunder on shadows high up the mountainside. Hawkins turned away, chiding himself for the momentary lapse. He wasn't necessarily unnerved, but he was hopped like he had never been on motivating fear and racing adrenaline. The only way was straight ahead, shooting and scooting, dig them out, put one between their eyes. The ex-Ranger had seen and survived countless missions, even when all hope looked lost, with the other members of Phoenix.

This was something else altogether. This was, he thought, a new war. Normally they operated on their own, independent of other U.S. Special ops, but their side was pulling no punches. The best of the best were in this shadow war for the long and savage haul.

All for one…

Closing, Hawkins spied a break in the rubble, caught several moans from somewhere in the shadows beyond. He armed a frag grenade, gave his teammates a look and a nod to let them know he was tossing in a live one.

A sharp pitch of the steel egg, autofire stuttering from the shadows, driving Hawkins back, and the blast ended all groans and shooting.

Now the tough part, he knew. He drew a breath, took the lead as he charged into the smoke, weapon fanning the cloud and beyond.

It took time, a dangerous chore, splitting up and combing the ruins, but McCarter gave the all-clear over the com link a few minutes later.

"Let's sweep the grounds, fan out, skirmish line, move east," McCarter ordered. "By the way, step lively."

When Hawkins heard the brisk update of what the Delta colonel had in mind, he knew time was running out fast. He didn't want to believe it, their side prepared to uproot the whole mountain in a nuclear cloud, but after what he'd seen here in Afghanistan, he believed anything was possible.

Anything that would tip the nightmare scale closer to the edge of Armageddon.

CHAPTER NINETEEN

The Colonel's nuclear threat kept the commandos of X Force moving ahead, but with a little more sense of urgency in their hunt. As if they needed any motivation to keep advancing, weeding out any wounded possums, McCarter thought, and had to start hoping they didn't run out of ammo, since the body count since they'd landed was of biblical proportions already, and they hadn't even entered the first cave. They were all hopped up on superadrenalized alert, ready to mow down anything that even twitched, the Briton damn near feeling his own eyes bugging out of his head, scoping the smoking moonscape for targets, even as the crackling firestorms shot superheated wind his way and singed his eyebrows and drew the sweat down his forehead. It was risky, sparing even a heartbeat to swipe the moisture off his face, but it was better than being misty eyed from burning sweat at the worst possible—fatal—moment.

The ex-SAS commando figured ten minutes they had been combing the hellgrounds since fragging the bunker on the way out of the PT grounds. He resisted the urge to check his chronometer, hated to be on anyone's clock, much less an angry warhorse who was prepared to irradiate half of Afghanistan, the Briton aware, though, the clock was winding down.

McCarter checked anyway. Thirty-eight minutes, and there was still a lot to do. There was a bloody good chance they might have to skip going into the caves, but it looked as if Grimaldi was cleaning up what he could, the black gunship maybe six hundred feet up the slopes, the chain gun hammering once every few seconds to keep the militants honest.

Or slaughter a few more who might think they could crawl out of their holes and maybe pop off an RPG and score one for the Taliban. Good news, Striker was en route with a CIA black-ops squad to add some more muscle to their war machine. Beyond this belly of the beast, McCarter knew a major strike against the Taliban's heroin cash cow was in the wings. Basic logic told him that without drug money, handed off by the Russian Mafia, the Taliban's resurgence might not have come about. The Russian Mob, in its lust for the almighty dollar, never giving a damn whom it bartered with, had also, most likely, funded a number of terrorist operations with its bargain with the Taliban devil.

McCarter lost sight of his troops every dozen or so yards. On his order they were spread out in a marching line, north to south, heading east, something like forty yards between each of them. The inferno still raged all over the grounds, tanks nearly melted down to their tracks, the god-awful stench of roasting flesh so thick in the air, McCarter nearly believed he could walk on the stink alone. And wafting clouds of smoke, so fat, towering and thick that they could wrap themselves around a strip mall, he figured, would boil over his commandos, or they would melt into the billows, eventually rolling out the other side of their black shrouds.

Autofire sounded every minute or so. As ordered, each kill, or kills, was to be reported to McCarter. Encizo and Manning seemed to be checking in more frequently than Hawkins or James, which didn't mean Hawkins or James, he knew, were slacking off.

So far, eyes scanning the shattered hulls of T-62 tanks and pulverized antiaircraft batteries, McCarter wasn't turning up any live ones. If it twitched, wriggled or moaned, he would put a round through it.

No questions, no hesitation. Whatever they nailed today was one less headache for the free world tomorrow.

The Briton came to a crater and lurched back just as three pairs of eyes that seemed to shine firelight, brimming with anger, hatred and pain burned his way through the shadows down below. The howls came first, followed by a triburst of autofire. How they had survived or where they'd come from, he couldn't say, didn't care. No point in dawdling, since he was on the Colonel's nuclear timepiece, so he armed a frag grenade, lobbed it over the edge. The detonation tossed up a mangled body minus an arm. The Briton came in on the crater from another angle of attack. Two were down, but number three was scrambling across the crater, huffing out of fear. The al-Qaeda fanatic turned back just in time to watch his personal doomsday unload. The ex-SAS commando zipped him up the spine, slamming him facefirst into the other side of the crater.

McCarter patched through to Grimaldi. "X-J, bring it down here. We need to at least have a pop at whatever tunnel rats are buried up there. How many are you turning up on your thermals?"

A pause, then Grimaldi said, "One hundred and change."

McCarter whistled. Suddenly the Colonel's idea of blasting the place off the planet with one well-placed nuke was sounding better. "Round us up."

"On the way."

Unfortunately, another six precious minutes were eaten up as McCarter encountered shadows as he cut a course for his commandos. Two came at him, staggering out of the smoke, hands up. The Briton dropped them in their tracks with a sweeping burst of autofire to the chest. Two more burst out of deep trenches, charging him in blind rage, and he dropped them as soon as they were off the starting line.

They had played, and now they paid the price.

He found Encizo dumping a C-4 block down a hole in the ground, autofire rattling out of the black maw. The ensuing blast was brilliant, hurting McCarter's eyes, telling him Rafe had dropped a block that was laced with white phosphorous. The screams seemed to carry themselves on the smoke curling out of the hole, then there was blessed silence moments later, more toasted flesh riding the smoke churning toward McCarter.

The Phoenix Force leader patched them on the frequency that tied in only the five of them. "It's a wrap, mates. X-J's coming down. The mountain's next on the hit list. Let's shake a leg."

The Predator's rotor wash swept away several acres of black smoke as it touched down in an area miraculously free of rubble or bodies.

Another burst of autofire, and James informed McCarter, "Three more to put on the scorecard."

"Let's go!" McCarter shouted, waving on Encizo, Manning and Hawkins, forging into the rotor wash.

The Briton gave it all one last look. If there was anything out there still breathing, he wanted to meet the bastard and personally shake his hand, then shoot him.

AFTER GETTING AN UPDATE from Grimaldi, Bolan moved for the fuselage hatch, peering into the rotor wash. He stood there as the pilot lifted them up the mountainside, taking in the mind-boggling devastation of the camps, or what was left. He had to figure two to three square miles had been cratered by the air strike, seas of fire still raging, a glowing umbrella outlining too many corpses to bother even with a guesstimate.

It was nearly a done deal here, but the caves could prove a whole other ball game.

Alpha had already laid out the holes they would hit, using their thermal imaging to tally up hostiles and their positions burrowed inside the mountain. The way it looked to Bolan, his M-16 cocked and locked, a thermite charge down the M-203, they were slated to get dumped off on a series of three caves just inside a ledge. One hole in the mountain was sitting on top of the two other maws in a pyramid shape, the imaging turning up hostiles moving through the rocky passageways, which joined together, a hundred yards back but on the rise.

X Force, Grimaldi informed Bolan, was already off-loading, going in, hard at it.

The Executioner was turning, looking for Alpha when he found him hauling a modified three-barreled M-197 20 mm Gatling gun from a steel container. It was already belted, a linkless feed curling up from a steel storage drum that Alpha hung over his shoulder.

Alpha showed Bolan a mean smile, told his troops to fall in, then looked back at the Executioner. "Any questions? No? Let's rock and roll."

X Force hopped out of the Predator, McCarter and Encizo taking the lead as they landed and began to climb up the rocky slope. Ten yards above, and the hole in the mountain was already alive with hostile shooters. Autofire was raining over the Stony Man team, rounds skidding off stone, flaying chips everywhere, driving them to cover behind a ring of boulders. Then they rode it out, holding off for a few heartbeats as the Predator rose, loomed and started paving the way inside with a sustained pounding of chain-gun fire.

McCarter was up and climbing, eyes fixed on the maw, as dust and blood took to the air, a gory mix that looked set to create some sort of seal on the entrance.

The Briton hit the ledge, Encizo on his heels. Manning, James and Hawkins had angled across the slope, finally topping out and flanking the maw across from McCarter and Encizo. Crouching, hearing the scuffling of feet and the shouts of the enemy in both flight and pain, McCarter wheeled around the corner. Two gunners trailed six more extremists, the duo dragging a hapless militant whose legs were drenched in blood.

Tapping the trigger of his M-203, the Briton launched a missile that zigged for the pack of runners. It blew in the heart of the pack, the thunderclap bowling them down, flinging what looked to McCarter a few severed arms and legs down the passageway.

"X-J!"

"I've got you covered, X-Mac. Nothing on your six or your flanks! Feel free to announce Johnny's home to the bad guys."

"Not what I mean! Have Bonzo rip up the floor with a nice long blanket of Vulcan fire. I want to see if there are any surprises waiting for our charge."

Grimaldi copied, swung the Predator out and around, edging the gunship dead center of the entrance. The door gunner cut loose with a half-minute leadstorm. The Briton strained his ears, tuning in for the sound he was listening for beyond the rotor wash and churning Gatling. Sure enough, McCarter made out the faint crunch-pops of land mines.

McCarter waved at Bonzo to cease and desist, shot him a thumbs-up, then led the charge into the cave.

THE EXECUTIONER TAGGED an RPG gunner as soon as he dropped to the ledge. The enemy missile flew high and wide of their gunship, sailing off into the night, destined to blow somewhere out in the inferno below.

The black-ops shooters were climbing for the solitary hole above the soldier, Bolan wondering when and where Alpha had given them that order to strike out on their own. Alpha's firemen trailed the pack, gun nozzles fisted and ready to start the next round of horror for their enemies.

No matter what Alpha's standing orders to his shock troops, the Stony Man warrior had his hands full right then. They were driving extremists back into the caves with sustained bursts of weapons fire. Alpha's Gatling gun smoked and churned, dicing up two militants in the closest maw, flinging them out of sight. Good news—militants were right around the corner, scurrying deeper into the cave, which meant Bolan and Alpha could give chase, free of worry over land mines, since the extremists didn't have time to plant antipersonnel mines, not that quick.

The soldier knelt at the corner's edge, palmed a thermite grenade and hurled it into the cave. When it blew, a number of shrieking voices lashed the air.

For good measure, Bolan rolled out into the maw, cranked out another thermite round from his M-203, catching sight of runners fleeing the burning scarecrows bouncing off the walls.

The white phosphorous blast washed over another half-dozen militants, lighting them up, dancing demons thrashing around before Bolan spared them a long mercy burst.

Above, the Executioner heard the ceaseless stammering of countless weapons, the reverberating racket seeming to reach him from some distant point ahead, around the corner. If that was the case, then these caves did in fact intersect.

The war for the mountain was under way.

Bolan and Alpha marched into the cave.

McCARTER AND ENCIZO blasted the rocket militant off his feet, flinging him over the edge and off into some bowl-shaped depression, but not before he loosed the RPG's warhead.

"Hit the deck!" McCarter told his troops, bracing himself as the warhead slammed into the ceiling. The blast rocked the floor under him, hunks and slabs of stone raining down, pelting him head to toe, the concussive thunder driving the din deep into his eardrums.

One heartbeat too slow, and McCarter knew they

would have been cooked by one lousy terrorist with an old piece of Soviet hardware.

The Briton heard them beyond the ringing in his ears, extremists shouting and scrambling beyond the raining dust, a large group, it sounded, down there in some arena of rock. It had been a two-hundred-foot march down into the bowels of the mountain, their original entry point slashing through another cave where one of Grimaldi's Hellfires had scythed apart maybe thirty militants.

"Frag them!"

McCarter led the five-man toss of steel eggs, lobbing his first through the smoke and over the edge. Four more hellbombs punched through the cloud, disappearing.

As soon as the five roaring explosions sounded, McCarter led the charge. He hit his belly on the edge, weapon out, his teammates flanking him on their bellies. McCarter took in the carnage below.

Jackpot.

He skipped counting all the dead. There were too many, black turbans still fluttering to rest on bodies, blood streaming down the walls. There might have been some narrow passageway out of this circular enclosure where a few might have made it out, but as he listened to the silence, making out the faint, distant sounds of autofire somewhere to the east—Striker's point of engagement, Grimaldi told him—they had mopped it up as best they could.

He was checking his watch when, lo and behold, the Colonel was buzzing him.

"We're going to set off a few thermite goodbyes for the finishing touch," he informed McCarter. "What we don't burn down, we'll seal the cave entrances on the way out."

"Does that mean what I think it means?"

"If you're asking am I calling in an air strike, the answer is affirmative, but I'll pass on the big one. What's your status?"

"Wrapping it up, but there's still a few hostiles running around."

"Finish it. You're free to go to your next phase. Good work, X-Mac, pass that on to your men. And good luck. We'll take it from here."

"Aye, aye, Colonel. Pleasure doing business with you."

"Maybe I'll see you around."

"If that happens, the suds are on me."

"I'll hold you to that."

McCarter passed on the Colonel's job-well-done. "Let's move it out, mates. See if Striker needs a hand. Keep your eyes peeled and, by God, try and retrace the same steps you took on the way in."

"Yeah," James said, falling in with his teammates after giving the slaughter zone one last grim search. "Getting eighty-sixed by a land mine on the way out wouldn't exactly make my day."

JUST AS BOLAN HAD suspected the top passageway joined the two lower caves. He was coming around the corner when he saw a group of extremists tumbling down a jagged set of steps. They were shot to hell from above, an explosion ripping through the howling throng next, flinging them Bolan's way, shredded missiles that hardly resembled anything human after being sliced and diced by countless steel bits. Two, then three came flailing and shrieking into the descending mob as Bolan heard the whoosh of flamethrowers. There were so many militants, armed and wheeling all around, searching for somewhere to go, that Bolan didn't bother with a head count. Not that he could, and not that it mattered.

The Executioner hit a knee beside Alpha, hugged the corner and went to work sealing off any fighting withdrawal.

It was pure slaughter, the enemy trapped in a cross fire of bullets, bombs and flames. The smoke and blood thickened as it filled the air, a gruesome shroud that hung over falling bodies, wet meat slapping the walls, heads erupting in thick, gory sprays of muck. The extremists dominoed in pockets, attempting to fire on, but were mowed down, burned up into shrieking demons next as they were torched by Alpha's firemen. The din of weapons fire was nearly drowned by the wailing of men being burned alive. Where Bolan could, he spared a mercy burst. One clip emptied, the Executioner filled the M-16 with a fresh magazine, fired on.

They spun under the torrent of lead, some driven to the floor of the cave, hollering, then trying to stand only to be hammered even harder by another hurricane of autofire from above and behind.

Alpha was snarling something, but Bolan was busy concentrating on sweeping survivors off their feet. The Gatling gun was a definite plus to have for this engagement, Bolan saw, spitting out a couple hundred rounds at least, blowing them to spewing sacks by the fours and fives and more.

When it was over, Bolan rose from his crouch.

"We're clear!" the soldier heard Alpha bark into his com link.

The Executioner waded into the smoke as the black-ops shooters came down.

"We'll take a walk around, Stone, but something tells me we're finished here. We'll mine all caves and bring the walls down on the way out, just in case. Whatever we've missed, there's another air strike due in about sixty minutes."

Bolan nodded, keyed the button on his com link to check in with McCarter.

CHAPTER TWENTY

Yuri Boldirov took one look at the major's hangdog expression and considered shooting the man on the spot, tossing him off the ramp then commandeering the Antonov his own damn self. It was almost too much to bear watching, all that was riding on the line, twenty metric tons of heroin to be picked up, and he was staring at a man who acted as if he'd just been sentenced to thirty years' hard labor in a Siberian gulag. For Boldirov to even consider having to waste one more breath, haggling and trying to soothe Major Mokaravlic's nerves, assure him everything would be fine, might push him over the edge.

The last of the crates was rolled off the wheeled tracks by the soldiers, static line yanking open the chute. There, the goodwill part of their mission was accomplished, plenty of bread and beans, bottled water and winter clothing dropped to keep the Afghan government happy and blessing their Russian brethren when the sun rose and they bowed and scraped to their God. Little did the government know, Boldirov thought, that he was actually aiding and abetting their hated enemies.

Boldirov snugged the AK-47 higher up his shoulder, glanced at his own soldiers, seven of Moscow's finest assassins, extortionists and headbreakers spread out in a staggered line beside him. Where the major and his men were clean-cut, shaved and crisp in their military uniforms, Boldirov and his soldiers of the Ruskavka Family were mostly bearded or goateed, longish in the hair and styled in knee-length black leather trench coats.

"Close it, Major," Boldirov snapped, one of the uniforms hitting a button, the ramp coming up to shut off the freezing blast of air sweeping in from the night sky. "Your mission of mercy is over. Now it is time for real business."

The major told his uniforms they were dismissed. Boldirov and his men stood their ground, hard faces watching the soldiers, forcing them to squeeze past on their way out of the cargo hold. In a way, he could appreciate the major's jangled nerves, his career all but on the line if this operation was discovered, and they were arrested by, say the SVR, once they returned to their base in Uzbekistan. The major huffed and puffed and stamped his feet a little. To some degree Boldirov understood the man's predicament, but the major had long since signed on, making, as the Americans were fond of saying, his own bed. The major loved his gambling and his vodka and his prostitutes, gifts bestowed upon him by the very Ruskavka Family he now worked for. Strange, Boldirov thought, how life took men down certain dark roads they never saw coming until the stop sign hit them in the face. Much as the Americans had known there would have been a major terrorist assault on their own soil, how had Mokaravlic blinded himself to what the tea leaves had been trying to show him, ignoring all the warning signs, no less? Those envelopes he had too willingly accepted while frollicking the drunken hours away in a gentlemen's club, for instance. Who had he believed was picking up the tab for all those merry nights in Moscow anyway?

Still, Boldirov knew this mission was fraught with peril.

He well understood the dangers of entering Afghanistan, whether as friend or foe, allied with the American forces or not. No one was ever truly welcome in Afghanistan. As a veteran of the ten-year Soviet-Afghan conflict, one of the first of the eighty-five thousand Russians to invade the country, Boldirov had firsthand experience in dealing with the various war and drug lords and tribal chieftains. Back then, if they wouldn't sell him heroin, he would shoot them, or burn them down with nerve gas sprayed from helicopters. It had been that very experience during the war that had enabled him to establish a pipeline, safe windows of passage for drug shipments, with, of course, help from Viktor Ruskavka, who had been third in line, years ago, to the top man of the KGB. The current government was powerless to do anything about the drug trade, despite help from the Americans.

"I sincerely hope," Boldirov said, showing the major a cold grin, "you are not going to start bellyaching once more about the great risk you are undertaking, how the Americans will find out what your plane is really doing, and will shoot us down in the sky."

The major chuckled, a strange mirthless sound that hardly matched the grim worrywart stare. "Oh, but you are the smart one. You have it all figured out. In Viktor Ruskavka's gangsters we must trust."

"Yes, I do have it all figured out, Major, and I would watch your tongue with me. We knew two days in advance about the American attack on the terrorist camp. Certain channels," he said, referring to his CIA counterparts, "were reached and they, in turn, reached out even further and informed others we were leaving on a mission to help the northern tribes. All air traffic is confined to the southeastern part of the country."

"And you do not find that strange?"

"How is that?"

"I am saying, what if there was a leak? What if we are being set up? Our radar screens show, that, yes, their bombers and fighters are moving in a corridor that fits your scheme. What happens when we land in this Taliban-controlled drug mecca?"

"What of it? Their planes, their satellites will only see a bunch of villagers loading up our plane with

U.S.A.-stamped burlap sacks, 'wheat surplus' that will be flown to the northern tribes."

"Very clever, I must admit."

"Thank you, I think so myself. A war effort, if you want to look at it through the eyes of a soldier."

"Whose effort? Whose war? Do you take me for a fool? You do not think I know what is really in those sacks?"

"But of course you know. And you also know that you will be a rich man when that shipment of 'wheat' reaches Moscow."

A dark look fell over the major's face as he looked away from the Russian gangsters. "A man sins, he darkens and stains his soul before God by his own foolishness, but that does not mean…"

Boldirov felt a terrible rage swell his chest when the major fell silent. What was this crazy talk about sin and God? What foolishness?

"Major," he said, taking several steps toward the man, "you are beginning to anger me. You do not want to anger me. Look at me!"

The major slowly turned his head, met the fierce look in Boldirov's eyes, unflinching.

"You are beginning to sound like one of those Arab fanatics. There is no God—there is no sin. And there is no turning back. You, if you choose to believe in this soul, have been bought and paid for. Should you waver, should you not pull yourself together, I will be forced to become your judgment day. Are we clear?"

"We have an understanding, yes." The major paused, then said, "If you will excuse me."

Boldirov watched the major walk away, brushing one of his soldiers on the move. Insolent bastard, he thought, and told his soldiers when he was out of earshot, "Watch him closely. Viktor is depending upon us to deliver. This is the largest and most profitable run of them all, perhaps our last, until the situation in this miserable country is resolved, or it is back to business as usual."

COMMANDER ALPHA LOST two more soldiers on the way out of the caves.

The Executioner was gathered with the men of Phoenix Force, all of them grouped around the war table, watching in solemn respect as Alpha zipped up the second black body bag. The dead soldiers didn't look much older than thirtysomething to Bolan, and he could venture a guess as to what they really were. Delta, Special Forces, Army Rangers, they were all over here, aiding the Afghan government against Taliban militants, fighting for freedom and also avenging the blood of the innocent, hoping in the process to restore some sanity to the country. Land mines had claimed the latest casualties, Bolan thinking and hoping the soldier Alpha was kneeling over would have made it. He had lost a leg, just below the hip, but shrapnel had practically eviscerated him. He had held on, Alpha clutching his hand as he was hauled into the gunship, telling the soldier to hold on, make it, fight to live.

Bolan and Phoenix Force allowed Alpha his moment of silence. Including Alpha and his shooters, they were fifteen strong as they flew on in the Predator for Dharwhar. The ballpark figure by intelligence put the enemy numbers in the drug stronghold at thirty to forty, but the Taliban goons hunkered down in the village hid for the most part in the main hovel where the bulk of the heroin was housed. There were al-Qaeda shooters believed to be guarding the poison, and Alpha earlier claimed to Bolan he had an informant inside Dharwhar who had been filling in the blanks on the coming drug deal.

Alpha rose. At the table, he began spreading out the sat imagery of the village, the surrounding valley. Silently he stabbed the AIQs, circled in red. Finally he looked up, scanning the faces of the Stony Man team. "The Russian gangsters are on their way. They'll land before we do. I've got them painted on radar. We set down in a valley two klicks southeast of this rise, leg it in, NVD goggles. These brazen bastards, according to my birds presently watching the area, don't even bother to put out the sentries. Clear sailing, going in, all the land mines have been removed by the UN long ago or blown up some camel or kid before this real estate was swept." More finger stabbing. "Our flyboys stay put until they get the word. Game plan. Let them start loading up the dope, then blast the plane off the dirt landing strip with our gunships. Maybe let them only get half the load on board, bastards thinking they're home free, dropping their guard—I'll call it when we're in position. Our gunships fly on, blow these labs off the face of the earth. Simple. All we have to do is execute, bore in and start lopping heads. Any questions?"

Bolan heard Encizo speak up. "How come you know so much about their operation?"

"What the fuck is that supposed to mean, soldier?"

"Hey, hey, easy, mate," McCarter said. "We're all in this together, right? We're all on the same team, eh?"

"If you say so, 'mate,' but I don't like your man there implying I'm not one of the good guys."

"That's not what I meant," Encizo said. "It was just an honest question."

"I'm CIA, and we're the next-closest thing to God. We know all, see all. How's that for an honest answer?"

"Works for me, Commander," Encizo said, spreading his arms.

"Hey," McCarter said, "we're sorry you lost some of your men, damn fine soldiers, I can be sure."

"Don't patronize me."

"Very well. This thing has us all a little jumpy. What say we just go ahead and do it like you laid out. Blast them, burn them and blow them off the earth. No problem with your plan."

"All right, look," Alpha said, heaving a breath, "I didn't mean to jump down your throats."

"Enough said. Let's move on," Bolan told them all. "Save all this bad energy for the bad guys."

"Right," Alpha said. "Let's nail down some of the

particulars, because we'll be knock-knock-knocking on hell's door soon enough."

BROGNOLA WAS STARING at the red phone, silently willing the Man to call, drumming his fingers on the table when Price said, "Staring at it, Hal, won't make the Man call and tell us Able's a go."

"Tell that to Carl. I can only imagine he's bursting out of his skin about now. I mean, we have Walker and Ruskavka painted on sat imagery, practically standing a stone's throw away from Spectron, and we're waiting in limbo. Not only that, but what the hell is with those Russian subs? Three of them, docked in plain view, sitting pretty in the ice floes, not a damn care in the world. It's as if the Russians, Walker, the Taliban, everybody is standing under our recon planes and satellites and shooting America the middle finger. All the bad guys out there, swaggering around, got the U.S. by the short hairs, laughing in our faces."

"You can scratch the Taliban and al-Qaeda off that list," Price said.

"Yeah, something goes right for a change. Thank God, at least our guys didn't bite the dust."

"According to Striker and David, it was messy, nasty and down-and-dirty at the Ramadan camp. We can count our blessings—somebody up there is on the side of the angels."

Brognola fell into his usual routine to take off the edge. He stood, went and poured a cup of coffee. He washed down four antacid tablets with the swill, then unwrapped a fresh cigar and stuck it in his mouth. He paced, he steamed, he glowered at the phone, he muttered a curse, then went and sat at the table.

"We followed the money trail to its sources and back," Price said. "We have the identities of traitors within the State Department, Exxon, Shell, among a few high-ranking intelligence agents in the NSA and DIA."

"Right," Brognola groused. "Dirty bastards. Problem is, I want a confession, I want the truth, I want to hear from Rutgen who he or Walker or Ruskavka greased. I want Lyons to play bad cop on this guy. I want to cut Able loose. The thing is, even if the Man calls and has a special-ops team set to go on the Spetsnaz base across the Beaufort, it could take a day or more before they get into position to make a move."

"Maybe not, Hal. Maybe the Man has been hard at work without letting on yet that he has a black-ops team en route. With the fluid situation in Afghanistan, he has a heavy load. He hasn't forgotten about us. Keep your fingers crossed—could be it's already in the works."

Brognola grunted, sipped his coffee while Price went back to scrutinizing the latest intelligence gathered by their cyber team. He looked at the mission controller, Price opening her mouth, then the red phone rang.

For the first time in days, Brognola almost smiled as he picked up the receiver. Almost, because he was dreading the possibility of a thumbs-down from the Man.

"Yes, sir?"

THE EXECUTIONER watched the ridgeline through the NVD goggles, hunched and moving, dead center of the Phoenix Force advance, McCarter on his left, James on his right flank. So far so good, no sign of sentries, all of it laid out just as Alpha swore. It was broken scrubland, ripped by trenches in parts, and Bolan, here and there, made out the small craters where mines had gone off. There was no sense in dreading the worst-case scenario. Not only would an overlooked land mine take one of them out, but it also would alert the enemy to the coming hammer-down.

Com link in place, he gave the other half of the strike force a quick look. Alpha and his shooters were moving in from the west, paralleling their own march. If Dharwhar was laid out as both sat imagery and Alpha said, and there was no reason to dispute that, they were looking at a good-sized village. There were noncombatants, Pashtun tribesmen with families, and Bolan had to wonder how the fierce warriors would react when the blitz was on. No matter, if it was armed it was going down. Women and children, he hoped, would just hit the deck, make themselves scarce.

M-16 leading the way, the soldier and the other Stony Man warriors began the haul up the slope, alert for any movement on the ridge.

All clear.

Two minutes and change later, they topped out, then flattened out on their stomachs.

The Executioner spotted the massive Antonov transport, parked out on the flat dirt runway. They were just north of the village, flares lining the landing strip. And they were hard at work, armed shadows hauling burlap sacks from the bed of a canvas-covered truck.

Bolan took in smack central. Like most of Afghanistan the courtyard walls and many of the stone hovels bore the scars of the Soviet invasion. Half of the village looked to be little more than rubble, walls broken down by past shelling. From the main warehouse, donkeys, laden with still more sacks, were trudging for the Antonov. The big transport's turboprop blades were spinning, which told Bolan the Russians weren't planning on overstaying their welcome.

Timing was everything in life, Bolan knew, and that was especially true of a planned and massive assault on the enemy. He still had many questions, like Encizo, about how Alpha knew so much, could get it down to minutes like this. He didn't think Alpha was one of the snakes, the big man having laid it on the line too many times up to that point, too much anger and grief over the loss of his men, among other things. Nothing to do but go with the program, the warrior knew, watch his back and the six of X Force.

Bolan kept scoping the layout, tallying up armed militants wandering about the store. Figure ten milling about, watching their fellow extremists hard at work. Trench coats, seven in all, were near the transport, had to be the Russian gangsters supervising the labor detail.

Count up the smattering of turbans and uniformed Russian soldiers, and Bolan concluded Alpha's plan looked solid, given the numbers. Get the bang started out there with the two Predators dropping the roof.

This, the soldier knew, was where they could do some serious damage to the thriving Taliban and al-Qaeda partnership, strike a blow against the fanatics ever regaining power in Afghanistan. Heroin was the bread and butter that kept the terror machine rolling, as was the case from Colombia to Southeast Asia. The province of Helmand, farther to the south, was where, Bolan knew, they grew the vast fields of poppies. The gum was then shipped to labs to be refined, but with the Taliban regrouping, hoping to oust the new government, the exiled leadership hoped to hide its stashes, moving them to newer warehousing and transshipment points among loyal villages.

Dharwhar was the latest case in point.

Bolan looked at McCarter, shed his NVD goggles, stowed them in a pouch. There was enough light burning around the village, torches, kerosene lamps, fire barrels and headlights from trucks and the flares on the runway to go in and clearly mark the opposition. Phoenix Force followed Bolan's line of thinking.

The soldier's com link buzzed, and Alpha said, "Let's move in. Shake and bake, guys, and start blasting out of the gate. I just gave Thunderbird the word to lift off and let it rip."

Bolan and Phoenix Force rose and moved down the hillside.

It was about to get messy, Bolan knew, the sky falling and the evil ambitions of gangsters and terrorists set to go to hell.

CHAPTER TWENTY-ONE

Vasily Mokaravlic stood with his soldiers, watching as what he considered nothing more than terrorists, cold-blooded murderers, those evildoers, as the American President called them, hauled the U.S.A.-stamped burlap sacks of poison up the ramp and into the cargo hold.

There was a face to evil, and Mokaravlic knew he was looking at it. It was everywhere. He was surrounded by evil, terrorists, gangsters, trapped, nowhere to go, but in its face he felt strangely brave and somehow at peace with it. It made him sad to some degree, just the same, seeing these men who wanted nothing but money and power, who gained the world through deceit, duplicity and staining their hands with blood, a lot of it shed by the innocent as they paved their road to hell, unaware they were marching straight to their own doom and damnation, until it was too late for the evildoers, nothing left to do but wail and gnash teeth or attempt to take as many with them into the great beyond as possible, since they came to realize their cause was unjust, an abomination, in fact, in the eyes of God. They were so enslaved to their evil, they seemed almost ignorant, and perhaps that was their bliss, he thought. Not knowing or caring just how vile they were.

Evil was their armor.

Well, he hadn't led what he considered a good life by any stretch, and his heart had been heavy for a long time with the crushing weight of his own guilt, sorrow, shame, having for so many years before now been unable or unwilling to control his own desires for the world, "chasing the wind," he thought, as King Solomon had so wisely put it.

Recently he had returned to his church in Moscow, a Russian Orthodox, reestablishing some connection to his faith and praying to a God he had forgotten over the years, imploring the Almighty to have forgiveness and mercy on his wretched soul, even when he knew he was cornered by evil men into his darkest hour, falling prey once more to his own weaknesses, waking up, again, too late. He wasn't sure if that counted for much in the final and true analysis, praying and asking his sins be forgiven, but it gave him comfort, hope that all was not lost, even in his waning, lonely years, aware he wasn't far off anymore from being a tired, sick old man, sitting alone in an apartment in Moscow, wondering where was God anyway, and how he could have come to be such a miserable wretch. No family, no friends, but, oh, he would have money to chase the wind.

As if it mattered.

He would have given every cent he was about to earn from this evil for the blinding light, instant conversion. It pained him to think he had even allowed it to go this far, that in some way he was a coward for not standing up to these gangsters. What was he so afraid of anyway? His own death by their hand if he didn't cooperate? Or maybe it was something else, a whispering voice in the corner of his mind, a hope that he would be there to watch, even participate in their demise?

He knew what he had been over the years before he had fallen into the clutches of these evil men. A drunk, a gambler, a whoremonger, a twenty-first-century Rasputin but in uniform. But wasn't the Bible laden with stories of sinners who turned it around? How many of those saints had been sinners first, he thought, before they forsook the darkness they had mired themselves in for so long? Perhaps too many to count, but they had only been human, after all, like himself, trapped in the flesh while at war with some other deeper calling buried within. His abysmal failures as a father and a husband, created by his own hand, had been part of the reason—no, he corrected—*the* reason why his wife had slowly drunk herself to death, a once beautiful woman growing old and haggard and sad before his eyes because he hadn't the first clue as to the meaning of love.

And why his three children wouldn't have anything to do with him, even to this day.

So his sins had caught up to him, ensnared by his own hand, swept up in the net of evil men who knew how to find and prey on the weakness of others. Strangely enough, he no longer cared if he lived or died, believing he had come to peace with himself and his God. If he was found out to be helping these gangsters by his superiors or the Americans or whoever, he would simply confess and allow himself to be marched off to a gulag. Repentance and thus salvation were gained only by terrible suffering anyway. That was the Russian way back to oneself, their soul, back to God. Not seeking the world and its fleeting glory through crime, like the face of evil he now watched.

They would never, could never understand.

Let it be.

He looked up at the sky, clear and dark, the air cold, crisp and clean. Still, something felt wrong about the night, and he couldn't quite put a finger on it, wondering if it simply wasn't some nagging fear of the unknown out there, those American fighter jets and bombers he had mentioned to Boldirov, swooping down, sealing their fate in bombs and bullets, their scheme uncovered at the last minute, the hand of God coming down to smash them all. And would that be such a bad thing? If the worst was to happen, dying in Afghanistan, then he would die on his feet, not grovel for mercy from any man, but asking God on the way out to see he wasn't forgotten or forsaken.

He saw Boldirov suddenly looking his way, scowling. "May I ask you, comrade, what is so amusing?"

Mokaravlic shook his head, muttered, "I am afraid you would not understand."

Boldirov looked set to pursue the matter, but something jolted his attention next, the gangster's head whipping toward the village.

Mokaravlic smiled, heard them shouting and pointing at the black winged birds of prey streaking for them. They were running everywhere, his soldiers included, Boldirov barking out orders for them to board the plane.

He stood his ground, smiling at the mass panic, believing right then that good did triumph over evil.

Any shred of doubt was erased in the next instant as the Antonov began disintegrating under a pulverizing line of explosions.

The evildoers, he knew, were about to get "done."

MANNING COUNTED the enemy numbers inside the large stone hovel on the handheld thermal-heat-imaging monitor. First glance at the digital readout, and he knew it wasn't going to be any cherry pickings.

No problem, since none of them had come to Afghanistan looking for quick, clean kills on a stroll down easy street.

Bolan and McCarter had divided the forces down the middle, and it was up to Manning, Encizo and James to smash and burn the heroin storehouse.

Unless Alpha and his black-ops team bulled inside first.

Easier said than done, and Manning knew the terrorists would stand their ground, go down to the last thrashing, screaming militant. Bullets were drilling their overhead cover, flaying stone in hailstorms.

"Fifteen, no make that seventeen inside, running all over the place," Manning told James. "Nine closest to our point of entry, including the three trying to wax our butts at the door!"

At the far end of the shattered courtyard wall, the big Canadian saw Bolan, McCarter and Hawkins crouched and hard at work, nailing runners across the no-man's-land, dumping a few well-placed 40 mm blasts into groups of four and five militants, kicking them out toward the runway.

The Predators, Manning saw, were busy pulping the Antonov with Hellfire missiles, chain-gun and Vulcan Gatling firestorms pounding into the thundering march of explosions. Stem to stern, the transport bird was coming apart like a giant aluminum can, wings sheared off, cockpit smashed and blown out by a missile right down the gullet.

"Rafe! Bulldoze these bastards! We don't have all night to play games!" James shouted, lurching low around a hole in the wall, spraying the doorway where a trio of AK-47s blazed.

Encizo unslung the multiround projectile launcher, squeezed into a hole blasted out long ago by a Soviet shell and began hitting the trigger. Three crunching explosions, and the AK shooters were lost behind the flames and smoke, a terrorist fluttering down fast and hard, slapping the earth with a wet whap that told Manning it was still filled with pieces of the militant's skull and grisly portions of brain.

The big Canadian shot a look down the dirt stretch running in front of Dharwhar's hovels. Commander Alpha, lugging the Gatling gun, was leading the charge for a doorway midway down, two of his own rocket men imitating the 40 mm entry to begin crashing the party.

Manning and Encizo fell in beside James, the ex-SEAL spraying the smoking hole in the wall of the drug house as some brave but stupid soul attempted to charge outside in a kamikaze surge. He was down and out before he capped off two rounds.

Now the hard part, Manning knew, flanking the hole, peering through the smoke—going in, and not getting waxed off their feet two steps past the hole.

Manning couldn't believe what he found at first. The militants were still stuffing white bricks, wrapped in thick plastic, into sacks, which were stamped U.S.A. It boiled Manning's blood for a second to think the Russians and the Taliban had devised an angle, using the American relief effort, to get their poison moved.

There was no cover except a long table, piled high with more sacks. First they had to clear away the drug smugglers, but luckily they were paying more frenzied attention to the dope than they were to the trio of Stony Man commandos not more than twelve feet away.

At the other entryway, Alpha beat them to the punch, hosing down a group on the run for the back door with a hammering wall of 20 mm pulverizers, the wave of heavy slugs seeming to burst a few of them apart like sacks of gore, one of the militants howling as his arm was blasted off just above the elbow before Alpha silenced his screaming and thrashing with a head shot.

Manning, James and Encizo cut loose in unison, a triburst of M-16 autofire that began scything apart the terrorist smugglers.

They spun, splashed blood over the white poison, dropped from sight, and the trio of Stony Man warriors charged in, began searching for fresh blood.

THE AIRFIELD and its mauled and stunned survivors were the chore belonging to Bolan, McCarter and Hawkins. The Executioner took point, flanked by the ex-SAS commando and the ex-Ranger, all three selecting targets on the run, sweeping bursts of autofire in all directions, bowling down runners, shouters, anything that turned up.

The Antonov, Bolan saw, was swathed in leaping flames, trench coats flailing about, some standing, some crawling, some rising and looking to save whatever they could of the night.

Fat chance of that, Bolan determined.

A few of the Russians' Taliban flunkies opted to run for the hills to the west. No problem. One of the Predators was already banking away from the smashed Antonov, chasing down those who had no stomach for this kind of fight, and weren't these the same guys, Bolan thought, who had called Americans cowards. A nice long thunderous barrage of chain-gun action, and maybe ten Taliban and al-Qaeda gunners were burned down, nothing left out there but lifeless corpses.

The labs in the valley were next on the hit list, Bolan knew, but the standing order was to mop this up first, fly on as a group, torch the crucibles of modern-day alchemy.

The Executioner, McCarter and Hawkins fanned out, giving one another a wide berth.

Two crawling moaners were treated to a Bolan burst of autofire. Three more armed militants, one of them trying to chase down a pack camel, were swept away in crimson showers as the three Stony Man warriors spared no one, not even the animals. All dope was to be torched, and Alpha, Bolan recalled, let it be known they didn't have all night to waste running around the desert to chase down a frightened donkey or camel laden with a few million bucks' worth of smack.

Good enough.

The Executioner picked up the pace, skirted the billow of smoke roiling his way and marched into the slaughter bed.

The hammering of triple death went on pounding the drug smugglers and the terrorists.

The Executioner was pleased to find it was shaping up to be a bad night for the enemies of America.

THE SCREAM of outrage was the last thing Yuri Boldirov could recall. That was right before he watched, frozen in horror, as his plane and his heroin went up in flames, two gunships, Apaches or variations thereof, streaking in from nowhere, no warning, unleashing missiles. Wreckage flew, and the concussive shock waves had bowled him off his feet, hurling him through the air like a rag doll.

How bad was it? he wondered. The din of weapons fire was close and coming closer, the stink of cooking flesh and burning fuel cloying his nose, pulling him back to reality.

And a nightmare was what he found.

He stood somehow, shaking from head to toe with murderous rage. Whatever Taliban and al-Qaeda lackeys were left were scurrying all over the place, a few them crying out in sharp pain, spinning and falling next as—

Three men in black were materializing through the smoke, shooting anything that moved.

And coming his way.

And where were his vaunted so-called soldiers? How about that weasel of a major?

Suddenly the trio of attackers was locked in an engagement near the flaming ruins of the canvas-covered truck which—

He cursed.

Figure two-thousand-plus bricks of white gold in there, now burning up.

He found and grabbed up an AK-47. There was

plenty more heroin out in the valley, two labs, in fact, choked floor-to-ceiling, wall-to-wall with bricks the Taliban had squirreled away for a coming offensive against the Afghan government.

Well, to hell with that. This battle was not over.

He could still turn the tide, if he could drop those three bastards who had crashed his party.

Boldirov made a beeline for a shroud of smoke near the shattered tail of his plane, opting to hide there, wait for them to come to him.

CHAPTER TWENTY-TWO

He knew he was dying. Vasily Mokaravlic had but one regret, annoyed, even as he crawled through his own blood, senses swimming in nausea, that he wouldn't see the utter defeat of the evildoers.

He hadn't been quick enough, or perhaps hadn't cared, one way or another, when the Antonov had been blown to flying scrap. A piece of wreckage had razored out, as he held his ground, smiling around at the shock and horror on the faces of the gangsters and the terrorists being drubbed by bombs and bullets. It had taken his right leg off, just above the knee.

So he was bleeding out fast, the pain strangely gone as a cold numbness settled in, wanting to take him away, floating out of his body, free at last. He looked up, the shouting and the shooting seeming to come from miles away. Through the mist, he saw the tall shadow in the black trench coat, striding through the wall of black smoke, a face of rage.

The face of evil.

The voice barking out orders belonged to Boldirov. Somehow the gangster had survived the initial bombardment. But for how long would he last? The attackers, and he had to assume they were American commandos, hadn't come to Afghanistan for some R and R in the rubble of Kabul. These nameless attackers were here hunting, and they were taking the blood of the enemies of America.

And rightfully so, he believed.

It looked as if the gangster were attempting to rally what survivors of his horde were left standing, yelling at them to arm themselves, follow him.

What to do? Mokaravlic wondered. Lie there and die in his blood, or perhaps make sure he at least achieved a Pyrrhic victory, one final act of repentance? Killing bad men, he believed, wasn't an evil.

He scrabbled around, found an AK-74. They were coming his way. He looked up, lifting the weapon, felt the smile forming his lips.

"You stupid man!"

Boldirov fired first. He felt the bullets rip into his chest, but again there was no pain, not much more than a few bee stings at worst.

It was over.

He felt free.

Reality receded, a gentle dark wave, and then he was floating off into the great unknown.

NO POINT IN DAWDLING over a few militants, so Bolan pumped a 40 mm charge into the heart of the threesome. The enemy's autofire abruptly ended as they sailed from the blast, flying on and into the burning bed with its melting load of poison.

The Executioner spotted the trench coats beyond the smoke, racing for the flaming tail of the Antonov. They were armed with assault rifles, and Bolan figured they would lay in wait for him to go to them.

No sweat.

"David, T.J.," Bolan said, signaling they should proceed down the port side of the burning, shattered hull.

Bolan moved out, delivering mercy rounds to several wounded and downed gunners on the way with short bursts of autofire. A fresh clip racked up the assault rifle, and he peered into the smoke, angry flames reaching out with superheated breath to drench his face in free-running sweat.

Cautious, knowing they were there but not seeing them, the Executioner stepped ahead, assault rifle out and ready to rip.

They were quick, but Bolan had anticipated their play. He spied a piece of jagged wing that had fallen, impaling itself into the ground. Bullets drummed into the wreckage as the Executioner took cover. He went low around the left end, triggering a short burst, catching one trench coat in the chest, sent him flying back and out of sight.

The problem was, he was pinned down, the distance to where the other shooters were hunkered behind a wall of fiery debris too great to attempt anything other than trade fire.

It was up to McCarter and Hawkins, unless he wanted to expend another 40 mm bomb. He was running low on 40 mm bangers, so decided he could hold on for a few more moments and wait to get by with a little help from his Stony Man friends.

MCCARTER HEARD the autofire. Closing fast on the racket, he surged ahead, low, Hawkins on his right flank. A few more yards, and he saw four long-haired, bearded Russian gangsters blazing away, backs turned to the Stony Man duo.

One of them was turning, but it was too late, even as he swept his assault rifle around, bellowed a warning in Russian.

McCarter and Hawkins, marching ahead, hosed them down, left to right and back. They danced, one whirling human dervish jigging right into a wall of flames, screaming for a second or two as fire ate him up, then all was silent.

McCarter keyed his com link. "We're cleaned up here, Striker."

"Then let's get back to the village. Our guys may need a little assistance. Meet you up front."

McCarter turned toward the rubbled courtyard wall. The din of autofire was still raging from inside the dope warehouse, voices raised in pain and panic. He only hoped the dead and the dying didn't belong to them.

No fatalist or ever one to worry about his own skin when charging into combat, McCarter knew the gods of war sometimes stopped smiling, even on the good guys.

TWO TERRORISTS WERE using their militant brothers who were getting the slice and dice from Encizo, James, Manning, Alpha and company to make a sprint down a long hallway across the room.

It was a clean sweep so far as Encizo watched them falling all over the place, blasted off their feet, human bowling pins going down hard, Alpha advancing, the mammoth Gatling gun erupting militants into spewing sacks of blood and innards as if they were shoved through a meat grinder.

Strikes and homers everywhere.

Now they had to go dig a couple SOBs out of some room, Encizo knew.

"We've got them covered," James told Alpha.

Encizo, James and Manning charged ahead as Alpha ordered his firemen, "Torch it all! And give these bastards a funeral pyre while you're at it!"

The twosome in question didn't look so brave or brazen anymore to Encizo, not like those al-Qaeda press releases where they sat in some cave and launched hate-filled diatribes at America and Israel.

In fact, they looked damn near terrified, ready to wet themselves, Encizo thought, giving chase, hugging the corner wall at the end of the hall. Funny how that happened, he considered. The day of retribution had come calling to claim their filthy terrorist hides, and they didn't want to give up the ghost.

"Dammit!" James growled, flanking the other side, as the terrorists slammed the door at the end of the hall.

"I'll kick it down. You guys frag them!" Manning said.

Manning led the jaunt, Encizo watching the other doors they passed. He pulled up beside the door, looked over his shoulder, nodded.

Encizo and James plucked frag grenades. He held up three fingers, counting down, and they pulled the pins. Up and out, the big Canadian drove a boot heel into the doorknob, sent it crashing open as autofire exploded from inside the room.

They were awkward throws, Encizo and James forced to toss them in at an angle as the barrage of lead hit the doorjamb, tattooed the wall across the way in a stitching drum of divots. The double thunderclap hammered the autofire into sudden silence.

Manning crouched, peering low around the corner, weapon out, as Encizo and James bolted into the smoke, splitting up to the side, one high, one low.

"Clear!" James called back to Manning.

"How you looking out there, Stone?"

"The floor's mopped, spick-and-span. We're on the way," Bolan replied over the com link. "Thunderbird's ready to move us on to the next pit stop. Just say the word."

"Okay."

Alpha was marching for the far door, looking out at the funeral pyre that was the Antonov, turning back, his firemen washing long fingers of white flames over the white bricks when—

He couldn't believe what he saw at first, stunned into indecision for the first time he could ever recall.

The boy, a damn kid, no older than ten, was running through the front door, screaming his lungs off, something in Arabic but there was no mistaking he wanted them dead.

He was mummified in wrapped around bundles of dynamite.

"Holy—"

Alpha saw his shooters whirling toward the kid, assault rifles blazing, but he already knew it was too late, as the little SOB pushed a button on the doomsday package and achieved his martyr's wish.

Bolan shot McCarter and Hawkins an anxious look, then broke into a sprint as soon as the blast roared. It was a big one, and the back walls were punched out by the fireball. McCarter was cursing, and Bolan feared the worst, didn't even want to think...

The Executioner bored into the smoke hitting him in the face in thick, coiling balls. He heard hacking, wanted to feel hope.

"Cal! Rafe! Gary!" McCarter hollered, whirling this way and that.

It was utter devastation, and Bolan saw the blast had taken out maybe six or seven of their guys. Slabs of stone had fallen over the dead, most of whom were so mutilated it would be damn difficult to ID.

More cursing and coughing, Bolan turning to find Alpha rising from the dust and smoke near the back door.

"Little son of a whore! Walked in here and blew himself the fuck up! A goddamn child!"

McCarter looked frantic to Bolan as he began checking the bodies, shouting for their guys. Then Bolan saw one, then two figures shoving away a beam, clambering over a mound of stone. Number three was James, all of them swatting at the smoke, hacking.

"I want this village swept!" Alpha raged. "I want every last one of these—"

Bolan knew where the CIA black op was headed, and stepped up to the man. He could well understand the sort of rage that would drive Alpha over the edge, unleash a demonic fury to strike back, line them up against the wall, old men, women and children, and mow them down.

"No," Bolan told Alpha.

"No? No! I just lost another half dozen or more of my guys. If that was your men got blown to shit, you think you'd do any different than burn down every last living thing here in this hellhole?"

"He's right," McCarter said. "We're not here to murder unarmed civilians."

"Civilians? You even consider these Stone Age bastards human?"

"Yes, we do," Bolan said. "We start wasting noncombatants—"

"Yeah, yeah, makes us no better than them."

"Took the words—"

"Right out of your mouth. Screw it!" Alpha found one of his firemen still in one piece. "I want you to burn every last brick. If it's on a camel or a mule, burn them, too. Fuck! Fuck! Okay, Stone, we sweep the village, but if it's got a gun, if it even holds something looks like a stick of dynamite, I don't care if it's an eight-year-old girl, it's dead. We'll do it your way."

Phoenix Force and the Executioner trailed Alpha toward the front door.

"That was close, guys," Manning said. "If we hadn't been chasing—"

"Forget it," McCarter said. "Sometimes you luck out."

Alpha shot his dead troops a long angry eye, then told his standing men, "Get them loaded up. We don't leave our guys behind, not even a missing arm or leg. Get it all!"

THE SWEEP of the village turned up four shooters in hiding. Alpha, Bolan recalled, seemed to take pleasure in being the first one through every other door and making sure he was the one who shot them up. With twenty to thirty 20 mm rounds apiece, there wasn't enough left of the bodies to feed a buzzard. All heroin was torched.

At least the poison back at Dharwhar.

They were flying on, Bolan watching as Alpha stood over the fallen bodies—or remains—of his latest casualties, scowling.

The order for the pilots was to go in, firing away, thoroughly soften up the target area. Bolan, like Alpha, wanted it wrapped up with as little trouble as possible. At every turn new dangers were rising, even suicide bombers—kids—charging out of nowhere.

The Executioner waited as the Hellfires began flaming away beyond the hatch, the Vulcan door gunner opening up with long concentrated bursts on whatever was on the ground.

"How you looking up there?" Alpha hollered at Grimaldi and Beavis.

Bolan heard the thunder below, glimpsed one, then two of the sprawling stone buildings going up and out in great roaring balls as the firestorms mushroomed from the valley floor.

And there were still plenty of armed fanatics down there, running around in all directions, firing up at the gunships.

He heard Grimaldi give him a report, then Alpha was back with the Stony Man team. The gunship lowered, touched down.

"All of them are going down here, Stone, armed or not, kid or not."

What could he say to that? Bolan looked away as Alpha shouldered past him, lugging the Gatling gun, fresh box hung around his shoulder, and hopped out the hatch.

McCARTER HAD TO WONDER if he would have been consumed by the same murderous rage as Alpha if he'd lost even one of his guys. Sure, he would have grieved, burned with raw fury, looking to lash out at the closest enemy, maybe even a groin shot or two to make it last.

Maybe not.

He was a warrior, not a sadist. He was a cold professional, and he knew he wouldn't sink to the same animal level as the terrorist scum they hunted.

The Predators did quite the number on the labs, a few Hellfires having smashed the stone structures to smoking rubble. No doubt there were precursor chemicals in those ruins, he knew, now burning and adding to the inferno he and his teammates closed on.

Toyotas and canvas-covered trucks were burning now, as they had already received 40 mm thermite grenades from the M-203s of Bolan, James and Hawkins, while Encizo advanced, unloading Little Bulldozer. Enemy shooters were still flying about, racing out from behind burning wreckage or clambering from the rubble of the pulverized labs. With both Predators scissoring back and forth over the valley, choosing entire groups of targets and cutting them down, it didn't take long to drop the curtain on the slaughter show.

Alpha was on a rampage, McCarter saw, the Briton triggering his M-16, hitting a pair of al-Qaeda goons to his two o'clock, flinging them over boulders and rubble that now lined the valley floor. Five Taliban militants came out of the ruins, coughing, their hands up. They were speaking rapidly in Arabic, but there was no mistaking the tone for mercy.

Alpha cranked out the 20 mm execution.

McCarter read the distaste on Bolan's face as the Executioner turned away, M-16 fanning the dark pockets carved into the granite walls of the gorge.

IT TOOK a little over an hour to walk through the valley of death, comb the rubble for any hidden shooters or wounded, walking or otherwise. It they were wounded and couldn't fight, Bolan knew, that was their tough luck. This war wasn't taking prisoners.

Two trucks were found heaped with white bricks, and Bolan did the honors of pitching in thermite grenades. He stepped back, watching the gold that fueled the terrorist murder machine burn.

No more friendly casualties, no more surprises.

Bolan gathered with Phoenix Force near their grounded Predator. All of them stood, scanning the devastation, the sweeping blanket of bodies on the valley floor. They appeared grim, even amazed at the sight of so much death handed out so quickly.

They also looked exhausted to Bolan, and he could well appreciate they needed about two straight days of sleep.

"It's over for you guys," the Executioner told the five commandos. "You've done your part. Phone home, then go grab some R and R on a beach someplace."

"Sounds like you've got something on the back burner, Striker," Hawkins said, a wry glint in his tired eyes.

"I do." Bolan watched as Alpha headed their way. "It concerns a few CIA snakes up in Uzbekistan."

"I heard that, Stone," Alpha said. "You're right. Our work's not finished. And this last piece of butcher's business you can damn well believe I'm going to really enjoy."

"What a surprise," Encizo said, then cracked a grin when Alpha scowled at the Cuban.

CHAPTER TWENTY-THREE

"It's a go, Carl. The Man says take them out."

"About damn time."

It was the best possible news, since Carl Lyons wasn't the patient sort, not when the enemy was practically walking around in the same neighborhood. With his guns oiled, cleaned, locked and loaded, it had been all Lyons could do to keep from crashing down the opposition's door on his own. Holed up in their cramped quarters at the Spectron Oil Reserve, Lyons, Blancanales and Schwarz had done the recon already on the lodge where Walker and Ruskavka and his fresh crew of fifteen Moscow imports were hiding—out in the open, under their noses, a twenty-minute drive through the woods. They had already gone over the strike plan, provided, of course, their quarry didn't up and leave the north slope.

This time, no one on the opposition walked away, he determined.

Lyons shot his teammates a thumbs-up.

Lyons looked away from them, dropping a cold eye on their prisoner. Rutgen, his hands bound by plastic cuffs, looked hapless and defeated, sitting as he had for the most part on his bunk, staring at nothing, thinking whatever gloomy thoughts, or maybe conjuring up some angle that would get his head out of the noose. He had nearly admitted to his treasonous involvement as soon as Able Team flew in, rounded him up, and Lyons fell into his bad-cop routine, no "Hello, Mr. Rutgen," just a backhand across the chops. He still wouldn't give up names, but Lyons had been more concerned with getting the green light to move on their enemies before he concentrated on another round with the traitor.

"And our boy Rutgen?"

"He's all yours," Brognola said. "If you can get a few names out of him that would certainly help. We've followed the money trail to a few power players here in Wonderland, but a confession would really make my day."

"Oh, I'm sure I can get him to talk. I'm sure I can become his worst nightmare."

"Yeah, I'm sure, too."

"Now that you've cut us loose, I can let some of this dammed-up testosterone out of my system. You know, you have to kind of admire the stones on all these guys. We've been watching Walker and Ruskavka since we got here. I can almost walk out the door and shout to them, they're that close. I mean the opposition isn't hiding in some cave where we've got to wade in and smoke them out. Then you've got these Spetsnaz black ops, three subs parked right in our faces. They act like they're untouchable."

"I trust you'll show them they're not. Oh, by the way, you have three hours to finish up with Walker and Ruskavka."

"How's that?"

Brognola explained a black-ops team from an undisclosed branch of the military was en route from California in an AC-130 Spectre. Three B-2s would be called in during the ground assault and sink the subs.

"First-name basis only," Brognola said. "You-guys, use initials, CL, like that. The CO is Major Ben. He's bringing forty shooters. Before you start bitching—"

"Me?"

"Yeah, you—before you start bitching, Barbara had to call in some markers just to get you guys on board. Their ETA to land there is 2000 hours."

"Let me guess. This Major Ben says if we aren't on the tarmac he flies on without us."

"I got that impression from Barbara."

"They're going to sink nuke-powered subs in the Beaufort? Doesn't sound like anyone in Washington's too conservation minded these day."

"Not our call. This is war, Carl. The Russians, whether it's a renegade operation or not, hit us first."

"Anybody run this by Moscow?"

"Their president and naval commander have been apprised of the situation, I understand."

"Denying any involvement."

"The usual, but who knows, what with the Russian Mob having taken point on this operation."

"Okay, we'd better get busy. I'll keep you posted."

Lyons signed off, stood, walked up to Rutgen and drew his .357 Magnum Colt Python. He aimed it Rutgen's crotch.

"I'm not going waste any time, Rutgen. I want names," Lyon said, and thumbed back the hammer. "Sing now or sing soprano."

"That won't be necessary. I'll talk, but what do I get in return?"

"You get to keep the family jewels."

MAX WALKER FELT as if he were waiting for the next terror strike, the sky falling, the world going up in fire all around, and no way to stop it. He didn't know when or where; he just sensed it was coming.

Soon. Any minute.

It felt like forever since they'd fled Seattle, scurrying on, whipped dogs with their tails tucked between their legs. And with seconds to spare, jetting away just as he'd looked out the cabin window and spotted the three bastards in black doing their damnedest to blow the Learjet out of the sky.

The problem was primarily the big delay.

Walker couldn't stand sitting in his upstairs room

any longer, thinking dark thoughts, brooding how all might be lost...

And eating his own fear, wondering just how tough he really was. Not to mention the knowledge that he had pretty much cut and run in the face of danger, the sight of men dying still making him question if he could cut it.

He found the Russians in the massive living room, Viktor, of course, at the bar, sipping on vodka, smoking a cigar. There was a strange, distant look in the boss's eyes, nothing there really he could pin down, but he just stared at his satlink, as if urging it to beep.

Night was falling again, and incredible as it looked, the boss's lodge was planted smack-dab in another ring of wooded hills, just like his Seattle digs by the water. This time, though, the fifteen shooters weren't lollygagging around, watching porn. As grim as hell, they looked ready to kick some major-league ass.

Could be, Walker thought, Ruskavka had tightened up this new bunch. It would appear, on the surface, Ruskavka had things under control, but Walker wasn't sure of anything these days. Twelve shooters, he counted, most of them standing, watching out the windows, with a foursome at the kitchen table, playing cards, three out front, he assumed, patrolling the perimeter. No smiles, no chatter, with assault rifles and machine guns slung around all shoulders.

All ready.

But for what? And when? And where?

It was time to broach a few subjects, Walker decided,

taking a stool beside Ruskavka, who grunted, staring into his drink.

"Yes, Max? I smelled you coming."

What the hell? Smart-ass at this time he didn't need. The aftershave, he thought, that was it. He was keeping up appearances, despite the anxiety and waiting for it to hit the fan, showering, changing clothes, a few hours of working out, stretching, some kicks and punches, staying loose, getting...

Right, getting ready.

"Not your aftershave, either. Your fear."

Walker felt resentment coil his guts. "And, I suppose, you are as cool as the air outside your lodge."

"Not especially. We have problems, Max."

"No shit. That's why I figured we need to talk. For one, I found out from the plant manager my man is under arrest. And do you know by who?"

"The three cowboys."

Cowboys? Now that was a new one. Figure Viktor had been watching too many Eastwood flicks, or maybe not. There was some—no, a lot of truth in what he stated. Those guys gave new meaning to badass Men with No Names, only they wielded a lot more than a six-shooter or a repeating rifle and some bad attitude.

"So, Viktor, why are we still in hiding?"

"We are not hiding."

Walker felt his anger mount as Ruskavka didn't bother to explain himself, sitting there, faraway look, sipping his vodka, smoking.

"You care to elaborate, Viktor?"

"Your money. The submarines."

"Goddammit, Viktor, don't treat me like one of your flunkies. Talk to me!"

Ruskavka didn't flinch, budge, just chuckled. "They must remain where they are across the Beaufort. There is much American ASW activity suddenly in the vicinity."

"Meaning no pickup."

"Not yet. I am seeking other alternatives. I am considering getting out of the oil business."

"Not me."

"No, not you. You are a man of vision. Speaking of which, I will require fifty million dollars if you want certain merchandise. Cash only."

Walker nearly squawked at the price. With the assets and numbered accounts scattered around the world, it would take time to get his hands on that much. Time was something he didn't have.

"Can you get that much, Max?"

"When we get to Moscow."

Ruskavka smiled as if enjoying some private witticism he was dying to unload.

"Did I say something funny, Viktor?"

"Hardly."

"We're waiting around for some reason?"

"Yes."

Another pause, and Walker growled, "Which is what?"

"The three cowboys."

"We just sit here, bull's-eyes painted on our backs..."

"Why are you so afraid of them?"

Walker balked. The boss had him pegged.

"Your silence speaks volumes. You see, Max, I come from a much different country, very different background than yours. I was former KGB. I know men, I know how to stand up to them, I know how to take what I want. I know when it is time to walk away, when it is time to fight. I am not a soft American businessman, sitting around, counting his money."

"You—"

"Watch your tongue with me, Max. I was not necessarily referring to you."

"That's big of you to say, Viktor."

"We stand our ground and fight."

"Wait for them to come to us."

"You could say that. Until they are dispensed, we will never be free men again—we will always be looking over our shoulders. You see, they know we—or you—are nervous, sitting around, wondering when it will happen. Myself, I can wait. When they come I will arm myself and do what must be done. You see me all the time, as if I am some king of leisure. That is not true. I did not become boss by letting others do all the dirty work."

Frustrated, Walker knew the conversation was over, aware suddenly he was on his own, cut off from resources, no backup. Squat. Zip. Zero.

"Why don't you go to your room and get some rest."

"And leave any fighting to the real men?"

Ruskavka's silence infuriated Walker even more. He nearly blew up, but figured a temper tantrum would just have the boss chuckling. Disgusted, feeling terribly, miserably alone and afraid, he was off the stool, heading for the stairs when it happened.

It was a recurring nightmare, freezing him up, just as it had back in Seattle.

Why wasn't he shocked? It was so awful, it was damn near funny, he thought.

The first two, maybe it was three explosions, started bringing down the roof, the front window blasting in again, a déjà vu of flying bodies and a cyclone of glass, wood and stone. He was searching around for a weapon, Ruskavka's soldiers up and moving, when he heard Ruskavka laughing.

"Those fucking cowboys again."

BLANCANALES KNEW they were on a tight schedule if they were going to return to Spectron and catch their Spectre ride. When Lyons gave the word over the com link, he let Little Bulldozer announce to the enemy they had returned.

It was one hell of way to tell the enemy hello.

The distance was something like a hundred yards to the lodge. Perched on a hilltop, covered inside a patch of birch trees and shrouded in darkness, Blancanales began his assault by peppering the front porch, then dumping three rounds through the roof. Lyons and Schwarz were advancing through the woods to the north right then, looking for live ones. Gadgets adding explosive fuel to the firestorm with his M-203, one missile after another blowing down the north wall. By the time they were finished pulverizing the lodge with explosions, Blancanales would be amazed if anyone was left standing. Still, they would go in there, wade through the mess, knee deep in bodies and blood, no doubt, and finish them off.

No other way.

The motor pool consisted of three 4WDs, Sno-Cat, a stretch Mercedes limo for the big Russian cheese. Three more rockets, and Blancanales fairly obliterated any escape, a wave of wreckage slamming through the front wall, bringing down beams, wiping out the porch.

A few Russian shooters ventured outside, staggering through the smoke, squawking then running in several directions when his teammates announced themselves with well-placed head shots.

Blancanales sent one more round arcing for the roof, watched it touch down, impact fuse lighting up the missile in a saffron flash, then broke from cover. Little Bulldozer going around his shoulder, he took his Uzi to go in search of walking wounded or any opposition that was clinging to the edge of oblivion.

LYONS BULLED through the wreckage of what he assumed was a side door. Schwarz, as ordered, had split off, going in through the back, while Blancanales, he knew, would come marching through the front. Two

Russian shooters were running through the smoke and falling plaster at the end of the hallway when Lyons held back on the subgun's trigger, drilling them down a short flight of steps that led to God only knew where.

It was pandemonium around the corner, figure three, four voices barking in Russian.

Crouched, smelling smoke then hearing that a fire had started upstairs from one of Blancanales's bombs, Lyons knew he had to pick up the pace. He didn't want to check his watch, but no way in hell would he miss that ride across the Beaufort. They had taken it this far, and he wanted to be at the finish line, or he'd wake up tomorrow with a vile taste in his mouth.

Assuming, of course, he walked away from Viktor Ruskavka's Alaskan digs.

He was coming around the corner, two black-clad figures vanishing beyond some fallen beams and walls of debris where the ceiling had collapsed when—

He glimpsed his attacker at the last possible second, the elbow flying for his nose, out of nowhere. Twisting his head, he took the spearing blow just below the eye. White-hot pain exploded through his skull. He was stumbling down a hall, wondering what the hell, swinging his subgun around when a wall of fury descended on him. The next thing he knew, he was flying through the air, all flailing arms and legs.

And minus his subgun.

He slammed down on his back, his bell rung, but

heard, "What did you call me back at that restaurant? I think it's time I gave you a little attitude readjustment, friend. Come to Max, pal. Don't run away."

Walker.

Lyons jumped to his feet, reaching for his holstered Colt Python, then found Walker charging him out of the smoke and flickering flames above his head. The steel tycoon was empty-handed, Lyons wondering where his subgun was, when Walker drilled him in the chest with both feet. Sailing on, Lyons rolled up in what appeared a sprawling stainless-steel kitchen. From some great distance, weapons fire rattled on.

Lyons was on his feet, saw the roundhouse kick aimed for his skull, meant to crack bone like eggshell, drive splinters into his brain. He ducked, the foot sweeping on, clattering like a gong through hanging cookware. Lyons knew *Shotokan* karate, but decided to go strictly down-and-dirty, feeling a mean urge to mess this guy up beyond messability before he finished him. Walker left himself open for a split second, so Lyons came up like a human grenade and piledrived a fist into the family jewels. That took some of the starch out of Walker. The guy bent over, whoofing, eyes popping, Lyons rising and hammering a headbutt off that nose. Funny how intense pain and a mashed, blood-spewing schnoz will turn the tide, Lyons thought. Still Walker came back, seemed to feed off his agony, in fact, a windmill of arms and straight kicks. Lyons took one in the gut, the ribs, a fist off the jaw, Walker's eyes shining with sadistic glee.

Enough of this crap, Lyons thought, reaching for his Colt Python, only to find air in the holster. A slashing kick to the jaw, and Lyons saw the lights wanting to wink out. Another roundhouse, off the side of his face, and the Able Team leader toppled on his back. Somehow he clawed onto reality, Walker standing over him.

Laughing.

"Maybe you're getting a little too old for hand-to-hand, pal. Maybe you're not such a cowboy, after all, maybe you're just a big bag of wind who can only throw around a bunch of grenades in a sneak attack."

The few seconds bought Lyons a little time, the cobwebs washed away by raw anger and something jabbing in his spine. He knew what it was, thrown to the floor during the explosion, he guessed, a hole in the wall near the obliterated sink, a shattered pipe spewing cold water, now rushing under his shoulders.

"No gun, pal. Too bad, so sad. You know what they say about grabbing the bull by the horns?"

Lyons rolled up on his knees, then felt Walker kick him square in the ass, driving him ahead, but not before he scooped up the large butcher's knife.

Lyons was vaguely aware someone else was in the vicinity. Great. Deal with Walker first, then get gunned down by a gangster.

"Here, pal let me help you up. Show you what a sport I am."

That sealed it.

Lyons felt Walker dig his hands into his shoulders, haul him upright. He whirled, and plunged the blade deep into Walker's groin. Staring into the eyes of shock, Lyons wrenched up on the blade until he grated breastbone.

"You should have kept on running," Lyons said, then shoved Walker away where he toppled on his back. "'Sport.'"

Lyons was about to reel from exhaustion and pain, then lurched to his side, aware of the presence in the shadows. He expected bullets to come tearing into him, instead...

"Not bad."

Schwarz stood there in the shadows, grinning.

"Enjoy the show?"

"Immensely."

Lyons nodded at Walker. "Ever dream at night of trying to fill that asshole's shoes?"

Schwarz held the wry expression. "Only in my dreams, Carl, only in my dreams."

Lyons led the way out of the kitchen, searching then finding his Colt Python and subgun. Schwarz on his heels, covering their six, and Lyons heard the long stuttering of autofire from the trash mound that was the living room.

He clambered over a fallen beam, just in time to see Viktor Ruskavka dancing to the stuttering tune of Blancanales's Uzi.

"STEP ON IT, Pol!"

"What do you want to do, Carl? Get out and shoot the tires out on that bird?"

Lyons saw the Spectre lumbering down the runway, storage tanks blurring past as Blancanales floored the four-wheel-drive Jeep, racing ahead.

"What's with you two these days?" Lyons gruffed. "Every time I say something I get the smart-ass routine."

"Must be the company we keep," Schwarz said from the shotgun seat.

Lyons cursed, but Blancanales charged past the mammoth gunship, sluicing the Jeep onto the runway, straightening, tapping the brakes, then jumping ahead. "Whoever this Major Ben is, he jumped the gun. We still had thirty-plus minutes."

"They can't take off, so I'm sure you'll get to introduce yourself to the good major," Blancanales said.

Sure enough, the monster gunship was forced to slow down.

Lyons was the first one out the door, war bag in hand. He was jogging down the side of the gunship when the hatch in the fuselage opened up.

"You're late."

Oh, but did he already like this guy, or what? Lyons thought, staring up at a bald, bullet-headed white suit scowling down at him as if he'd just swallowed a huge turd, or believed he was looking at one.

"Major Ben, I assume."

"You don't assume on my team, mister."

"By the way," Lyons said as Blancanales followed Schwarz after pulling the Jeep off the runway. "We still had a few minutes before you bailed on us. Or am I assuming again?"

"Don't push it. Grab a seat and hold on."

CHAPTER TWENTY-FOUR

Carl Lyons reformed his opinion about Major Ben when the man walked them through the briefing, just the four of them at the war table, amidships, the white-suited commandos hunkered down on the benches nearby, checking gear and weapons, not paying Able Team even a passing scrutiny.

Every time Major Ben growled and scowled them through the particulars of the assault, Lyons piped up with questions he really needed answers for. He realized the guy was a major asshole.

"Why haul the hostages, who will be tired, scared, hungry, all of us maybe hunted by these Spetsnaz shooters, ten klicks to this inlet where you 'assume' one of our subs will be on hand to pick us up and take us home sweet home?"

Major Ben scowled. "Because of the B-2s taking out their subs in the only decent docking on this goddamn ice floe, that's why. This was the only other available docking site."

"You might want to make sure all of us are safely snugged and tucked belowdecks before you irradiate the North Pole," Lyons said.

Major Ben bared his teeth. "They'll let the smart bombs fly when I tell them to."

"That's comforting," Lyons said.

"What is your major malfunction, mister?"

"Other than the fact we parachute from a mere thousand feet, and, by the way, we'll rig our own chutes, if you don't mind, then leg it in through six feet of snow, a four-klick jaunt, and don't you think these sailors have radar, by the way…"

"You're starting to really irritate me."

"I couldn't tell."

"That's it. You going to go with the program or would you like to stay behind and be a Monday-morning quarterback?"

Lyons had a few remarks set to fly, but could tell he'd pushed the guy far enough. "We'll go, if just to hold your hand and make sure those hostages don't catch an errant bullet from one of your guys."

"You son of a…"

With that, Major Ben stomped off.

When Able Team was alone, Schwarz quietly asked, "So, what would you have done, CL?"

"Well, HS, I think an insertion by an attack sub, say right up their butts, put you in their faces, would be the quickest way. Forget blowing the subs out of the water. We've got sat imagery telling us maybe half of the Russians are a half klick, little more, up the snow, sitting around in their tents, hostages, Spetsnaz, with most hands on board the three subs. Silent approach, sound-suppressed side arms to nail any roving sentries. I have to believe there are a few sailors, maybe even an officer or two who are having doubts about their Spetsnaz keepers and the Russian Mob deolaiing wai on Spectron. Sure, I'm thinking someone will attempt to use the hostages as a human shield, but let's see if any nervous feet dance our way, want to give it up."

"That doesn't sound like the bulldog we all know and love," Blancanales said.

"Sometimes you have to temper your urges, use a little diplomacy. Use the threat of force."

Schwarz shook his head, grinning. "Before this gets any deeper, what say we go check our chutes."

"Amen," Blancanales said.

YURI ZHABKOV KNEW there was only way to save his career, and his life.

Mutiny.

But how? He was under what he assumed was house arrest, two armed Spetsnaz commandos just outside his tent. His crew was detained aboard his sub, while Kirchenko went off to his C and C tent, doing whatever he was doing. This was, no doubt, a rogue Spetsnaz operation, and it left him wondering how far up the chain of command this conspiracy to sabotage American oil reserves on Alaska's north slope went, meaning just whom could he trust? Kidnapping American scientists alone was just the tip of the iceberg of this madness. The destruction at the oil fields wouldn't be forgotten, much less forgiven by the Americans. Somehow he needed to radio the naval high command.

If he could get his hands on a weapon, but then what? When the other two hunter-killer subs docked, they had disgorged another thirty Spetsnaz troops, and the word from Kirchenko was that the crewmen of those subs seemed more willing to oblige the madman, going along with whatever his schemes.

Zhabkov had to believe the reason for the delay, not setting sail and shoving off for Chukchi, was simple enough. There were ASW contingents in the Beaufort, possibly American air traffic, B-2s or F15Es about to…

Well, he feared reprisal, a Bosnia or Afghanistan type air attack on this frozen snowy hell. He could almost feel the nerves around him, occasionally hearing voices outside, whispers in the icy moaning wind of this wasteland, hinting that an attack was all but imminent.

He was about to brazen his way past his guards, heading for the tent flap, when Kirchenko marched inside.

"Going somewhere, Commander?"

"You must have been reading my mind."

"Really? I take it you do not like being stripped of command, and that you were coming to see me to insist I return your sub to you."

"As I said, you are a mind reader."

"Our radar screens are showing air traffic, sonar indicating a number of American submarines in the vicinity. If what I believe is about to happen…I ask you now. If I arm you, will you fight beside us?"

"But of course. It is my duty to protect my vessel."

"You have no qualms about engaging American commandos?"

"No. I have…well, I am how would the Americans say?—in too deep."

"Aren't we all." Kirchenko barked an order over his shoulder.

Zhabkov watched as a Spetsnaz commando swept inside, held out an AK-74 and two spare clips. He was taking the assault rifle, trying to keep his expression neutral, his intent to turn the weapon on Kirchenko, when the first of several massive explosions ripped into the compound. The look of naked fear on Kirchenko's face nearly made him laugh out loud.

THE HOSTAGES WERE the main and only concern for Able Team, and Lyons had hammered that point home before the jump.

It was hard, slow going, and Lyons found himself cursing the whole setup. As ordered by the major, the three white-parkaed, white-ski-masked commandos stuck to the far right flank of the advancing line of shock troops. Figure the good major, Lyons thought, was looking to lead his guys into the heart of the compound, hell-bent to grab the brass ring, maybe cut them out of the loop.

No sweat, let the major have his fifteen minutes of fame, if that was his bent, because the guy struck him as a glory hound, more interested in padding his résumé than results or the lives of his men.

Lyons hadn't struggled and shot and blasted and cursed his way this far just to see the gloomy sights, which weren't many.

In fact, it was a white frozen desert. And cold. Thermals and gloves helped to ward off the bitter freeze, but Lyons wasn't feeling too hot as it stood. He ached, head to toe, jaw, mouth and skull sore and bruised and battered. He wished Max Walker the hottest seat in hell.

They slogged on. Across grinding ice floes, over ice ridges, wending through minivalleys of ice rubble. NVD goggles guided the way, the Able Team warriors going with the standard issue M-16/M-203 combo like Major Ben and his shock force. Blancanales had insisted on taking Little Bulldozer along, getting a scowl and a muttered oath, something about him "hot-dogging the play," from the major.

Lyons was starting to feel winded, the freezing air burning his lungs as he tried to keep up the hard pace, the shock troops double-timing klick after klick. He had the mental lay of the compound, and it wasn't much. Radar installation, several large tents, snowmobiles, Sno-Cats, ammo depot made of ice blocks.

"This is Omega Leader to CL."

Lyons reached a finger inside his hood, keyed his com link. "Yeah, what?"

"Just over the next ridge. In about thirty seconds the bombs will start falling."

"And those subs?"

"What about them, mister? They're getting blown the hell out of the water on my say-so. How many times I have to tell you that?"

Lyons shook his head, kept moving, beginning his climb up the ice ridge. "It's your party, pal."

"Just don't muck this up."

"Meaning stay out of the way?"

"Do your job."

"Count on it."

The Spectre, Lyons saw, was thundering in from the north, but as he fell in beside Blancanales and Schwarz, he heard the air strikes were already hammering the compound. Laser-guided smart bombs, he reckoned, unloaded from the B-2s out to sea.

"No point in malingering, guys," Lyons said, topping the rise and beginning the charge down into the compound. "We're on our own."

"We always were," Schwarz said.

"You can say that again."

THE CRUISE MISSILE slammed into the ZSU-23-4 cannon, obliterating the multibarreled antiaircraft gun in a fireball that lit up the night. AK-74 in hand, Zhabkov watched as Kirchenko burst into the tent, heard the Spetsnaz man begin bellowing for the hostages to get outside.

Then he saw them.

He figured thirty, no forty white-suited commandos were charging over the rise, spread out in a racing skirmish line, firing away already. And he could well believe they weren't there to arrest any of them.

Could he do it? Turn the weapon on Kirchenko, show the Americans he wasn't part of this insanity? Shoot as many Spetsnaz commandos as possible? If he began firing on the commandos, he knew his life would be numbered in seconds. There were simply too many.

Kirchenko and ten Spetsnaz commandos hustled and shoved the American scientists out into the glow of halogen lights.

Autofire began lashing the air, close by, as maybe two full squads marched out to engage the American commandos.

"What are you waiting for, Zhabkov? To the subs!"

They were dead men, he knew. Once they dived... then again, maybe not. Maybe the American subs would let them pass, unmolested, if they held on to the prisoners.

Zhabkov fell in with Kirchenko, ignored the bleating cries of the terrified hostages. He was moving, still breathing, still hopeful he could find a way to save himself.

THE ICE WALL PROVIDED cover for Able Team as autofire blazed from the northern edge of the compound. If nothing else, it would be easy enough to pick out the Russians, since the commandos were in dark parkas, the old Soviet red star patched on their shoulders.

Major Ben and his commandos began unleashing an endless torrent of autofire and 40 mm missiles that raked the line of resistance. Sno-Cats, snowmobiles and bodies began taking to the air on sheets of fire.

Then the Spectre swooped down, hammering the grounds with cannon fire, decimating whole pockets of Russian shooters. The ammo depot blew in a brilliant supernova of flames, missiles or flares or something, Lyons saw, spiraling out of control, plowing through runners.

The Russians, Lyons noted, were still boring ahead from the direction of the smoking tents, armed and picking up where their downed comrades left off.

He wasn't sure what possessed him to do it, but Lyons, having shed his NVD goggles, took his field glasses from his nylon pouch. He lifted them, focused on a large group running south.

In the direction of the subs.

One look, noting how the armed contingent snatched and jerked their haul along, and Lyons knew the Russians were bent on using the American scientists as a human shield. If they made those subs, or even came close to ground zero when those B-2s unloaded the works…

They were all toast.

"Hey!" Lyons barked at Schwarz and Blancanales, who were hosing down entrenched commandos with autofire. "Let's move out! They've got the hostages and they're looking to boogie out to sea is my guess!"

THE FIGHTING GREW more intense as Blancanales marched beside Lyons and Schwarz, sticking to the western edge of the camp. It was shoot and scoot, popping off a 40 mm grenade on the fly, hurling up bodies and waves of snow with each blast. Spectre was busy thundering away, unloading on the grounds with Bofors cannon, blasting the radar dish to smithereens.

"Hey, you three!"

Blancanales heard Lyons curse, hearing his own com link buzzing with the wrath of Major Ben.

"Yeah, what?" Lyons snarled back.

"Where the hell you think you're going? We're under heavy fire over here!"

"Doing our part for our country," Lyons roared back, triggering a one-handed burst at two shadows reeling from a wall of shimmering flames, dropping them in their tracks.

Blancanales chanced a look back. The commandos were beginning to leapfrog ahead, but there was too much open ground and he saw them taking casualties, Major Ben cursing as maybe three, no, four of his guys, Blancanales saw, were toppling from return fire.

The word was obviously passed on to the Spectre to bear down and mop it up. The sky began raining explosive death from above, the monster flying battleship soaring over the compound, hammering pockets of Russian commandos, clearing the way for Major Ben and company to advance.

Blancanales picked up the hard run, falling in with Lyons and Schwarz to go for the hostages.

"What's the plan, Carl?" Schwarz wanted to know.

"Cut 'em off, then start sniping the bastards!"

"Is that what you call tempering those urges?"

CHAPTER TWENTY-FIVE

Yuri Zhabkov became more infuriated and desperate the more distance they put behind the camp. The freezing cold didn't help his mood much, either, nor did Kirchenko's constant haranguing of the prisoners do much to calm his nerves. It was as if Kirchenko were looking to take his anger, even his resentment and hatred of America out on the prisoners. Several of the prisoners stumbled, falling, crying out as they began slogging through a narrow corridor where ice ridges ringed their grinding march.

"Get up!"

They didn't move very fast, so Kirchenko found it necessary to kick an elderly scientist in the ribs. A scuffle broke out, until two Spetsnaz commandos jumped in and shoved the muzzles of assault rifles under the jaws of would-be heroes.

The Commander tallied up the numbers of Spetsnaz. Eleven.

He wasn't sure he could or would do it, then another moment of utter horror changed his mind, sealed his and the fates of the Spetsnaz commandos.

As he watched the destruction of their only hope going up in flames, beyond the distant ridges where their ride was docked, he figured it somehow all fit.

Justice.

The triple explosions lit the blackness, a triburst of rising fireballs that were brilliant, hurt nearly as bad as staring straight into the sun.

"No!" Kirhchenko roared.

The subs, Zhabkov knew, were going up in flames, more cruise missiles, his men going down with the vessels.

It was more than he could take.

Zhabkov chuckled, then swung his AK-74 at the closest commandos and began spraying them with autofire, deciding it was long since way overdue to bring justice home to these criminals.

ABLE TEAM LEGGED IT in on the Spetsnaz commandos, climbing the ice ridge, gaining high sniping ground just as the B-2s buried the subs at sea.

And Lyons, sighting through the crosshairs of his infrared scope, saw someone down there in the narrow walk had gone berserk.

What the hell, he thought.

It was what he had anticipated, one of the Russians pushed over the edge, or maybe hoping to restore some sanity with this act of madness, going against his own, jumping the sinking subs, as it were.

The problem was, some of the science crew began scattering for the ice ridges when the shooting started, which meant they'd have to go...

The hell with it, Lyons decided. The pell-mell charge gave Lyons, Schwarz and Blancanales a clear field of fire to begin pumping rounds—head shots all—into any armed hooded parkas.

The crazy man shaved the odds, sweeping a long burst of autofire down the line of commandos, a few of them stunned into immobility long enough to be chopped down.

One, two, three, four, and Able Team had it down to a few commandos, wheeling around, wondering where the killing shots were coming from.

Ponder no more, comrades, Lyons thought, and slammed another bullet home.

Berserker, Lyons glimpsed, was tagged by some Russian howling out a stream of profanity.

Lyons took care of that problem, coring a single round through the parka, slamming him facedown into the snow.

Then Major Ben started screaming in his ear, throwing off his aim.

"What the hell is going on over there! Goddammit, talk to me!"

Lyons keyed his com link, left it up to Blancanales and Schwarz to finish it up as they selected the final few targets, switching to full-auto slaughter. The trio of commandos left were riddled with lead, twitching, toppling to the snow.

"What the hell's going on, Major," Lyons snarled, "is we're going to round up the hostages."

"What?"

"I said the hostages are free and clear."

"I tell you what, mister…"

Lyons waited, but the empty threat never came.

"I got work to do, Major. See ya."

Lyons led Able Team down the ridge. "We're Americans," he called out. "You're safe, you're going home."

Several shadows stepped out of the cracks in the ice wall, while others stood, shaking, two of them exclaiming their thanks and appreciation.

Lyons heard the groan, feared one of the science detail was down, then took a head count of the standing shadows.

Seven.

He let out a breath, walked up to the tattered scarlet ruins in the snow. It was the berserker.

"Why did you do it?" Lyons asked the Russian, crouching beside him.

"Why not…it was wrong, what they did. I am a commander of a submarine, not…a murderer…kidnapper… these Spetsnaz…they were little better than common criminals."

Lyons nodded, looked up as Blancanales and Schwarz gently corralled the Americans, asking if anyone was hurt.

All good to go, not a scratch.

"What's your name?"

"Zhabkov...Commander..."

And he died.

Lyons brushed his eyes shut. Many questions, he knew, would never get answered. Such as why the oil reserve had been attacked to begin with, but he could venture some guesses. Walker probably wanted to rebuild the reserve, using his materials, reselling them.

No, the man had more money than God. Terrorism, then? Taking over the Spectron Oil Reserve, then Prudhoe Bay by force, extortion? Or was the scheme larger? Worldwide?

It didn't matter now.

"Carl, heads up, here comes the asshole," Schwarz said, nodding to the wide break in the ice ridge as the white suits came running.

Lyons grunted, stood.

"We'll take it from here," Major Ben growled, rolling up to Lyons and putting the evil eye on Able Team. "I don't know who you hot dogs are, but I hope to hell I never have to lay eyes on you people again."

"You can be sure the feeling's mutual," Lyons said, and led Able Team away.

BOLAN DECIDED to go with Alpha's straight-on blitz of the CIA outpost. This last killing chore, he decided, was definitely being done for the home team. War, Bolan knew, always created profiteers, those who skulked in the shadows, lining their pockets while the heroes were out there in the trenches, doing the fighting, and often the dying. It sickened him to know the hyenas were hiding in the dark, feeding off the lion's killing efforts, but he was there now, and there would be an answer.

It had been a long, grinding wrap in Afghanistan, the soldier and Phoenix forced to hunt down a few more snipers in the hills near the demolished heroin labs. Then burning the rest of the poison.

All of them had choppered to a secure base where weapons, material, food, clothing and fuel bladders had been dumped off. At the American air base in southern Uzbekistan, Bolan told Phoenix Force to stand down, go home.

They had.

It was just Bolan and Alpha now, donning black leather bomber jackets to fight the bitter cold of the rugged landscape. Uzbekistan was as bleak as Afghanistan, only Bolan didn't see the scars of war on dreary, stone buildings. There was plenty of razor wire, though, and Alpha was let in at the gate by what Bolan assumed were American soldiers.

Their names were Killian, Smart and J. J. Smitty, SOD boys, gleaning intelligence for special ops while at the same time courting the Russian Mafia. Alpha gave Bolan a quick brief on the trio of traitors before heading out in the 4WD Jeep. They were bringing side arms, and mini-Uzis to the party. The word was, the three traitors were holed up in their C and C stone digs at the far north end of the base. Just in case a few more snakes were in the nest, and had to be smoked out, the Executioner had one frag, one flash-stun on hand.

"Let me do the honors of blowing down the door," Alpha said, producing a golfball-sized gob of plastique with radio-activated primer. "I go in first. I want one live squawker to put a few questions to."

"I thought you already had all the answers."

"That's what I need to find out. Hey, I can't be perfect all the time."

Alpha swung the Jeep between what looked like two nondescript stone hovels.

They were out and shadowing through the night, closing rapidly on the CIA C and C. One radar dish on the roof, no one wandering the perimeter, but it looked dark inside, blacked out, abandoned.

Or as if, Bolan thought, they were expected, an ambush on the other side of the door.

Combat senses flared up, and Bolan legged it in beside Alpha.

Alpha placed the charge on the doorknob, palmed his radio box, drew his mini-Uzi. The soldier fell back, waited until Alpha sent the door crashing down on a crunching miniblast.

They were about to break into the smoke, when autofire rang out, raking the doorjamb.

Falling back, Bolan wasted no time, armed a flash-stun and chucked the steel egg in the direction of the weapons fire, three guns, it sounded like.

Bolan and Alpha, flanking the opening, rode out the tremendous senses-shattering thunderclap.

And in they charged, going low, Bolan's mini-Uzi up and tagging a shadow in black, a blind, deaf and dumb black-suited gunner reeling near a bank of monitors. The Executioner sent him flying back, jerking frame slamming into green screens, sparks showering past his toppling frame.

Alpha's mini-Uzi was flaming at something dead ahead, but Bolan sighted a blind shooter going for broke in the far corner of the room, an M-16 pounding out wild autofire. A long burst of minisubgun fire, and the soldier waxed number two off his feet.

Horrible groaning slashed the smoking air, the sounds of someone in pure agony. Bolan turned, watched as Alpha drilled a short burst up the wounded CIA man's legs.

"A few questions, Smart, then we're gone. Beyond your Russian buddies—all of whom are dead, by the way, meaning no heroin, no fat payday for you—who else in the Company is sleeping with the enemy?"

"No one...you fucking ape."

"A what? Come on, you can do better than that? Names!"

"If you got the Russians, that's it."

Alpha pulled his Glock, shot the man in the shoulder. Another round of yelling and cursing, and Bolan had seen enough.

"You're lying!"

"I'm not."

Alpha was lifting his Glock when Bolan walked up and pumped a mercy burst in the man's chest.

"It's over," the soldier told Alpha as the man wheeled on him, a face of rage staring back.

"That's not your call, Stone. I decide when it's over."

"It's over."

And the Executioner walked away.

EPILOGUE

Brognola felt his eyelids drooping as if they had weights attached to them. He was alone in the War Room, nodding off.

"Hal?"

He jerked awake, embarrassed to be caught napping as Barbara Price walked in.

"Why don't you go get some sleep?" she said. "Phoenix is on the way to Diego Garcia, then they'll catch a military flight back to Reagan. Striker and Able checked in. It's a wrap on their end."

"Yeah, maybe you're right. Sleep. It'll be restless, if it even comes at all."

He felt troubled and saw Price peering at him, sympathetic.

"What's the matter?"

"I'm not sure, Barbara. We only won a round or two. This thing, this new war as it's called."

"It's an old war for us, Hal."

"That it is. I have a lot of questions that will never get answered."

"Like?"

"Like why Walker and the Russian Mob apparently decided to spill a few hundred thousand gallons of oil into the Beaufort, just for one."

"There's a lot we'll probably never know. All we know is that Phoenix, Able and Striker did their part."

"Yeah. Maybe that's enough."

And maybe it was, he thought.

"This one, though," he said, "something tells me we're headed for more messy, dirty and perilous battles. The future doesn't look so bright from where I sit."

"No, it doesn't. But as long as a few good people are willing to go to the mat to fight to turn it around, we have a chance."

Brognola smiled, nodded. "Amen to that."

James Axler
Outlanders®

ULURU DESTINY

Ominous rumblings in the South Pacific lead Kane and his compatriots into the heart of a secret barony ruled by a ruthless god-king planning an invasion of the sacred territory at Uluru and its aboriginals who are seemingly possessed of a power beyond all earthly origin. With total victory of hybrid over human hanging in the balance, slim hope lies with the people known as the Crew, preparing to reclaim a power so vast that in the wrong hands it could plunge humanity into an abyss of evil with no hope of redemption.

Available November 2004 at your favorite retail outlet.

Or order your copy now by sending your name, address, zip or postal code, along with a check or money order (please do not send cash) for $6.50 for each book ordered ($7.99 in Canada), plus 75¢ postage and handling ($1.00 in Canada), payable to Gold Eagle Books, to:

In the U.S.
Gold Eagle Books
3010 Walden Avenue
P.O. Box 9077
Buffalo, NY 14269-9077

In Canada
Gold Eagle Books
P.O. Box 636
Fort Erie, Ontario
L2A 5X3

Please specify book title with your order.
Canadian residents add applicable federal and provincial taxes.

GOUT31

THE DESTROYER

NO CONTEST

The Extreme Sports Network is the cash cow feeding off America's lust for blood, guts and sex disguised as competitive athletics. From Extreme Rail Surfing to Extreme Nude Luge to the excruciatingly gory Extreme Outback Crocodile Habitat Marathon, it's ESN's life-or-death thrill ride to high ratings. But why—an outraged international community demands—do Americans always win and Europeans…die?

The answer, Remo suspects, lies in Battle Creek, Michigan….

Available January 2005 at your favorite retail outlet.